Caroline had been kissed before by men whom she had longed to injure with the nearest blunt instrument for taking such liberties. Lord Marchton's recent unwanted embrace had been but the latest on a long and lamentable list. Kissing certainly was not an activity she had ever enjoyed.

Caroline knew of the lies that Marchton had spread about her. She knew that Guy Constant had heard them. Thus, it came as no surprise when he took her in his arms.

What surprised her was the kiss itself, gentle at first, tender—then something much more, as he dragged his lips from her mouth and kissed her throat, her cheek, the lobe of her ear, before returning with heightened passion to her lips again.

But what surprised her even more was her response, as her palms did not press in protest against his broad chest, but instead her arm stole around his neck. . . .

Yuletide Match

YULETIDE MATCH

by

Margaret Westhaven

A SIGNET BOOK

SIGNET
Published by the Penguin Group
Penguin Books USA Inc., 375 Hudson Street,
New York, New York 10014, U.S.A.
Penguin Books Ltd, 27 Wrights Lane,
London W8 5TZ, England
Penguin Books Australia Ltd, Ringwood,
Victoria, Australia
Penguin Books Canada Ltd, 10 Alcorn Avenue,
Toronto, Ontario, Canada M4V 3B2
Penguin Books (N.Z.) Ltd, 182–190 Wairau Road,
Auckland 10, New Zealand

Penguin Books Ltd, Registered Offices:
Harmondsworth, Middlesex, England

First published by Signet,
an imprint of Dutton Signet,
a division of Penguin Books USA Inc.

First Printing, December, 1993
10 9 8 7 6 5 4 3 2 1

1

"TEASING JADE!" Lord Marchton's prominent eyes nearly started out of his head in angry disbelief. "Vixen!" Hopping on one foot, he clutched his injured shin. "Slut!"

Caroline did not draw herself up in indignation, nor did she object, as any woman of breeding might, to the young man's colorful language. Hers was the less complicated response of the cornered animal. She was only a governess, after all. She had no right to play the outraged young lady. Instead she acted as shy and stupid as she could manage, keeping her eyes downcast, continuing to edge her way to the door of the schoolroom. Her attacker's face was less livid now, and he was no longer nursing his leg. At any moment he might lunge for her again. Reaching behind her, she groped for the door handle and freedom.

The door opened at that moment, slamming into Caroline's back. She cried out in pain and pitched forward into the arms of her enemy.

"Miss Percival! What is the meaning of this?"

Those ringing tones belonged to Caroline's employer, Mrs. Brangley. Caroline twisted in Lord Marchton's grasp to look around and wondered, in an odd, detached sort of way, how she had ever come to work for such a woman.

Mrs. Brangley had once been very handsome and even now carried her substantial bulk with the confidence of a beauty. Her golden curls had not faded with time; quite the contrary, they had grown brighter with prosperity and access to the best cosmetic aids. Mrs. Brangley's eyes habitually gauged how this or that person or object might best be used to her advantage. On this occasion Caroline noticed their expression mingled the glint of calculation with a sly touch of triumph. Caroline struggled harder to free herself, hating to be in such a powerless position for Mrs. Brangley's entertainment.

The young nobleman who held Caroline prisoner was taking the opportunity to handle her with the liberty she had just kicked him in order to subdue. She wrenched herself away with all the strength she possessed, applying her half-boot this time to his instep. She ground the heel in hard, glad for the second time this morning that she was not wearing her soft kid slippers.

"Ouch! Bitch!" Lord Marchton glared into Caroline's face. For one instant she saw the raw malevolence of a thwarted masculine pride, an expression she had seen more than once in her life when repelling an unwanted advance. In that moment she knew real fear—a fear of something primitive she did not really understand.

Then the young lord recovered himself, and so did his intended victim. He was only a silly aristocrat who thought much too highly of himself, Caroline realized as she watched him turn from her to do the pretty with the lady of the house.

Straightening his coat, Marchton put on a well-bred smirk in greeting. "Ah, how do you do, Mrs. Bangtree. I fear you find us in a lamentable state, ma'am."

"I can see that, Lord Marchton." Mrs. Brangley smirked back, appearing not to notice that he had misremembered her name. "You needn't be gallant, sir. The girl must have led you on. I have not the least doubt of it."

"I told you so, Mama," remarked a little voice from the folds of the lady's skirts. Caroline was not surprised to spy her charge, Amanda, a diminutive child who bore a strong resemblance to a cherub. The little girl was giggling in derision. Her message delivered, Amanda sped away down the corridor.

Was the seraphic Amanda the one responsible for directing young Lord Marchton to the schoolroom where her governess was spending a rare half hour alone? Caroline was certain of it. How else could a casual visitor even have known where the schoolroom was?

Lifting her chin, Caroline tried to salvage something from this wretched morning. "I regret to inform you, ma'am, that this gentleman intruded on my solitude with the express intention of forcing himself on me. I have never given his lordship cause—indeed, I have scarcely seen his face before today."

Mrs. Brangley sniffed. "Come now, Miss Percival, you cannot expect anyone to believe Lord Marchton sought you out. You, of all people! Your looks are hardly such that—"

"I know all about my looks, ma'am," Caroline interrupted. She also knew she had no hope of convincing a former beauty that a young woman who was not striking could come by male attention without begging for it. But whether Mrs. Brangley would believe it or not, men had no exacting standards of beauty when the female target was vulnerable. The position of governess had unfortunately made that clear to Caroline more than once.

"How dare you interrupt me, you little . . . " Mrs. Brangley caught herself on the point of saying something very unladylike, Caroline was sure. Perhaps she would have repeated some of Lord Marchton's earlier words had not the gentleman still been present.

"I beg you, madam, do not be too harsh with the girl," the young viscount put in, speaking in the slightly nasal, insinuating voice he had used on Caroline when trying to ingratiate himself with her. "I leave town today. She will have no opportunity to repeat the assault."

This, Caroline supposed, was kindness of a sort. She felt her fists clench as though directed by another power. Resolutely she kept the right one from connecting with Lord Marchton's long nose. Nothing she said or did would make a difference, she reminded herself. Nothing. To show spirit would be to lose any hope of a reference. She assumed she would lose the position; that much was inevitable given this absurd tangle.

Marchton bowed to Mrs. Brangley. "I must leave you now, ma'am, but rest assured I will be in touch with you soon, you and your husband, on a little matter which might be of interest to you. You might tell Mr. Bangtree that."

"Oh!" Mrs. Brangley was evidently flattered by such condescending treatment from a member of the peerage. She preened as she replied, "How kind of you indeed, sir. Mr. *Brangley* and I will look forward to the pleasure."

"Brangley. To be sure, Brangley. Your pardon, ma'am. Wretched memory for names, but I engage to remember yours," the young man said with a pointed look.

"Dear sir, your mistake was quite natural. There are some Bangtrees who live in Berkeley Square, and we are often confused with them."

Caroline was astonished as the insipid exchange went on. The Brangleys were Cits, and rather poor examples of the class at that. Why would someone with the evident self-consequence of Lord Marchton wish to continue the acquaintance? He had a very sly look, too; she only hoped he had no plans to harass her again by calling on the Brangleys another time. Well, he would have no opportunity. For this infraction she would certainly be dismissed.

How, indeed, had the chance arrival of this distressing young man in the Brangley household brought her to such a pass? Caroline looked from one uncaring face to the other as Mrs. Brangley and Lord Marchton exchanged parting civilities.

Lord Marchton, a narrow-faced young man not long down from university, had come visiting the Brangley household with his older brother. A half brother, Caroline assumed, for they had different names, and the younger was the one with the title. Marchton's older brother happened to be the guardian of a child in the Brangley's care.

Some evil had seen to it that Caroline, setting out upon a walk with the little girls in her charge, was noticed by Lord Marchton, who, bored with his elders' conversation, was lolling about in the Brangley's drawing-room window.

He trailed after her and the children to the park. Caroline knew the game, for she had played it many times in her career. She treated him as coldly as she dared, repelling each gallant advance. When the interminable walk was over, she hoped the incident could be filed away in her memory as simply one more uncomfortable hour in service.

And so it would have been, had not his lordship returned to the house today, in the spirit of deviltry, and invaded the schoolroom. He had managed no more than a clutch at Caroline's waist and a whispered offer of compensation when she connected her half-boot with his shin.

And for defending herself she would lose her position! Caroline sighed, mentally reckoning up the amount of her savings. She would not be able to afford much time in lodgings before her situation grew desperate.

"Miss Percival." Mrs. Brangley's voice broke into Caroline's gloomy thoughts. "I shall deal with you later." And she swept away, a grinning Lord Marchton in tow.

Caroline gave them time to descend the steps to the floor below. Then she ventured into the corridor and to her own room.

This simple chamber, an attic really, overlooking Upper Wimpole Street, had been Caroline's home for two years. It was sparsely furnished and cheerless, and she had considered it her prison. Now the room looked unwontedly cozy and comfortable; well, so it was, compared to the uncertainty of the outside world.

Caroline was never one to wait until the last minute. She removed her trunk from its place under the narrow bed and began to fill it with the meager contents of the wardrobe.

She was folding the second drab gown when she heard a timid tap at the door. She knew at once who it must be.

"Come in, Harriet."

A small child with dark braids and speaking hazel eyes slipped into the room. "Oh, Miss Percival, Amanda says you're leaving!" The little girl dashed to Caroline's side and burst into tears.

"Oh, dear." Caroline patted the child's back and sat them both down on the bed; there was nothing resembling a chair in the minuscule room. She wouldn't like to leave Harriet; indeed, she would miss her quite dreadfully. The quiet child, shoved aside in the home of her uncaring cousins, had touched Caroline's heart.

Harriet Deauville was an orphan. Her guardian had never paid the little girl the slightest attention. Caroline understood that Mr. Constant had been out of the country when Harriet had lost her parents and come to live with the Brangleys; still, Caroline couldn't call that an excuse for allowing a sensitive little girl to languish with such an overwhelming and vulgar family.

Worse, when Constant had visited the house a couple of days before, he had done nothing to alter Harriet's situation. He hadn't even seen fit to meet his ward. He must be insensitive to a remarkable degree not to see at once what an unsuitable situation this was for a little child.

Caroline reminded herself in all fairness that the circumstances would look most suitable to a man. Harriet was with wealthy distant cousins, including a girl of her own age. An outsider would see nothing amiss in that. And a bachelor guardian could hardly be expected to take a girl child into his own household.

Harriet would probably be fastened to the Brangley's for the entire term of her minority, unless she was lucky enough to be sent off to school. Any school would have to be better than this house.

Caroline detested her own position with the Brangleys, but it was a position. The next one might be worse, and she was beyond anything sorry that she wouldn't be in the house in the coming years to ease her little favorite's way.

"You *can't* go." Harriet was weeping into Caroline's lap. "I hate it here. It won't be bearable without you, ma'am."

Caroline stroked the child's hair, feeling an urgent rush of affection. Would she really never see her small pupil again? Such a thought was enough to make her cry herself; being an adult and a governess, she stifled the temptation. "Dear, you will bear it very well. You and I have something in common. I know all about living with cousins, for I did it myself for six years. And here I am, alive to tell the tale."

"You lived with cousins? But you have a mama. You've told me so," the child said, looking up through her tears.

Caroline shrugged. "My mama was ill and couldn't have me with her. After my papa died, we hadn't enough money to stay together. So I had to live with some cousins of his. And I stayed with them until I was old enough to become a companion to a dear old lady, and then, when she died, I got work as a governess. I eventually found my way here to be Amanda's teacher."

"And mine." Harriet gave Caroline a quick hug. She wriggled to a standing position and clasped her governess's hands. "And I'll never forget you, Miss Percival. I . . . I love you."

Caroline looked into the trusting eyes. "I love you, too, my darling child," she whispered, touching Harriet's face. She had not said those words for many years, nor had she felt the emotions that would warrant them. She had assumed herself incapable of being fond of any human creature save her mother. Yet there it was: she did love little Harriet, and she would likely never see her after today. Salty drops welled up in Caroline's eyes

despite the example of maturity she wished to maintain;
she blinked them back.

"Well." Afraid that the scene would degenerate into a
river of tears, Caroline decided to be brisk and gov-
ernessy. "Suppose you help me pack, dear. I could really
use the help."

Harriet brightened somewhat, and she was trotting
back and forth to the wardrobe to fetch her governess's
underpinnings when another knock sounded at the door:
this one a businesslike rap.

"Yes?" Caroline called over the patched petticoat she
was folding.

A housemaid peeked in. "You're to go to herself at
once, miss, in the morning room. This instant, she said."

The maid's interested gaze told Caroline clearer than
any words that the scandal had reached belowstairs.
Would everyone believe that she had lured that distressing Lord Marchton to the schoolroom as he claimed? Or
were the servants more canny than that?

Willing herself not to flush too deeply, Caroline nodded. "Thank you, Betsy."

She took Harriet with her and dropped the child off in
the nursery, where Amanda and her two older brothers
were engaged in a noisy game involving a battered
chamber horse and a whip. Harriet shuddered and went
straight to the corner where an oblivious nursemaid sat
over some mending.

The child was too retiring, Caroline was thinking as
she continued her descent to the morning room. The
Brangley children were hellions, but Harriet would have
to stand up to them if she were not to be subdued into
nonexistence. She must be brought forward somehow . . .

Caroline shook herself. This was no longer any of her
business. She remembered that she was about to be
turned out into the streets, and her step quickened. She
had no desire to prolong the agony.

Presently Caroline entered the ornately decorated
morning room, the Wedgwood Room, as its owner

styled it, in which all of the furnishings, the walls, and the china ornaments were in some shade of white or blue. Mrs. Brangley had picked out all the decorations herself, and the mix of tones was not a happy one.

Caroline schooled her expression into the proper blandness. She would not let her anger show; she would die rather than give her employer that satisfaction.

"Well, Miss Percival," Mrs. Brangley said with a sneer from her reclining position on the Delft-blue long chair. Behind her, aqua and sky blue cushions bulged. "At least you can still respond promptly to a summons, whatever your other failings."

"To be sure, ma'am," Caroline said with a curtsy. Raising her eyes, she let out a little gasp—she and her employer were not alone in the room.

Mrs. Brangley smiled flirtatiously—and there was nothing more repulsive, Caroline considered, than a flirtatious smile on a face that would be more useful at scaring children than at enticing men—and looked over her shoulder in the direction Caroline's shocked glance had taken.

A man stepped forward from shadow into light. He looked Caroline over with the impersonality of a dandy selecting a fob. "Ah," he said in a slow, deep voice, "so this is the temptress."

Caroline couldn't stop an angry flush and a look of indignation. She held her tongue and, folding her hands, submitted with a proper meekness to being stared at. She was rarely examined so carefully; this outrage was a novelty at least.

She had managed in a single glance to form an opinion of her new tormenter. The man was taller than Caroline thought comfortable. He had an angular face, a decided nose, and cool gray eyes; dark, curling hair completed the picture, and he carried himself like an athlete in clothes that Caroline assumed to be of the first stare of fashion. He was a handsome man, she decided; though none of his features were regular, they blended into a harmonious whole.

She could not imagine who he was; no one of *ton* called at the Brangley's, much though Mrs. Brangley wished she could puff up her husband's merchant status into social significance.

Caroline supposed the gentleman, whatever his identity, was seeing in her the colorless governess she affected; though she had begun to wonder ever more often of late years if she was pretending to be passionless and plain or if she really was. He would see what the world saw: smooth brown hair scraped back from a center part, small stature and a gown so unflattering both to Caroline's complexion and figure that it had won Mrs. Brangley's unqualified approval.

"Now do you see what I mean, Mr. Constant?" Mrs. Brangley's voice rang out into what had become an uncomfortable silence.

Caroline kept looking at her hands, but she started at mention of the man's name. So this was Mr. Constant, little Harriet's uncaring guardian. She had pictured him quite differently.

Mrs. Brangley was continuing. "As you may observe, your dear brother—his lordship—could never have been drawn to the girl. She must have made a bid for his attention. Shameless creature. And this is not the first time she has tried to entice a guest of mine."

Caroline kept her head down, but a most untimely smile was tugging at the edges of her mouth. The thought of herself enticing that vulgar, snuff-dusted old doctor who had called to treat Mrs. Brangley's vapors was amusing in the extreme. Even more amusing was the notion, which had occurred to Caroline at the time, that her mistress was angry when the doctor cornered Caroline for a quick pinch and pat because she had wished to flirt with him herself.

"Let me have a look at you, girl," Mr. Constant said.

Caroline's head was jerked up; even the thought of a smile was banished as she looked into Constant's cold eyes.

"Just as I thought," he said in a drawling tone. "My

dear young woman, I'm going to urge leniency in your case. I don't know you, but I know my half brother. He has not yet learned to control his high spirits."

Caroline's eyes widened in surprise.

"They are very blue, are they not?" Constant said thoughtfully.

"What are, sir?" Caroline's voice came out in a squeak, and she winced at the sound.

"Your eyes." He turned away from Caroline abruptly and addressed Mrs. Brangley. "Don't let me influence you, ma'am, in the management of your household. But this young person looks to be a most efficient governess, and I would lay you any wager that Lord Marchton's dealings with her were all his idea."

Mrs. Brangley simpered and, under cover of this, threw a disgusted look at the governess, which Caroline had no trouble interpreting. "Well, I do thank you, Mr. Constant. I hope we'll be seeing you soon again. There is still that point about Harriet's trust, and since dear Mr. Brangley was so unfortunately from home this morning—"

"I leave London immediately, madam," Constant interrupted the flow of words.

"Oh." Mrs. Brangley's mouth drooped at the corners.

"Naturally I'll be in touch with your husband regarding Miss Deauville's funds. You need have no fear that you'll be put out of pocket, ma'am."

"Oh, naturally not, sir, with you such a wealthy—"

"It is the child's wealth that concerns us, is it not?" Constant said with a pointed look at Caroline.

Mrs. Brangley followed his glance. "You are perfectly right, Mr. Constant. How vulgar of me to discuss personal business before the domestics. Miss Percival, you may go."

Caroline read an extra meaning into the last words and immediately returned to her room to finish her packing.

She tried, by slamming her belongings with undue force into various corners of her battered trunk, to release some of the fury she could feel building within her.

Mr. Constant, far from helping her cause, had merely given the situation a new dimension of horror. She had never felt so exposed.

To think of that gentleman, who evidently had no very low opinion of himself, gauging her with a glance, dismissing her as an "efficient governess." Efficient, indeed!

After years of trying to appear precisely that, Caroline was perhaps all the more naturally incensed that her plan had worked. She *was* a groveling, efficient, poor little dab of a governess.

Flopping down on her bed in a manner she routinely cautioned young Amanda Brangley against, she began to cry.

A knock sounded at the door, and before Caroline could gather herself, it opened. The same housemaid who had summoned her before stood there. "The mistress gives you an hour to be gone," she said with a look of pity, or sympathy, or something. Caroline nodded, and the door closed.

She stood up, straightened her gown, dashed the tears from her eyes, and marched down to the morning room with no further ado. Mrs. Brangley was still there, alone now, engrossed in a back copy of *The Lady's Magazine*.

"Madam," Caroline said in cold tones, "I must trouble you for my wages."

"Your wages? Are you joking?" Mrs. Brangley looked up from the pages with an amused gleam in her eye.

"Yes, you owe me for this quarter."

"I owe you nothing, you impossible creature! Get out this instant."

"If you would prefer me to take the matter up with Mr. Brangley, I am sure I can leave a message at his club . . . " Caroline let her voice die away on a note that promised endless embarrassment. First and foremost, she didn't think Mr. Brangley would care for his wife dismissing the governess at the start of the Christmas holidays, when a drudge was ever more necessary to hold the children in check. The boys were just down from school, and they were nothing if not spirited.

With something like glee, Caroline considered the Brangleys' plight. She hoped they would not find a replacement for her until well after the New Year.

"My wages, madam?" Caroline kept her voice calm.

A long moment of silence followed her words. Mrs. Brangley glared, and her plump features began to screw themselves up into what Caroline recognized as the prelude to a fit of hysterics. "You dreadful creature," Mrs. Brangley finally exclaimed. Hauling herself up off the long chair, she crossed to a delicate white table and jerked open a drawer. "This is nothing more than blackmail," she threw back over her shoulder as she rummaged about.

Before Caroline knew what was happening, some coins had hit her in the face. "I trust that will be sufficient?" Mrs. Brangley said with a mask of a smile. Folding her arms, she waited for Caroline to pick up her wages.

Caroline took a deep breath and did. She had no pride left, then, none whatsoever. She ought to have ground the coins beneath her heel and swept away, supported by her dignity. If it had not been for the little matter of food and shelter, she might have done so.

Her last impression of Mrs. Brangley was of a triumphant smile and a tapping foot.

Little Harriet was waiting outside the morning-room door. "Thank heaven you're still here, ma'am. Did she . . . are you going to stay?"

"No, dear. I'm to be gone within the hour."

As they talked, Caroline was taking Harriet by the hand and leading her back up the stairs. Another flight, another, and they were again in Caroline's room.

"What on earth?" Caroline surveyed the confusion in amazement. The kitchenmaid was on her knees in front of Caroline's trunk. Everything that had been in it was on the floor, unfolded or otherwise pulled apart. "Sal, what are you doing?"

The little maid looked up. "Mistress told Betsy to watch you didn't take nothing from the house, ma'am. Betsy ain't got time to see to you, so she sent me."

"I see." Caroline felt the rage building again, and she willed herself to remain serene. The wave of anger was succeeded in one instant by a most out-of-place amusement. She could not think of anything in the Brangley's entire residence that a person of taste might covet. "By all means, my dear, stay and watch me pack. It will be a little rest from your labors."

Harriet helped and Sal looked on as Caroline readied her trunk and valise for what she hoped would be the last time in this house. Then, putting on her outdoor things, she cast one look at Sal, decided it would be useless to ask the little maid's help, and began to drag her trunk out of the room single-handed. Harriet trotted behind with Caroline's valise as the box bumped down the stairs. The kitchenmaid disappeared by the back, but Caroline took the front stairs out of pure defiance, knowing her erstwhile employer would prefer her to use the servants' way for her departure. She rather enjoyed the sound of her trunk crashing on each step.

In the entrance hall the footman sprang to Caroline's side with a look she interpreted as sympathetic. "I'll carry it outside to the hack stand, ma'am."

"Thank you, Tom," Caroline said with a smile.

She turned to Harriet for the last farewell.

At that moment a shriek sounded from nearby, and the morning-room door burst open. Amanda Brangley and her brothers chased past and up the stairs, pursuing something very wet, very furry, and very muddy.

Caroline blinked. She had assumed the children were still in the nursery, torturing the chamber horse. Amanda still held the whip, Caroline had time to notice before the three turned a corner of the landing and were lost to sight. Their footprints left evidence of their passing on every carpeted step.

Mrs. Brangley, face purple with rage in unflattering contrast to the determined blues and whites of her room, appeared at the door. The hem of her gown was covered with dirty tracks. "Miss Percival!" she cried. "Those imps have brought a badger into this house, of all things. And where they found a badger in London I am sure I do not wish to know . . . "

"Ben brought it along from Winchester in his luggage," Harriet whispered into Caroline's ear under cover of giving her a farewell hug. "They've had it in the back garden."

"You little devil!" Mrs. Brangley noticed the whispers and rounded on the child. "This is all your doing, isn't it?"

Harriet backed away in terror.

Caroline was between the angry woman and the little girl, and she squeezed Harriet tightly, casting a disgusted glance at Mrs. Brangley. She decided to ignore the woman and spoke to the child. "Keep your spirits up, dear Harriet. I'll find a way to communicate with you, I promise. Good-bye."

"Miss Percival, you will go upstairs at once and see that those children and that . . . that thing are properly subdued," Mrs. Brangley said in her most imperious manner.

"Indeed I cannot, madam. I suggest you hire a governess," Caroline said sweetly.

Harriet, who had been momentarily forgotten, took the opportunity to slip away. She was quite good at stealing off and slipping people's minds, Caroline knew; the child would probably be none the worse for Mrs. Brangley's outburst. From the back of the hall, Harriet waved and blew a kiss. Tears were still sparkling in her eyes.

Caroline was mindful of the little girl's need to remain hidden, and she made no direct response. But she smiled all the more serenely at Mrs. Brangley.

"Tom," directed the lady, seeing that her footman had hoisted Miss Percival's trunk to his shoulder, "you will not lift a finger to aid that creature."

"Oh." Caroline looked startled, then contrite. "It was

my impression, ma'am, that you would wish me gone as quickly as possible."

Mrs. Brangley heaved a heavy sigh and slammed back into her sanctuary with only a parting glare for Caroline.

Tom had been visibly fighting his reaction to the badger episode. Now he let a choked laugh escape him as he opened the front door onto the wet day. "Where are you going, miss?" he asked.

Caroline straightened her shoulders and readied her umbrella. "I don't know." she said, giving him a smile—probably the cheapest lodgings she could find, in some dismal section of town near an employment agency. "But I don't doubt it will be more restful than this place—if slightly less amusing."

2

A LECTURE was taking place at one of the highly polished dining tables in that sanctum of masculinity known as White's Club. The sound of a cold December rain on the pavement of St. James's Street, when added to the low murmur of gentlemen's voices in the dining room, provided a sober background suitable to the severity of the talk.

Guy Constant took a deep breath, eyeing his brother over the rim of his wine glass as he signaled to a waiter to remove the plates. "To conclude my observations, you're despicable, Evan. May I hope that you'll mature someday into something halfway resembling a gentleman? I thought I'd come to town merely to extricate you from your latest dishonest wager."

"Dishonest? Upon my word, Guy, though you're my brother I'll have to call you out for that," Lord Marchton exclaimed.

Guy looked at the viscount steadily. "That horse was lamed before the race, and by your man's hand. I have the full story, so you may save the pose of outraged honor for someone more gullible."

Evan's face was sulky, but he said nothing.

Wound up to a high pitch of morality himself, the elder brother pursued his point. "Today was the last straw. Trying to seduce a governess, indeed! Have you no sense of propriety?"

"The bitch led me on," muttered Lord Marchton into his china in the instant before the servant changed it.

"Invited me up to the blasted schoolroom. Damn it all, Guy, a man's not made of stone!"

Guy suspected, on the contrary, that his younger brother was composed of something more resembling jelly. Evan looked it, with his watery eyes and elongated features; and his tall figure somehow gave the impression of wafting to and fro with every breeze.

Not for the first time, Guy marveled that his mother could have so forgot herself as to marry the lad's feckless father *en second noces*. And not only that, to have produced a son who was a butter-print of the original yet who, by virtue of blood ties, could not be conveniently misplaced and forgotten. Evan Dawlbury, Lord Marchton, must be a weight around Guy's neck to the end of his days.

"You ought to pass the Christmastide with Mother," Guy suggested, in an effort to put two of his problems under the same roof, and far away from him. The subject of the Brangley's governess was best dropped. Evan would never admit that he had been in the wrong; yet his less than doting brother had no doubt he had been. One could not buy off as many irate fathers and grasping courtesans as Guy had on Lord Marchton's behalf without coming to some less than flattering conclusions about the young man's character.

"Spend the holiday with Mother?" squawked Evan. "Ain't she gone to Wales? Godforsaken place."

"That is indeed the address of her latest candidate for the position of our papa," Guy said dryly. "Lord Effrydd claims to have the blood of the old Welsh princes flowing in him, of course, but I believe he's at least a baron. I met him here the other day; grizzled fellow who looked like he ought to be wielding a battle-ax in some medieval fracas. A regular hearty primitive, and completely under Mother's spell. It would seem that, once again, our esteemed parent believes brevity to be the soul of widowhood."

"Hope he's got plenty of the ready," Evan muttered, shaking his head.

Guy agreed. But there was really no fear to the contrary. Their mother, Lady Lambert in her latest incarnation, had started out with wealth when she married Guy's father. She had progressed to wealth and title with Lord Marchton, and she hadn't seen fit to lower her expectations in the years since. The recently deceased Lord Lambert had been her fourth consort; if Baron Effrydd was to be her fifth, he was bound to possess more than an interesting pedigree and an appreciation of middle-aged beauty.

"Mother would be glad of your company. You might help run this latest bachelor to ground," Guy said in an effort to sweeten the prospect of dull days in the Black Mountains by an appeal to his brother's streak of mischief.

Evan shrugged. "Don't sound half so promising as going with you, I'm afraid, since I lack the funds to remain at liberty."

"And how you can find yourself embarrassed, when your quarter's income would buy and sell most of your expensive friends . . . " Guy was beginning with a long-suffering expression when Evan forestalled him with an elegant raised hand.

"My dear brother, you know my opinion on that. *You* are my most expensive friend. Would that your expansiveness matched your wealth." The young man sighed, and a twinkle appeared in his eye in appreciation of his own bon mot.

Guy couldn't forestall an answering grin. His brother was weak and a perpetual irritant. Besides his womanizing, Lord Marchton did not mind being dishonest when the situation demanded, and Guy had caught him out more than once in nefarious financial schemes of one sort or another that had blessedly been cut short before an open scandal could occur. Yet Evan had his charms. Sometimes, when they shared a moment such as this, Guy forgot his many problems with young Lord Marchton and simply remembered that they were brothers.

The son and heir of his mother's first marriage, Guy

was in his tenth year as an only child when his mama and stepfather presented him with a sibling. He had been elated and taken to the role of older brother with a relish. Not only that, he had done his best to be a sobering influence in Evan's life when the boy's father died, and though he oftentimes resented this obligation, he knew in his heart that he had taken it on unasked.

That was no reason, though, to be a martyr to the cause. "Go to Wales," he urged one more time. "Broaden yourself with travel. You'll be able to say you've seen the other side of Offa's Dyke."

Evan showed a blithe disinterest in anything so esoteric as the building projects of an ancient Mercian king. "I'm better visiting the old duke with you. At least old Davonleigh lives near Bath; not much amusement there, I grant you, but better than what I could find in Wales."

"We won't give much time to Bath. I have business with the Duke of Davonleigh, and then we'll go on down to Somerset for a quiet Christmastide. The company of horses and dogs sounds delightful after an autumn in town."

"But we'll be with Davonleigh a day or two. Bath can't be an hour's ride from his place, and the duke won't notice if I'm there or not," Evan pointed out.

"True," Guy felt bound to admit. "Still and all, I must insist that you keep a grasp on the proprieties. If you accompany me, you must consider it your duty to dance attendance on the old boy. Davonleigh is one of the glummest old recluses in the kingdom, and the properest."

"Why does he want to see you?"

Guy had puzzled over this and come to a satisfactory conclusion. "He likely wishes to buy my Somerset place. There's a ring of standing stones on it, you know, and the duke is fascinated by such things."

"Will you sell it to him?"

"By no means," Guy answered with a smile. "I'm fascinated by such things myself; and the estate has been in my family since the time of Elizabeth. But I have no other plans for the next little while, and I enjoy sparring with the old curmudgeon."

"I'd watch myself," Evan said, eyeing his brother with an unexpected shrewdness. "Davonleigh might have you in his eye as a match for his daughter."

"As an untitled gentleman, I can have little fear of that," Guy said serenely, "but as a matter of fact, brother, you had better watch yourself. Perhaps I've been distinguished because of my grand relations. You may find yourself the candidate for the hand of Lady Georgiana."

Evan shuddered. "No, no matrimony until I'm ready for the bonehouse."

"Much easier to bed governesses," Guy let slip out, with a touch of satire, before he remembered that he hadn't meant to allude to the subject again.

"Why, yes. Except for that blasted one this morning, governesses have always been most obliging."

So! Evan was as good as admitting he had been the aggressor in the morning's unfortunate scene. There had never been any real doubt, so Guy decided to let it pass. "Do yourself a favor, my boy, and stick to housemaids. Governesses are not your sort. You haven't much experience with that breed of upper servant. I've never bought off a governess for you yet. And I believe the young woman this morning was a good example of the reason why a fellow would do better to dally elsewhere: prudish enough to be a problem. That class of person, you see, is brought up to rather a rigid morality. Helps in teaching the little ones, I'm certain, but it's a hindrance to such as you."

"But I did have a governess only last April, during that theatrical party down to Kent for the Easter holidays. Fiery little thing, too, as I recall," Evan said with a touch of smugness.

"An exception to the rule, I fear," Guy replied dryly. "The one this morning would have been trouble; an outraged virgin if ever I saw one. But those blue eyes were rather intriguing."

"Oh," Evan said with a snicker, "did she have eyes?"

Caroline's blue eyes were at that moment wide open, and the owner of them squeezed between two hefty gentlemen on an outside seat of the Bath *White Hart*. Caroline would not allow herself to drop off to sleep, exhausted though she was. The backward perch was precarious indeed, despite the protection of her two burly seatmates, and she was fearful of pitching headlong into the dark road. This was Caroline's first experience of an outside seat on a coach, and she could not say she would recommend it as a mode of travel; but it was better than staying in London.

Her decision to leave the metropolis had been rash, formed in a few sodden minutes on the pavement of Upper Wimpole Street. Tom, the footman, having abandoned her to her fate with a few cheery words of leave-taking, Caroline stood in the rain and contemplated her situation. She was only four-and-twenty, yet it seemed she had been governessing forever. In over six years of service this was her first time of being turned off in so humiliating a manner, but none of her other experiences had been of a kind to make her love the trade.

Surely she might try to find some other sort of post.

Then another thought surged forward, a thought tantalizing in its novelty, though a bit embarrassing at Caroline's advanced age. She wanted her mother.

Mama lived in Bath. In a flash the solution was clear to Caroline: she would visit her mother while trying to find a post at one of the Bath seminaries, of which she assumed there were dozens. From Bath she would write to Mr. Brangley and beg a reference; and she had other, older references from positions she had held before coming to the Brangleys. She would contrive.

She would contrive also to write to Harriet. Perhaps she could beg Mr. Brangley's indulgence in that particular, too. She simply had to communicate with the little girl, to urge her to bear with her fate. She must counsel courage and show the child that she did have someone in the world who cared about her—unlike that despicable, cold guardian, that insolent Mr. Constant.

As the coach rattled toward Bath, bouncing along the road at frightening speed thanks to the noble young whip who had paid to take the ribbons, Caroline wondered uneasily why her thoughts would keep returning to Mr. Constant. He was handsome, of course, and she saw few enough handsome men; in his careless way he had counseled leniency in her case, and she supposed his kindness to her was commendable in its way.

But his treatment of Harriet was infuriating! Rather, his lack of treatment. Nothing could excuse him from such a want of sensitivity to a little girl left in his guardianship. He might at least have bothered to meet the child, to see for himself how she was faring.

Caroline thought of Mr. Constant with resentment and disapproval, but she did think of him.

She woke up before dawn with a jolt, still squeezed between two greatcoats, and fought her way back to consciousness from a disturbing dream. How had she ever fallen asleep during this hellish ride? And, having done so, how could she have dreamed of Mr. Constant kissing her?

Yet she had. She had only seen that face once, but in her dreams it had drawn near to hers, those finely molded lips had covered hers . . .

Caroline carefully eased her arm out from beneath her seatmate's brawny elbow to put a hand to her forehead. Was she going mad? Why should she even remember clearly what a strange man's lips were like?

She shivered in the wind and rain. Reflecting that twenty-four hours ago had seen her in a warm bed, in a prosperous house, in a steady if dismal position that she had expected to hold until little Miss Amanda grew up and left the schoolroom, Caroline concluded that if she herself were not going mad, her world certainly was.

She put Mr. Constant and his disturbing effect on her firmly out of her mind. She would never see the man again. She wouldn't think of him.

The novelty of the journey soon claimed her attention. Caroline hadn't traveled much in late years; her entire childhood had been spent in Hampshire, and since she had been old enough to earn a living, fate had not sent her beyond Surrey and London. Her excitement grew as she came fully awake, and as morning shadows succeeded darkness, the coach bumped down the hill into the city of Bath. Caroline sat up straight and looked about her with great interest.

Through the driving rain she had a blurred impression of whiteness and grace; of noble buildings and graceful crescents and wide squares. The tower of Bath Abbey drew her eye, and she found the coach jolting to a halt in the yard of the White Hart, right across from the church.

Caroline had experienced before the treatment a poor and plain woman received from ostlers, from fellow passengers, from anyone. Still, it was a shock each time it occurred. All the gentlemen with whom she had been traveling outside jumped down in a hurry and went on about their own concerns, doubtless feeling that if they didn't meet the eye of a woman in need of assistance, she didn't exist.

She was used to it, and she even enjoyed, sometimes, being beholden to no one but herself. Within a short time she found herself safely down from the stage, no thanks to anyone but Caroline Percival. Her trunk was at her feet on the cobbles, and she was endeavoring to get a small boy belonging to the inn to assist her with the baggage.

The surliness of said boy was somewhat mitigated by the offer of half a crown that Caroline could ill afford, and he finally engaged to put the trunk in out of the rain until the lady should send for it. He also gave her some cryptic directions to her destination. She supposed there would be someone at her mother's address, Westgate Buildings, who could deal with transporting the box, and she didn't like to show up unannounced with her baggage in tow. Mama would be shocked enough as it was; and perhaps she would have no room to shelter her daughter. Caroline knew so little of her mother's living arrangements.

Squaring her shoulders, Caroline walked out of the inn-yard and into the wet morning streets of Bath. Despite her lack of real rest she was alert, looking about her like any tourist at interesting buildings and the occasional glimpse of green, sodden hills beyond them.

The rain continued to beat down, and in passing a shop window, Caroline spared a thought for her bonnet. The ugly thing didn't even look ruined; the uniform of a governess was so much more serviceable than one would wish. Her own appearance was dreadful, no doubt, though she could not examine it closely in the murky glass. The rain and cold, added to a nearly sleepless night, wouldn't have put her in her best looks.

She asked a rain-drenched milkmaid the way to Westgate Buildings, the inn boy's instructions having run out two streets from the White Hart. She stopped to buy a penny's worth of Christmas greenery from an old woman's basket.

Despite a growing nervousness of meeting her mother in this disgraceful state, despite her great fatigue, she found herself admiring everything about the city of Bath, from the new houses of gracious golden stone to the little alleys that must have dated from the Middle Ages.

At last she reached Westgate Buildings and found herself standing before a door in a shabby corridor. She was beginning to feel very shy. Taking a deep breath, she knocked.

The maid who answered the door was vaguely familiar, but Caroline didn't stop to speak. Her eyes were on the lady stretched out upon the sofa in a small shabby parlor: a thin lady with white-sprinkled brown hair under a widow's cap.

"Mama!" cried Caroline and ran forward.

The lady's blue eyes opened wide: she held out her arms with a look of incredulous joy.

Caroline embraced her, filled with a peace and contentment she hadn't known in twelve years.

"Why, my dear," her mother's soft voice said in her

ear, "you didn't grow very tall, but you are quite a pretty thing. I'm so very, very glad you're here."

Caroline had knelt beside the sofa to put her arms around her mother; now she sat back on her heels and looked earnestly into the face before her. She had a miniature of Mama, taken with Papa about a year before the accident, but she would have expected her mother to have changed more than she had in so many years. There might be more lines about her eyes than formerly, and the brown hair had certainly begun to show gray, but other than that Lady Percival was the same.

"Milady," a hesitant voice said, "is this little Miss Caroline? Oh, what a happy Christmas this will be."

Caroline looked up into the face of the maidservant who had opened the door, and full memory returned. "Binberry, how delightful to see you again. So you're still with Mama, are you?"

Binberry, a sturdy woman with snowy white locks under a voluminous cap, straightened her plump shoulders. "As if I'd be anywhere else but with Lady Percival. Really, miss!" Then her features creased into a smile. "So good to see you, Miss Caroline . . . Miss Percival, now you're all grown up."

Caroline smiled. "How gratifying to be among people who still think me young."

"Caroline!" Lady Percival gave her daughter a kiss and beamed on her. "You can't be twenty-five yet. I assure you I was quite young at that age. I didn't even have you. And now you're here—I'm so glad, but so surprised, that those dreadful people you've been writing of would give you leave to visit me."

"They didn't," Caroline said with a sigh. "I was . . . let go."

"Oh?" Lady Percival spoke the one syllable on a half note of query.

Caroline responded with an abridged account of her misunderstanding with Mrs. Brangley over a young gentleman visitor to the house; and her mother and Mrs.

Binberry were suitably indignant, managing to pick up quickly all Caroline did not say.

"They were ill-bred beasts, and you are well rid of them," Lady Percival pronounced with a shake of her head. "Upper Wimpole Street, indeed!"

Thinking of little Harriet, Caroline could not repress a sigh.

"And now to think of you working in Bath, where you might be near me," her ladyship continued, looking fondly at her child. "I could have wished for nothing better, dear daughter, considering that all higher paths are closed to us."

Caroline looked down to hide a smile at her mother's dramatic turn of phrase—so like her letters!

When Binberry bustled into an alcove to make tea, Caroline glanced about the apartment curiously. Apparently there were only two rooms. She would have to look for other lodging, then; would there be something cheap enough close by?

Her mother noticed her look and proved that the years apart had not lessened her ability to divine what her daughter was thinking. "I have my bedroom in back, my dear, which will take a cot for you. I should think we can hire one quite easily. Binberry has a little chamber at the top of the house. We shall be quite snug."

"Different from Willowdown, isn't it?" Caroline said wistfully, then wondered how she could have been so insensitive.

"Different indeed," Lady Percival answered with a nostalgic smile. Caroline was glad to see that the reference to their old home had not cast her mother down. "But you know, my dear, Bath will have its amusements for you. We'll pass a delightful Christmastide before you take up your new post. I know you'll find one instantly, so you must not begin to look too soon."

Caroline was surprised at how much pleasure the kind exaggeration gave her. "I wish I shared your optimism about the likelihood of a post, Mama." She got to her feet and set about putting the ivy she had brought with her into a glass of water, which she placed in the center of the small mantel shelf. She looked about her, really seeing the room for the first time. The furnishings of the little sitting room were mean and shabby; the one window looked out on the back of the building; yet there was an air of cheer. When Caroline's eyes rested on the wall above her mother's sofa, she saw a watercolor of Willowdown, executed by herself at the age of twelve, not long before the accident.

Willowdown, Papa's seat in Hampshire, the home of the Percivals for centuries. Papa had been the sixth baronet. Caroline had passed the first twelve years of her life at Willowdown in an atmosphere of luxury and love that was now vivid in her memory, now hazy as a dream.

The accident had put an effective stop to happiness. The same overturned carriage that deprived Lady Percival of her husband robbed her of the use of her legs, and she found herself that most expendable of creatures, an indigent invalid and a widow. She had brought no fortune to her marriage, and she and her husband had always spent their income rather than putting anything aside for so distant a possibility as the future. The jointure would barely support her, and she had no relations to turn to for help. As for the estate, it was entailed on her husband's second cousin, the nearest male heir.

There was no small house on the estate suitable for a dowager. Her ladyship removed to rooms at Bath, where the doctors thought the waters would aid her health. As for Caroline, she was allowed to stay with the cousins who had come into possession of Willowdown.

Caroline had been a proud and rather willful girl of twelve. She adjusted with difficulty to poverty and meekness. Such minor indignities as changing to a smaller bedroom in the less modern wing of the house were crushing blows to a child who was struggling with bereavement as well as the sting of lowered consequence.

The cousins were kind if offhand and saw to it that Caroline received a fine education alongside their own two daughters. She could not be considered the equal of her cousins, of course; the difference was always there.

Worst of all, in all the six years she had continued to live at Willowdown, Caroline was not permitted the expensive journey to Bath to visit her mother. Apparently it occurred to no one that a mother and daughter might wish for a sight of each other. And Lady Percival, an invalid whose state would make travel costly and painful, could scarcely come to Caroline even if she had been invited to do so.

Caroline could have been with her cousins yet. She had a clear memory of their shock at her announcement that she wished to earn her own living. A Percival of Willowdown to work for her bread! The family's good name could never bear the disgrace.

Caroline had been with her relations long enough to know a life spent accepting grudging charity would never suit her. As an indigent cousin, she would not be brought out into society, so escape by way of marriage was unlikely. She knew her mother's tiny income would not stretch to accommodate a daughter, which was a pity, for Caroline's first choice would have been to set up housekeeping in Bath with her dear Mama. The cousins could see no necessity of contributing to such an establishment when Caroline was so useful to themselves.

So Caroline found a position as a paid companion to a dowager who lived in Surrey and had made her acquaintance while visiting at Willowdown. Caroline assured the Percivals that no one need know she was from Willowdown, but they had not taken her defection well, and communications in the years since her removal had not been friendly. She doubted whether they would take her back into their household for any other motive than to save themselves from disgrace.

Not that she would go back. No, she had found an odd sort of pride which few of her class would understand, in fending for herself. She accustomed herself to the indignities of poverty, of meaning nothing to anybody. She found it helped not to be at Willowdown when someone treated her as a nonentity or offered her an insult.

The loneliness, the lack of loving guidance except through her mother's letters, the hopeless feelings that washed over her when she considered the future, all these were a severe challenge to one who tried very hard to be good-humored and optimistic. None of her employers ever gave her leave to go to Bath; and as she sent as much of her wages as practicable to her mother in any case, she could not have afforded the trip. Now she had finally made it, when she could afford it even less.

"I can't believe we haven't seen each other in twelve years, Mama," she said. "I simply can't credit it." The dozen years seemed to be fading to nothing now they were together, but such a stretch of time! Half her own life.

"Nor can I."

Mother and daughter were silent for a moment, thinking.

"Servants never get to go home," Caroline said. "No one thinks of it."

"My child, you were not a servant, and I won't have you brooding over your past in any case." Lady Percival spoke briskly. "This will be the most glorious Christmas season; I know it will. I will give you a day or two to rest from that dreadful coach journey, and then, as soon as we can contrive, we must go to the Pump Room so that I can drink my glass. I never go there as an ordinary thing, but with you to push my chair we'll manage quite delightfully. And naturally you must sign the book."

Caroline laughed, glad to be diverted. A glance into the corner of the room had revealed her Mama's Bath chair and reminded her of the tragedy of long ago. "Oh, Mama, I mustn't set myself up as a visitor. I'm here to look for work. I hope to become a resident."

"Whatever you say, of course, my dear, but you mustn't deprive me of my first chance in a lifetime to chaperon a pretty daughter to a public place. Now, we'll send for your baggage at once—the landlady's boy can go—and you must shake out your best and most becoming walking things."

Another peal of laughter broke from Caroline, and for the first time since glimpsing her mother she thought of her own appearance. She was still dripping from the weather, and she doubted her cloak or bonnet had changed for the better in the last day of hard use.

"My best things! Dear Mama, I'm afraid I'm wearing them."

3

LADY PERCIVAL never threw anything away. Her husband's property and the jewels she had worn as a matron were entailed, but she had brought all her personal belongings with her to Bath when she removed from Willowdown. Many of these were fripperies, ribbons and laces and shawls and furs, out-of-fashion gowns and shoes that would never be walked in again. The treasure was stored in a line of trunks in one of the attics in Westgate Buildings, and most of it had lain in lavender for all the years of Lady Percival's residence in Bath.

With the aid of these gifts from the past, Caroline was turned out to her mother's satisfaction when the two of them set forth for the Pump Room a few days after her arrival. Her durable gray bonnet was newly trimmed with cherry ribbons by Lady Percival's own hand. The serviceable pelisse had been altered in the direction of fashion to the best of Caroline's and Mrs. Binberry's ability and was enlivened by a small gray fur capelet. Caroline carried a matching muff, not so large as those currently in vogue, but passable.

The rain of the past several days had stopped during the night, and the morning was cold and cloudy with nothing more than an ominous dampness in the air. Caroline had no fear of the weather; the rain would simply not be so cruel as to come on again after so many dreary days. She wheeled her mother's chair along the streets with every expectation of pleasure in the outing. She was finding joy already in the fresh air and new sights, in nearly the first walk she had taken for years unaccompanied by squirming children.

After only a few days spent in her mother's society, Caroline was undergoing a metamorphosis of sorts. She felt herself becoming more the baronet's daughter, less the governess, with each passing hour. All the time they had been together, Caroline and her mother had talked until their tongues were weary, going over the many things that had happened in their separate lives and that no letter could do justice to. Caroline had found that, under the indigence and ill health, Lady Percival was still very much the lady of the manor; and what more natural than that a daughter should follow a mother's lead?

Caroline had been used to consider herself alone in the world. Now she realized fully that she did belong to somebody, and that if Mama, who was frivolous even in her state of invalid poverty, was not quite the steadying influence many mothers were, she was undeniably a doting parent. Caroline was first in Lady Percival's affections. Along with that distinction, she found herself accepting gratefully, but with a grain of salt, those kind notions of her mother's that set her up as much prettier and cleverer than she was.

In true daughterly fashion she wished she might live up to her mother's inflated opinion of her looks. She had allowed the cherry ribbons to trim her dismal bonnet; she had even done something more, let her brown hair free itself into soft curls rather than tame it back with braids in her usual unobtrusive style, designed to make her even plainer. Her color was better after a few nights of sleep, though on a rather hard cot; and Caroline regretted only that she had no new gown to set off her walking finery.

Her mother looked dignified, fragile, everything that a baronet's relict should be. Lady Percival's best walking things had not been much used in late years, and she and Binberry had managed to urge them into the current mode by a skillful plying of the needle. Caroline had noticed, as she helped with the sewing, that her mother possessed the light and knowing touch of a modiste, and a multitude of fashion knowledge culled from the periodicals that made up the largest share of her reading.

Caroline's unexpected arrival had set up Lady Percival royally, Mrs. Binberry had confided to the young lady when they had a moment alone one evening after her ladyship had been put to bed. Lady Percival was normally quiet and withdrawn and never went out for pleasure despite Binberry's pleading. That she wished to do so now was all due to Caroline, and Binberry's belief was that getting back into the world would do her mistress every good service. Caroline thus felt a pleasant sense of duty well done as she spent time with her mother in frivolous pursuits rather than immediately setting out to find a position in a seminary.

When Caroline first viewed the Pump Room over the rim of Lady Percival's plumed bonnet, she couldn't hold back a start of surprise. Accustomed to London, she was used to thinking of Bath as Londoners did, as a backwater of sorts, a place certainly second in fashion to Town: the quiet habitat of invalids like her mother rather than the leader of resorts it had been in years past. A place most renowned for its dowagers and schoolgirls could not be in the first stare of fashion.

Still, the loiterers and patrons assembled amidst the classical decorations of the Pump Room had all rather a daunting air. Caroline had never really been to a public place aside from the London parks, where the children clinging to her hands had marked her as a governess and beneath anyone's notice. Now she felt herself flushing as curious eyes turned toward her; even some male eyes, she noted in astonishment.

Could cherry ribbons do so much? She puzzled over this phenomenon as she wheeled Mama to the book of arrivals. Lady Percival wished to turn over the leaves, even if Caroline wouldn't sign, and so they did, Caroline staring unseeing at rows of unfamiliar names while her mother murmured at some, exclaimed at others. Lady

Percival had not kept up with her old acquaintances, lacking the means to appear in social circles. Also, Caroline had gathered that Mama had no wish for her friends' pity. For years her only outing had been into the warm baths near Westgate Buildings. But she knew quite a bit about her former world from a determined study of the newspapers, and Caroline's arrival seemed to have reawakened this interest.

By the time her ladyship had finished her perusal, Caroline was beginning to be more at ease. For one thing the dozens of faces that had been staring at her so intently had turned to the next arrival; and, for another, she was beginning to realize that she was no longer a governess and had as much right to parade about the Pump Room as any other creature. She would be a teacher soon, and there would end all her acquaintance with the social side of Bath; but for now, why shouldn't she enjoy herself?

As she wheeled Mama's Bath chair toward a likely wall where several other invalids' chairs were positioned, two females rushed up. Caroline brought the chair to a halt just in time to avoid a collision.

"Lady Percival!" cried the elder, a comfortably large woman in late middle age whose clothing proclaimed her to be rich if not overly refined. "I had heard you lived in Bath but never went out, and so I had no hope we would meet. How delighted I am to see you. This is my daughter Desideria."

The younger of the two ladies staged a sweeping curtsy much enhanced by the scarlet pelisse, trimmed in white fur, that twirled about her. She had raven hair and sparkling dark eyes and a statuesque figure that had so far escaped the less than elegant proportions of her mother's.

Caroline could not see her own mother's face, but a split second of hesitation from her told Caroline as well as any words that Lady Percival did not recall the acquaintance. She tilted her head to look at Caroline; a pleading look.

Caroline did her best to salvage the situation. Speaking up with more bravado than was her wont, she said brightly, "I'm Lady Percival's daughter, madam. I don't believe I've had the pleasure?"

Thankfully, the ruse worked. "Mrs. Dutton," the stout lady said, holding out her hand. "Dear me! A grown-up daughter of about my Desideria's age, I would say . . ." She scrutinized Caroline. "Or a little older. I do congratulate you, dear Lady Percival." With a fawning gesture she turned back to the lady in the Bath chair. Then she again eyed Caroline with a sudden, sunny smile. "But of course! I remember now. Miss Caroline, isn't it?"

"My daughter is my greatest comfort," Caroline's mother said in a careful tone. Caroline surmised that Mama still hadn't placed the women.

"As my Desideria is mine," Mrs. Dutton said, beaming. "I've been widowed since I saw you last, dear Lady Percival, and while Mr. Dutton cut up warm, you know—I have no complaints on that score—I find I miss his company more than I would have thought. Desideria has been like a rock, Lady Percival. A rock, upon my soul."

Miss Dutton grinned in a self-deprecating manner and shrugged fur-trimmed shoulders.

"Has your mother been acquainted with mine long?" Caroline asked the young woman as the two elder ladies exchanged some further civilities. She could sense Mama's continued ignorance of exactly who these people were and determined to help solve the mystery if she could.

"I must confess I've no idea," Miss Dutton replied. Her voice was melodious and carried a hint of a less than refined accent. "Mama knows so many people. You must come to see us, Miss Percival. I insist upon it. It must be very dull for you if your mother don't go out—and I don't see how she could in that chair."

Caroline murmured some noncommittal reply, smiling politely.

"Caroline," Lady Percival said at this moment, "I have

the most dreadful feeling I'm blocking people's way. If you could move me over to the wall, Mrs. Dutton and I might continue to converse in a little more comfort. I see a seat over that way for her."

"And I ought to fetch your glass," Caroline added, beginning to steer for the spot. This was the oddest predicament. She had felt a little pang on entering the room that they were likely to have no friends in the place, but the Duttons were so oddly intimate, for strangers, that she would almost have preferred not to have met them.

With a sudden shriek Miss Dutton turned aside to greet a group of young ladies, and Caroline continued to push the Bath chair while Mrs. Dutton trotted along beside it, still making conversation.

Caroline knew hers for a suspicious nature, and she was a bit ashamed of her own feeling that Mrs. Dutton must be a mushroom and a toad-eater, cultivating Lady Percival for some unknown reason. Why she had this impression, she could not say. Perhaps it was the way "your ladyship" dropped from the woman's lips with every sentence.

"I'll be right back with your water, Mama," Caroline said when she had settled the Bath chair, and Mrs. Dutton had plumped herself down upon the bench beside it. "Do you take a glass, too, ma'am?" she addressed their new acquaintance.

"Drink the waters? Oh, heavens no, child, they would be the death of me! I'm only in Bath for the company and to bathe," Mrs. Dutton said with a friendly nod.

Caroline set out for the pump and soon had a glass in hand. She was halfway across the room with this when someone caught at her elbow, causing her to spill some of the water.

She turned and found herself looking into the vapid face of Lord Marchton, which she had expected never to see again.

"Why, my dear," the young man drawled as he favored her with a look full of meaning, "I confess myself flattered. I don't often have a petticoat follow me quite this distance."

Caroline's surprise had caused a sort of paralysis of limb and tongue, but now she found her voice and tried to snatch her elbow away. "Are you mad, sir? Please let me pass. I fear you mistake me for someone else."

The remark was a lucky one; Lord Marchton was evidently slow of wit enough to be taken in and believe himself to be in error. His expression changed from knowing intimacy to puzzlement, and he dropped Caroline's arm. She walked quickly away.

"Some acquaintance, my dear?" Lady Percival was eyeing her daughter with interest as Caroline put the glass into her hands and settled in to stand beside her. Mrs. Dutton had excused herself for a moment to speak to two other ladies over the way, and Lady Percival wore a definite air of relief. "Quite an acceptable young man, I would say; not handsome, and not much countenance, but in our situation one mustn't expect miracles."

"The miracle would be if he doesn't approach me again to insult me," Caroline murmured. "He's the one, Mama, he's the one I told you about—the one in London."

"Oh." With an air of disappointment, Lady Percival scrutinized the young man through a quizzing glass. He was still looking at Caroline and wearing a thoughtful frown. "Somehow I had quite a different picture of a vile seducer."

"I'm sure his lordship sees himself in every bit as dashing a light as one could wish," Caroline said. "Unfortunately, he can't transform himself on the outside."

"The gentleman with him, now, is much more my idea of the rakish sort."

Caroline had been studiously avoiding the area Lord Marchton occupied. Now she glanced over. Mr. Constant was standing with his brother, and he appeared to be listening with great gravity as Marchton gesticulated wildly in Caroline's direction.

Before she could look away, her eyes met Constant's.

She resolutely cast her glance down and noticed, as though she had never seen them before, how scratched the buttons of her pelisse were.

Then a thought struck her. This sighting of Mr. Constant was not simply an embarrassment. It was an opportunity she wouldn't have dreamed of, and she must use it. Murmuring an excuse to her mother, she crossed the room, pausing before the two gentlemen with what she hoped was a distant yet friendly smile.

"Mr. Constant, good morning." Caroline was beginning to wonder at her own courage. She even managed another smile in response to his evident astonishment. "May I beg a word with you?"

The gentleman bowed, still looking at her as though she had appeared before him unclothed. "Go away, Evan," he said to his brother.

"I say," Marchton objected, "she's my conquest, you know, Guy. Ain't fair."

"I don't wish to speak to his lordship, sir; my business is with you," Caroline said, ignoring the younger man.

"Ah! Business. I understand." Constant gave her a keen look. "Well, then, madam. Shall we promenade the room? Evan, leave us. This will go much better without your aid."

Lord Marchton frowned, but his brother must have exerted some authority. He did as he was told, going to stand in a corner of the Pump Room and indulge in an evident fit of the sulks.

Once he and Caroline were alone, Constant did not mince words. "I find it difficult to credit that you have really followed me to Bath to extort money from me," he told her, speaking in an even tone as he led her down the room, "but I must believe the evidence of my eyes. Well, madam, how much is it to be? And what, precisely, is your threat? My brother didn't quite seduce you, as I understand it; is it merely because he tried that you feel you deserve some compensation?"

Caroline stopped walking and gazed at him, aghast.

"Why, you pompous and infuriating blackguard! How dare you say such things to me?"

Constant smiled—a world-weary smile that did not reach his eyes. "My dear young woman, did you not express a wish to discuss business with me? What other business can I have with someone of your stamp?" He touched the fur capelet that draped her shoulders. "Not so downtrodden as you appeared, are you? What do the Brangleys say to their governess's headlong journey into the west of England in pursuit of a man? On the trail of two men, I should say. And how the devil you discovered where we were going—"

"Do you seriously suppose that I knew you would be here—that any woman would go anywhere in search of you?" Caroline said through clenched teeth. "Good morning, sir. You are a conceited boor. Forget the business I mentioned. A man who could insult a female with so little regard for her feelings or the fact that this is a public place would never have a moment to spare to think of a little girl's comfort. I'll find some other way."

She turned on her heel and left him standing in the middle of the floor. The room was becoming more crowded by the moment, and Constant could not follow her without making a spectacle of them both. So much for her plan to ask the man if she might write a note to Harriet under his cover! She would find some other way; she would beg the favor of Mr. Brangley when she wrote to ask him for a reference, and that she must do this very day, for time and her savings were growing short . . .

"My dear!" Suddenly Miss Dutton was at Caroline's elbow. "Who was that devastatingly attractive man? Do present me."

"I . . . we aren't on good terms," Caroline said shortly.

Subtlety was wasted on Miss Dutton. "Oh, I could see that. Fancy, a disagreement with so eligible-looking a gentleman, and in the middle of the Pump Room. I wouldn't have the courage, I vow. Is he your beau?"

"Oh, heavens no," Caroline protested, reddening.

"Ah!" Miss Dutton eyed first Caroline, then Constant,

with an air of calculation. "Well, my dear, I must make my adieux, for Mama has been winking at me this age. I have a fitting in Milsom Street, and I fear we're late. Don't forget what I said. We're in Camden Place, and I quite depend upon you to call."

Caroline again made noncommittal noises and expressed her pleasure in the acquaintance. She made her way back to her mother's chair as quickly as she could.

"How was your meeting with those gentlemen, dear?" Lady Percival asked. "I take it the good-looking fellow isn't another man who insulted you?"

"Not in the way you mean, Mama," Caroline said, shaking her head. "I'll tell you all about it when we get home. Shouldn't we be leaving now? I heard someone mention it is coming on to an icy rain."

Guy Constant watched as that governess, whatever her name was, pushed a middle-aged lady's Bath chair out of the Pump Room. What was going on?

The chit was looking much better than she had that day in the Brangleys' house, he considered, remembering the plain young woman who had not wished to raise her eyes to his. Today she had stared him full in the face in her anger; curls he had not noticed before peeped out from under her bonnet, which, though a shabby affair, had a certain indefinable air of fashion. The furs were not something one associated with a governess, either, and added to his vague impression that the impudent miss was not quite who or what she seemed to be.

Most revealing of all, he had seen her pause to have what looked like a conversation about himself with a vulgar beauty, likely a fellow adventuress.

How in heaven's name had the girl found her way to Bath, and so quickly? She was obviously on the trail of himself and Evan; nothing could be clearer. He could guess that she had somehow heard of his business with the Duke of Davonleigh and decided to follow them. Her reasons had to be mercenary.

She must be a witch to have guessed he and his

brother would be stopping in Bath on their way to Davonleigh's estate; they wouldn't have done it if Guy hadn't given in to Evan's pleas for a look at what kind of society was gathered in the watering place. The boy was thinking of dashing back into the town as soon as he greeted the duke, and Guy didn't really blame him. Davonleigh had the reputation of being the stodgiest old man in England.

Both brothers had been shocked, though, to find the Brangleys' governess lying in wait when they strolled into the Pump Room.

Guy wondered in passing what those angry words of hers had meant—something about a little girl—he couldn't imagine. And why had she acted so outraged at his seeing through her plot? An adventuress should be more knowing than that; humor would have served her better than that self-righteous pose.

Her eyes were even bluer than he remembered. And her pelisse outlined a most tempting figure. One could understand Evan's attraction, Constant thought with the air of a connoisseur. The miracle was that his brother had seen through the girl's quiet looks, for Evan was not one to appreciate subtle beauty. The lad was usually enraptured by guinea-gold curls and bosoms full enough to be worthy of gasps and goggles from passersby.

Evan sidled up to his brother and said, in an undertone, "What did you tell the girl? She left as though you'd offered her a slip on the shoulder. Didn't, did you? I don't call that brotherly treatment at all. I say, I must be flattered that she followed me this far. Didn't think she had it in her. The little thing must be rewarded, don't you find? Advance me enough for a couple of days at a country inn, and I'll pay her well for her trouble."

"Evan, you are incorrigible," Guy said with a sigh. "I don't think . . . I don't know, but I can't think she came after you. I believe she's willing to spread the scandal of your attempt to dally with a governess and wishes me to pay her off. She can't know your reputation is already too bad to be worth saving."

"I say, are you going to pay her off?" Evan asked sharply.

"Never," Guy answered with a grim frown. "I rebuffed her, and I have no reason to suppose she'll be stupid enough to approach me again."

"I'll approach *her* then," Evan said, grinning. "I say, a great thing to have some interest for the days ahead."

"You might find a greater interest in the duke's daughter," Guy said. "Besides, we will not be staying in the region indefinitely. I've been thinking that Brighton might be gayer at this time of year, since you're so set against my country place and neither one of us wishes to hole up with some dull set of people in a great house." Brighton was a new idea; it had just this moment passed through his mind. No use giving that girl the satisfaction of running them to ground so easily. He would like to see her follow them down to Sussex; though if she did, he would have to give her credit for ingenuity and persistence.

"Brighton in December?" Evan shivered. "Whatever you say, old boy, you hold the purse strings. But I still maintain that governess would be worth my while."

"She's trouble and we're well out of it. Well, we've put our names in the book and had a look around. Shall we continue on our journey now and present ourselves at Davonleigh?"

"Suppose we have to," Evan said, shrugging. "I say, do you think Lady Georgiana is as dull as they paint her?"

"I could not really say." Guy spoke with a reproving frown. "I beg of you, Evan, don't ask her that to her face."

Lord Marchton raised his brows in astonishment. "Good lord, Guy, you act as if I've no address at all."

"Merely an impression I've picked up from your recent activities, my boy," his brother said with a sigh. "Governess, indeed." His eyes narrowed. "Before we go, remind me to have some inquiries set in motion."

"Inquiries about what?"

"About whom," Guy corrected his brother with a wise look. "Can you tell me what the governess was called, do you think? The Brangley woman mentioned her name, but I've forgot it."

"Something like Smith, wasn't it?" Evan squinted in an effort to recall. His eyes then opened wide, giving him a less sleepy look than he ordinarily wore. "You're going to find out about her?"

"If I can. Well, your memory is no better than mine, so I suppose I must start by introducing myself to that stout woman her companion was speaking with and begging the name of the lady in the Bath chair. That should be a start."

"Just so," Evan said with a shrug. "I say, brother, I shan't call it fair if you try to set the girl up for yourself. Not sporting, old fellow."

"Such an abomination never crossed my mind," Guy said serenely. "I am only trying to become informed."

"Always a busybody," Evan muttered.

Guy made no reply to his brother's insult. He was too much aware of the truth of the epithet.

4

"MY DEAR, I'm mortified, but I cannot place Mrs. Dutton," Lady Percival said, accepting a cup of tea from Caroline's hand once the pair had arrived back at their lodgings. "And I've met so few people in late years, I confess to some surprise at my own stupidity. She's not the sort of female one would forget. I'm dreadfully bad at names, of course, but surely I would have recalled such a manner."

"Perhaps it will come to you," Caroline said. "Her daughter asked me to visit. I think she was trying to be kind. But since we can't call them real acquaintances, I needn't go."

"Oh, my love, you must." Lady Percival put her teacup down on the arm of the sofa and clasped her hands in a dramatic gesture. "Only think, Caroline. I have not the means to introduce you to any sort of society, and though these Duttons were a little . . . "

"Vulgar?" Caroline suggested, feeling a bit ashamed of herself.

"Well, yes. I would not be surprised if the husband had had some association with trade. But they seemed altogether good-hearted, and I shall surely recall where I met the mother. If you go to see them, they might know people of more refinement than themselves, for they seem rich enough, and the females they were both talking to at the Pump Room looked respectable. And I would so like to have you go to parties, to see you live the life of a normal young lady for once."

Caroline didn't bother to give what had by now become her usual argument that she was too old to be a young lady; this line did not set well with her mother and was even beginning to annoy herself. She tried a different view. "Oh, Mama. You know I'm going to be looking for work starting tomorrow. I don't want to set up as a young lady, and I don't really have the time. When next we meet, I'll tell Miss Dutton that I'm a former governess, and I'm certain she won't pursue the acquaintance once she knows."

"Need you begin searching for a post at once?" Lady Percival said faintly. "Can't you enjoy Christmas first?"

Caroline had looked over the state of her purse that morning and was convinced that no time was to be lost in settling herself. She signed. "Mama, I'll have a much happier Christmas if I know I won't be starving in the new year."

"Oh, dear. Caroline," and Lady Percival's eyes filled with tears, "I can hardly bear to see you wasting your youth."

"I'm sorry," Caroline said. For some unaccountable reason, she felt guilty for having to earn her living, then resentful that Mama had led her to such a feeling, then guiltier than ever. She tried to hide these unpleasant sentiments by behaving with exceptional good spirits and, as usually occurs in such cases, ended by feeling genuinely cheerful.

By the afternoon of the next day, Caroline's heightened mood had suffered a setdown. She had visited four schools, none of which had an opening for a junior pupil-teacher, though the last place, Mrs. Havelock's in Pulteney Street, had held out half a hope if Caroline would be willing to work for half the normal salary.

Caroline sighed as she directed her steps across Pulteney Bridge. She had some errands in Cheap Street, and then she would go home. If she didn't know that Bath contained many more schools than those she had canvassed, she would be quite discouraged.

Wondering if the school-teaching project would have

to be abandoned in favor of a desperate search for another governess position, Caroline proceeded into Bridge Street once her shopping was complete. She was not quite ready to go home and meant to wander a little to cheer herself; she would have to show a bright face to Mama. She consciously straightened her back, and, hating the feeling of poverty that warred constantly with the secret, deeper sentiment, that she was a baronet's well-born daughter and ought not to be vexed with earning her own living, she stopped to buy a paper of hot chestnuts. Buying even so trivial an item gave her an illusion of prosperity. Mama had a delightfully juvenile fondness for chestnuts and a sort of childlike wonder at every treat. Caroline tucked the paper into her reticule in pleased anticipation.

Then, and not for the first time, a twinge of something like envy shot through her: envy for the young ladies she saw passing in carriages and on foot, fashionably dressed and looking quite at leisure. Whereas she was stealing a free moment, frivolously spending a penny on a luxury when it might better have been applied to a daily loaf . . .

"I must be daft," she murmured aloud; then glanced around to make certain she had given none of the passersby that very impression.

She knew what was wrong with her, or thought she did. For years she had molded herself into the perfect governess; she had grown comfortable in the between-stairs world of the upper servant. Yet give her a week with her mother, talking over old times at Papa's estate, and she was only a dissatisfied, shabby, displaced member of the gentry, dwelling on former glories instead of going on with her life. How could she be so weak?

Mama could not be blamed, or not altogether. She loved to talk of the past, but she didn't do so in a regretful way except in regard to Caroline. She never left off lamenting that her daughter, unlike herself at a similar age, would have no chance to meet and marry a gentleman of good family and adequate fortune.

This was the sort of maternal rhapsodizing that must be universal. Caroline could understand and take Mama's dramatic flights only half-seriously; but worse were the feelings in her own heart, the deep dissatisfaction with her lot, which proved her to be contemptible, not the self-sufficient creature she had taken such pride in believing herself to be.

Caroline's face was pensive as she turned into the High Street, and she wasn't seeing anyone. Thus, when a gentleman bowed before her, she stepped back with a start. Taking a good look at her accoster, she turned on her heel and began to walk quickly in the other direction.

"Your pardon, ma'am."

He was following her. She kept walking. If there was one thing she was not in the mood for, it was more insults from that cruel Mr. Constant.

A hand caught her arm—a damnably strong hand. Caroline stopped and stared pointedly at the gentleman's glove. "That is your brother's trick, sir. Do you propose to detain me in the public street while you take me to task for more of my imagined crimes? Or perhaps you mean to fetch a constable. Aren't there laws against the extortion you accuse me of?"

"Will you not look at me, ma'am, and perhaps stroll along in my company? We're beginning to attract attention." He murmured these words close to her bonnet brim.

"Oh!" Caroline looked about her, aghast. She had next to no acquaintance in Bath, but for the first time she realized that every strange woman she passed in the street could be the headmistress of some seminary and a potential employer. She forced herself to smile at Mr. Constant and to take his offered arm.

"Now," she said in the pleasantest tone she could manage, as they walked in seeming harmony past shop windows lively with Christmas greenery, "why did you accost me, sir? It was my impression that you wished never to see my face again."

Constant looked at her; she forced herself to meet his

steady gaze and wondered at the lack of malice in it. "It's quite simple, ma'am. I find I must apologize."

Her heart leaped. "Oh? For what?"

He laughed. "I admit I committed more than one crime at our last encounter, but I suppose you may choose among them. I've found out since yesterday, Miss Percival, that you came to Bath because your mother lives here, and that your meeting with me was quite an accident."

Caroline's steps slowed as she took this in. "You are telling me that you—or no, not you, probably some agent of yours—someone has been following me about and asking questions, invading my privacy in the most inexcusable manner. I wasn't even aware that you knew my name."

"Madam, you must allow that we met in the Pump Room in suspicious circumstances. I had seen you but once before, in London, and I believed you to be the object of my brother's mischief. Not a week later I come upon you in Bath, in suspiciously better looks, and you demand to speak to me on a matter of business."

Caroline took deep breaths as she forced herself not to rage at him as she had the day before. How could he have been so vain, so incredibly conceited as to believe she would follow him across the country, on whatever motive? He even found a way to insult what she knew was an improvement in her appearance. And now he had been following her, making her name a byword—he had as good as admitted it.

Constant seemed to discern that such thoughts were passing through her head. "I can only ask you to forgive me for everything. I am not a trusting man, Miss Percival."

"I should say not," she replied, with difficulty maintaining her sedate walk by his side. She was longing to run away from him. "So you made your inquiries and satisfied yourself that I came here by the coach the very day you saw me in London; that I am visiting my mother; and nothing else, I presume. There is nothing else to know about me."

"You're much too modest, ma'am." He hesitated. "I'm afraid I'd formed no favorable opinion of the Brangleys from my slight intercourse with them. I'm glad to see they granted you a Christmas holiday, especially after my brother's antics gave you such trouble with Mrs. Brangley."

She forced herself to nod and hoped her bonnet's poke would conceal her expression, which she feared was halfway between a grin and a grimace. He did not need to know about her problems.

"I accept your apology, sir," she said because there was really nothing else to say. Part of her wished to cause a scene, for his lack of trust in her motives was infuriating. Yet why should he have trusted her, a complete unknown from a class he doubtless thought of as amoral and grasping? She was suddenly desperate to end this encounter. "I turn here."

"What?" He peered down the medieval alley she had indicated. "Surely this isn't the way to Westgate Buildings."

"You know where I live?" Caroline burst out. "Oh, I forget. You've been sneaking about after me. Spying." She gave in to the temptation uppermost in her thoughts and walked quickly away from him.

He followed her down the alley. "My dear young woman, this is absurd. We can't part with your hating me."

"Why not?" Caroline spun around and looked a challenge into his eyes.

He was silent for a moment, apparently taken aback. Then he began to speak. "This is a season of forgiveness, a time when there is a softening in the most hardened of hearts, which I feel yours is not. It will soon be the new year, and with that will come a new beginning for all of us." He smiled and stared intently into her face. "Would you have me haunted by this experience?"

His change of manner was almost unnerving, but totally disarming. Much against her better judgment, Caroline smiled back. She had remembered something. For whatever unaccountable reason, this gentleman had turned friendly, and she could ask him that favor now. Or could she?

"I'll run the risk of your hating me all over again, Mr. Constant, and begin again on the subject I tried to open in the Pump Room." They were standing still now, in the shadow of the overhanging second story of an ancient shop, and Caroline steeled herself against his reaction.

"The business you mentioned." His voice was calm, and his expression didn't register disgust, though he did not look altogether pleased. "What is it?"

"May I write a letter and send it under your cover?" Caroline asked quickly, getting the words out before he could begin to berate her. "To your ward—to Miss Deauville."

"To the child? Of course. But why such anxiety? You'll surely be seeing her when you return to London."

Caroline cast down her eyes. She had forgotten that asking for his help in writing to Harriet would betray that she would not be seeing the little girl soon again. She would not have him pity her. How could she retrieve the situation?

"That's right. I can surely wait and give her my Christmas greetings when I see her later," she said with a laugh, trying her best to cover for her mistake. She had noticed before, from her experience with children, that lies were most often caught out when they became too elaborate. "I'm sorry to have bothered you for nothing."

There was a silence. Then, "You lost the position, didn't you?" he said with a penetrating look.

She had to glance away from those keen gray eyes, so full of . . . of what? Concern? How extraordinary. Pity? How embarrassing. "And if I did sir, it's my own business. I'm well provided for."

"Are you?" He frowned at her. "Then why were you a governess in the first place?"

Caroline swallowed. "I meant that I'm well provided

with the skills to find another post as soon as I wish one.
I've decided to change professions and become a teacher
at a school, you know. Bath is the natural place to look;
there is a young ladies' seminary on every corner, and
I'm waiting only to pass the Christmas with my mother
before I set to work again."

"Oh." His frown relaxed, but he still looked serious. "I
feel in some measure responsible for the fix you're in,
ma'am, for it was my devilish brother who got you into
your employer's bad graces in the first place.

Caroline shrugged. "You can hardly control your
brother's actions. And Mrs. Brangley wasn't much of an
employer, but I did love little Harriet. So, sir, if I might
write the child a line and send it by you, I would be most
grateful. I'm certain, you see, that Mrs. Brangley would
tear up any letter from me, but nothing would be more
natural than for you to write to your ward."

"I've never done it yet," he said, shaking his head.
"And even more naturally the Brangleys would open any
correspondence that arrived for such a young child, and
your secret would be out."

"True." Caroline hadn't thought of that. "Well, here is
another idea. Would you simply send Harriet my love
and a Christmas message from me when you do write to
her? She's the dearest little thing, and so alone; I do recommend that you get to know her."

"You really were fond of the child, weren't you?"

"I was. I am."

Constant found himself wishing for some odd reason
that he had indeed taken a look at the little girl when
he'd been in London. He hadn't thought it at all necessary at the time; a small female child could have nothing
in common with him, and she was well placed with
cousins who included a girl of about her age. She could
require nothing from a guardian but the straightforward
administration of her trust.

Harry Deauville had been a friend, and a good one.
When he and his young wife met their untimely deaths
from putrid fever, a local epidemic that strangely spared

their child, Guy hadn't been shocked to find that he had been named their daughter's guardian. Deauville had always laughed at Constant for being a staid and sensible fellow, and the couple had no near relations.

Their distant relations, if the Brangleys were any example, were not the trustworthy sort. Mrs. Brangley was a terror, and her husband, though jovial in manner, had the reputation for shady dealings upon 'Change. But these facts hadn't bothered Guy with regard to Harriet's living situation. The Brangleys were established in comfortable style. Children, if Constant's memory served him correctly, rarely spent time in the company of their elders anyway.

Now, for the first time, Guy thought with a pang of his dead friend and wondered if he had been somewhat less than attentive as a guardian. Yes, he would certainly meet the child when next he was in Town. He might bring her a toy; she would bob a little curtsy, and his conscience would be clear.

"I've thought of something," Miss Percival said, breaking into his thoughts. "If you would but write a letter to the butler, Mr. Howes, that would get my message to Harriet soonest. The Brangleys will be gone away by now. They always pass the Christmas with Mrs. Brangley's brother in Croydon."

"And Harriet?"

Caroline sighed. "Last year she was left alone with me. We had a very happy Christmas, in point of fact. This year I suppose they'll take her with them unless they leave her with the servants."

Guy frowned. He would definitely have to look into the matter.

"I'll write a letter to the butler," he promised, giving Caroline a reassuring smile. "As soon as you like."

"Oh, famous." The schoolboy expression slipped out, and Caroline offered him a smile in return, exposing a bewitching dimple in one cheek. "I'll compose a message and send it to you at . . . may I ask the name of your hotel, sir?" The last words were spoken with a blush.

"The White Hart, ma'am. We're fixed there for a number of days, my brother and I. My business here is taking longer than I expected."

In point of fact he had visited the Duke of Davonleigh on the day before, had a good-natured quarrel over his Somersetshire property—for that was indeed the purport of the duke's summons to his distant connection—and was now free. Lady Georgiana, whom he had feared would be thrust into his company or that of Evan, had not materialized. She was on a visit and not due back for a few days.

The whole thing had been simplicity incarnate. Guy had told himself that his entire reason for staying in Bath was Evan's desire to attend a Christmas ball at the Upper Rooms. His inquiries regarding Miss Percival—rather a nameless female who went about with a lady in a Bath chair—had been laughably easy, as effortless as his visit to the duke. Miss Caroline Percival was nothing less than what she claimed to be.

She was rather more, now he thought of it. "How did a baronet's daughter ever become a governess?" he asked curiously.

Caroline drew in her breath; then she gave him a strange look. "Are you wishing for entertainment at my expense, sir? Surely you know I didn't simply select teaching as an interesting career."

"I'm sorry." He was; he knew without asking that need must have motivated her. He had been insensitive again. She seemed to bring out that thoughtless side of his personality.

"It's a simple story," Caroline said. "My father's estate was entailed; he died an untimely death and hadn't yet provided for my mother and me beyond her marriage settlement, which was quite modest. My mother had no private fortune, and her jointure was not enough to keep me, too. That is all."

"And your relations? Could they not provide for you?"

She took a deep breath. "Sir, my family is a private

matter. Naturally there are hundreds of poor relations being supported in shabby gentility all over England. Perhaps you support some yourself. I simply didn't choose to be one of them. I wished to direct my own fate."

"But you—"

"Sir, I've already said too much."

"I see." But this time he didn't really see; there was more to her story. There had to be all those little details that set each similar tale of hardship apart from the next, and he wished he knew hers. He could not be so ill-mannered as to insist, though, when the subject evidently caused her pain.

He looked at her, trying to penetrate her facade, wondering why he was so curious about this young woman. She was only an ordinary creature, not so plain as she had been at first sight, but still nothing out of the common way.

Why the deuce was she arousing a most uncommon interest in him—he who had always steered clear of entanglements with females?

As he considered this, and she walked by his side, cheeks flushed to a becoming hue, they emerged from the alley into Milsom Street.

"Miss Percival!" shrieked a feminine voice, and they both looked toward the sound.

Caroline sighed. Desideria Dutton was waving her handkerchief from the window of a large carriage painted a bright blue and silver. Caroline waved back and would have gone on, but Desideria erupted from the vehicle and ran up to them on the pavement.

Her fine dark eyes were sparkling, and she clasped Caroline's hands with the freedom of a lasting friendship, not a mere day's acquaintance. "My dearest creature, you must let me take you up. Since you haven't a carriage—I mean, my mama told me you and your mother live in Westgate Buildings, in the most modest style—I cannot let you walk all the way back there."

"It isn't far," Caroline protested.

"Oh, but it is. A shocking distance," Desideria said, simpering in the direction of Mr. Constant, "and dear Lady Percival must worry so if you are really walking about alone, for I don't see a servant . . . "

Caroline knew a hint when she saw it, and she knew no way of avoiding the introduction. "You are right, ma'am. I have no servant with me. This gentleman and I met by chance only a moment ago. Do let me introduce you. Miss Dutton, this is Mr. Constant." She could add nothing by way of clarifiers; she felt it would be dishonest to claim Constant as a friend, and she didn't wish to exaggerate and say that Miss Dutton was.

"I believe I met your charming mother yesterday, ma'am," said Constant with a bow.

"Oh, yes! Now I recall." Desideria's expression grew even brighter, if possible, as she remembered that she already had a connection with the gentleman. For why else would he have spoken with her mother if not to make inquiries about a certain lovely daughter?

Caroline looked sharply at Constant. Here, then, was the origin of his queries about her. She might be self-centered to think he would not approach Mrs. Dutton but for information, but there it was . . . she didn't believe he would have.

"I adore the Percivals, don't you, sir?" Miss Dutton cooed, with a fond look at Caroline. "Such a fine old family; what a shame they've come upon hard times. But as my mama says, it's our duty to aid them in their hour of need, those of us who are in luckier circumstances, and so I thought a carriage ride . . . "

"You are charity itself, Miss Dutton," said Constant with a bow. "And now let me leave you ladies to the business of your day. I must be on my way, but I'm delighted to have met you, ma'am, and most grateful to you for taking care of Miss Percival. Caroline"—and he gave the latter lady a pointed look—"we will be in touch."

Caroline felt her cheeks burning. Why had he used her Christian name? That is, she knew he was trying to establish an intimacy for Miss Dutton's benefit, but for what reason?

"Mr. Constant. Mr. Guy Constant," Desideria Dutton said thoughtfully, gazing at the gentleman's retreating back. "Mama says he's one of the richest men to come to Bath in years. She was quite set up when he presented himself to her in the Pump Room. If only he would stay! Does he make a long visit, Miss Percival? Is he a very old friend of your family?"

"I'm a friend of his six-year-old ward," Caroline said, feeling that this was the most innocuous impression she could give of her relationship to Mr. Constant. That it happened to be the truth was a fitting touch.

"Oh, how sweet! A little child," Miss Dutton said with a sugary smile. "Boy or girl?"

"Girl. I was her governess."

Desideria's eyes opened wide. "My word! I had no idea. I am so sorry, my dear, that you must earn your bread. And why aren't you with the child now?"

"I lost the position." Caroline was watching her new friend intently, expecting Desideria to turn cold and distant in the wake of her news. Surely no young lady of fashion would willingly be seen with a governess.

"What a shame! Well, I shall tell Mama, and she will look out another situation for you, for I would wager you'll need to find something as soon as possible." She smiled in what Caroline chose to interpret as a condescending manner, but Caroline could hardly blame the girl.

"Thank you, Miss Dutton."

"Oh, no. We must and shall call each other by our Christian names. You will call me Desideria, won't you, Caroline?"

Caroline was properly grateful for Desideria's kindness.

"As for the little girl Constant has in his care, I must thank you for the information. I'll ask him all about the sweet, dear mite when next we meet. And now do let me take you up. Unless you would like to go into my modiste's with me? I have another tiresome fitting for some gowns."

"I'd love that," Caroline said honestly. The last time she had been inside a fashionable modiste's, she had been a child allowed, as a great indulgence, to accompany her mother. Mama would be so pleased to hear all about a visit to a house of fashion.

During the next hour, while Desideria swirled in and out of muslin, silk, and merino, Caroline sat thinking dreamily of her encounter with Guy Constant. He had had her followed, or watched, or at any rate asked questions about her! He must really have been concerned about his brother falling into the hands of a scheming adventuress.

If Caroline had been Lord Marchton's brother, she would have left him to the toils of the supposed adventuress and serve him right. She suspected Mr. Constant was much too protective of the viscount, and that Lord Marchton would perhaps grow in wisdom and character if left on his own to be chased and blackmailed and all the rest of it.

At any rate, Guy Constant now knew all there was to know about Caroline's problems, thanks to her unguarded comment about the letter to Harriet. Well, only a misguided pride had made her wish he didn't have to know of Mrs. Brangley's cold decision. She would try to be glad that he knew. She ought to be practical and use him if she could; perhaps he had friends who needed a governess. She somehow felt that she would prefer friends of his to any acquaintance of Desideria Dutton's mama.

Yet she had the definite feeling that it would be better for her peace of mind if she never saw Mr. Constant again.

As Guy walked into his comfortable sitting room, the best the White Hart afforded, his mind was still on Caroline Percival.

So preoccupied was his brain that he was taken aback

when a lady rose from the best seat by the window and advanced toward him, arms outstretched.

"Mother!" he said in astonishment. He noticed that Evan was also in the room, seated at Guy's own desk and looking damnably comfortable. As his eye lit on the desk, Guy frowned. Had he left the papers in quite that condition?

Evan apparently noticed the look and began an elaborate pretense of searching for something among the papers, finally coming up with a pen wiper, though no pen. He smiled his most vapid smile.

Guy continued to watch his brother, suspicious. He had noticed this streak of nosiness in the past and hardly knew what it could portend. Evan had no access to Guy's finances and no interest in business concerns as dull as those Guy engaged in. Lord Marchton's style ran more to extravagant wagers at Newmarket and shady investments than to consols. Why, Guy asked himself, should he feel this creeping discomfort at a little brotherly curiosity?

"We thought you were in Wales," he said to his mother, realizing that her ladyship had been left ignored for some minutes—or was it only seconds?—while he considered the extent of her other son's dishonesty.

Lady Lambert made a little moue of dissatisfaction. She was a pretty, diminutive woman with the dark hair and gray eyes Guy had inherited, and at the moment she resembled more a petulant child than a female of a certain age. Her elegant bonnet and swansdown-trimmed pelisse in the first stare of fashion were not at all what one associated with a holiday in the Black Mountains.

"Oh, Guy, don't mention that dreary place," she said with a sigh, presenting her cheek to be kissed. "It was a shameful take-in, the whole thing. You know"—and she allowed her elder son to lead her back to her comfortable chair by the window, which commanded a view of the street—"I can confess this to my dear boys, since you understand me so well. I was more than half convinced that by inviting me to Wales, Govan—Lord Effrydd—

was initiating some sort of impropriety which would likely end in marriage."

Guy found himself smiling, as he often did, at his mother's phraseology, and Evan barked out a laugh.

"But the old screw wiggled out of the trap, Mama says," he contributed, swinging his quizzing glass by its ribbon.

"Evan!" Lady Lambert directed a look of reproof at her young offspring. "Well, I suppose he did. Much to my grief, Guy, I found myself deposited in Castell Tarren, which is an amazing old ruin of a place, all rock and dead moss, perched high upon some crag or other in the middle of a forest, and beside a bog, and not far from a river. Lord Effrydd provided a chaperon, if you please, his deaf sister who must be rising eighty, and there I sat with her every day in a most gloomy silence while he went about on his merry way. This was not the man I had flattered myself was mad for love of me."

"Poor mother," Guy murmured, trying not to smile.

She sighed. "I had pictured a wild ride to his secluded hideaway, perhaps even a forced marriage—you know the sort of thing. He does look so romantic."

"His scowl was indeed the next thing to Byronic. Well, these things take time. Perhaps when you see the baron again—"

"But I wish never to see his face as long as I live! And I'm unlikely to, since I much doubt he's even noticed I'm gone. He was forever striding about this property in the cold, accompanied by a troop of strange, wild-looking dogs. He . . . he made me eat seaweed." She brought out the last statement as though confessing some dire impropriety.

"Seaweed?" yelped Evan. "I say, Guy, I'd call the fellow out for that. As elder son, it's your place—"

"Merely an old Welsh dish," Guy said. "Laver, it's called, not so, Mother?"

Lady Lambert shuddered. "I have no wish to know what it's called. He ate it for breakfast, fried in oatmeal.

I . . . I took a piece one morning without knowing what it was. Oh, there's no end to his sins, boys."

Guy nodded seriously. "And so you've come to Bath."

"Yes." Lady Lambert had been frowning quite dreadfully as she considered the transgressions of her Welsh lover, but she now gave a maternal smile. "I heard from your man of business when I passed through London that you were here, son, and I instantly decided to join you."

"You came from Wales to Bath by way of London?" Guy asked in astonishment.

"Well, I wasn't too certain that I wouldn't stop in London, but I found it sadly flat at this time of year. The Christmastide docs drive everyone of quality into the country, you know. And so I came on to Bath; it took scarcely more than a day to get here from Town, for I never mind travel. We'll have a family Christmas together, and you may help me open my house."

"House?"

"Yes, poor Lambert's house in the Crescent here. I've never even seen the place, as it happens, but his late mama was very fond of it, and it's said to be an acceptable residence."

"Famous, don't you think?" Evan put in with a grin. "Our duty to stay with Mama now, you know, what with the holidays and all."

Guy thought he could interpret the evil glint in his younger brother's eye; the sprout was probably thinking of another try at Miss Percival. Well, he would catch cold at that scheme.

"It will be our pleasure to pass Christmas with you, Mother, and I, for one, think you should put Lord Effrydd out of your mind."

"I already have," Lady Lambert said with a toss of her head. "I have another idea entirely."

"Do you?" Guy noticed that the gleam dawning in his mother's eye was remarkably similar to Evan's look of a moment before.

"Indeed." Lady Lambert smiled. "I have a great curiosity to meet your friend Davonleigh and his dear daughter, Georgiana. I hear that the poor girl lives much out of the world, and I feel it to be my duty to cultivate her acquaintance and take her about, if she so desires. I do detest girls being kept out of the social scene for no more reason than a father's indolence."

"I see," Guy said with a sage nod.

"Why didn't I think of it myself?" Evan cried. "Mama, you're a great gun. A duchess, b'gad! That ought to be worth some credit in town, don't you think?"

"Not for you," Guy said with a frown in his brother's direction. "You're an impoverished peer with no connection to Davonleigh, no matter where he marries. Best think on repairing your own estates."

"Now do tell me, Guy," Lady Lambert said, ignoring this byplay as she leaned forward in a businesslike attitude, "exactly how decrepit is the old gentleman?"

Guy sighed, resigning himself to the inevitability of a family Christmas and a seat in the stalls at his mother's assault upon his friend the duke. "I had best let you discover that for yourself, Mother. Now shall we go out and see over your house?"

"Do let us be off," Lady Lambert agreed, smiling sweetly. "I'll have such a lot to buy to put it in order, though I have every reason to believe the place is furnished."

Evan coughed and began to beg off the coming excursion. He would be glad to take up residence in the place, but he'd be dashed if he'd spend his valuable time in looking at it.

"Don't be cross, my dear," his mother trilled. "I know Guy will take all the trouble on himself. He always does."

Guy winced. He always did, didn't he?

Then he remembered that staying in Bath would mean seeing more of Miss Percival, and his mood brightened immediately. "The trouble is nothing, Mother. This is a lucky visit of yours." He regarded Lady Lambert in approval, as though she had thought up the Davonleigh scheme for his own convenience and acquired a house expressly to shelter him.

"Dashed lucky visit," Evan remarked, favoring their mother with his most engaging smile.

Guy remembered what Evan might be planning with regard to Miss Percival and shot a stern look at his brother. Evan didn't notice.

"Indeed," said Lady Lambert, "I can think of nothing more comfortable than a little quiet cheer with my family. This will be a delightful Christmas, my boys."

Would it? Guy thought of Caroline Percival's honest blue eyes. Perhaps it would.

5

"I CAN'T GO, Mama," Caroline said.

"But why not?" Lady Percival scanned the invitation that had just arrived in the morning post. "They will send a servant for you, and it's only a small party, so Mrs. Dutton writes. A little gathering of intimate friends, some music—quite the thing to start you off."

Caroline shuddered. She had never attended a party, and though she knew the Duttons meant to be kind, the idea of going into society for the first time at the age of four-and-twenty terrified her for reasons she was ashamed to admit, she who had spent so many years posing as the all-powerful oracle on deportment to the children she had taught.

But how exactly *did* one behave? She had entered drawing rooms full of company many times in her life, but she had been always sheltered behind the small figures of her charges. And after a half hour or so of the little darlings showing off before the company while Caroline stood in the most unobtrusive spot, she was always dismissed, along with them, to return to the nursery.

"I have nothing to wear," Caroline said, clutching at a straw, and not such a very light straw, at that.

Her mother had that martial, modiste's look in her eye. "No matter. There is a white muslin in one of the trunks, and it will do very well. It has no trimming at the hem, to be sure—it is a dozen years old—but we can remedy that with some ruching."

"White muslin! Oh, Mama. Not at my time of life.

Surely a quiet poplin would be better; I have my brown that I always wear to church. It's nearly as good as new."

Lady Percival shuddered. "No, Caroline, you are not going as a governess, but as Miss Percival, late of Willowdown. And you needn't worry that the muslin is too juvenile. This is a dress I had made shortly before Papa—that is, before I went into mourning. It was made for a dashing matron, not a young miss. Everyone wore white muslin in those days, but white is still the most elegant choice. Skirts are shorter this year, but you are a trifle taller than I, so it will work out perfectly. Trust me, my dear."

Caroline gave her mother a hug. "Oh, I'm certain you were the most dashing matron of all. But isn't the fabric a trifle thin for this time of year?"

"We shall contrive," Lady Percival assured her daughter. "Now do you fetch my stack of fashion papers, dear, and my box of trimmings. There's no time to waste. How I do love a project of this kind."

Another comfortable morning was spent ransacking the old boxes. Though Caroline couldn't quite reconcile herself to the prospect of going to the Duttons' party, she did like sewing and speculating by her mother's side, watching how Mama could turn even the most unpromising rag into something special. Not that the white muslin gown could be called a rag. Evidently expensive in its day, it had never been worn, and, as Lady Percival had said, it was not a ruffled and modest young lady's costume, but that of a woman who had been out in the world. Its problem was also as she had said: the gown's simple Grecian lines were undeniably outmoded according to the latest fashion plates.

Lady Percival set Caroline to sewing clusters of white ribbon around the hem, to stiffen it, made some slight alteration in the sleeves, and gave herself the important task of mending a tear in her best Norwich silk shawl, which Caroline must wear for warmth as well as decoration. After Caroline tried on the dress, her ladyship looked at it with narrowed eyes, then, to her daughter's surprise, actually detached the bodice and shortened it a bit, quick as a flash.

"There!" Lady Percival said in satisfaction. "I've observed that waists are higher than ever this year. And we'll put that bit of velvet ribbon here under the bodice, for a sort of sash, which will also serve to hide that I've done anything at all."

"Whatever you say, Mama." Caroline glanced at the small mantel clock. In a matter of a couple of hours, if all went according to plan, the Duttons' footman would arrive to escort her and she would be off to a party—in white muslin! No, surely it was all a mistake.

When at last she was wrapped in her mother's old evening cloak—a trifle too short, but it would not be noticed in the dark—and walking ahead of the Duttons' liveried footman down the streets that separated Westgate Buildings from the Duttons' hired house in Camden Place, Caroline still doubted the reality of this situation. How could she be going to a party? The time for this sort of excitement had surely passed her by, and she was in imminent danger of making herself ridiculous in her twelve-year-old muslin gown. She was only glad that she had resisted all Mrs. Binberry's efforts to thread a ribbon through her hair.

The Duttons' front door opened onto a blaze of light, and Caroline noticed that the butler was relieving her of her concealing cloak. She wrapped the Norwich shawl more securely around herself and hesitated at what seemed to be the drawing-room door. Talk and laughter came from behind it, along with the tinkling of an instrument.

"I will announce you, ma'am," said the servant, and flung open the doors.

Caroline stopped herself just in time from asserting that she had known, of course, that she would be announced. She must look as awkward and unsure as she felt. She gave her name.

"Miss Percival," rang out into a silence as all in the room turned toward the new arrival. There were pleasant nods, and then the music and talk resumed, to Caroline's infinite relief. She could feel her cheeks burning and hoped this would pass as an attractive high color.

Miss Dutton broke from a circle of young people, male and female, and wound her arm about Caroline's waist. "Dear Caroline, I'm so very pleased you could come. Did Freeman collect you in good time? I'm so glad it wasn't wet, or I would have insisted on sending the carriage. As it was, though, Mama thought you would not want it."

"Perfectly true," said Caroline, a little overwhelmed. Desideria was a picture in the sapphire silk Caroline had watched her being fitted for the day before; her dark curls were done up in an intricate knot from which artful little ringlets escaped. She wore sapphire earrings and carried a silver fan.

"I do thank you for inviting me." Caroline made mental notes on every detail of the other girl's costume to tell her mother later.

"Oh, my dear! The very least we can do is bring a little fun into your life. It is Christmastime. Now I must take you to Mama." Desideria squeezed her friend's waist. Bestowing bright smiles on all and sundry as she passed along the room, she conducted Caroline to the sofa nearest the fire, where Mrs. Dutton was holding court among a flock of ladies of about her own age.

"Miss Percival," Mrs. Dutton said warmly, holding out her hand. She addressed the other women. "Dear Miss Percival is the daughter of Lady Percival. The Hampshire Percivals. Her dear mama does not go out. The poor thing is a sad invalid, quite unable to walk, but she was kind enough to spare her daughter to us this evening."

The surrounding females buzzed with excitement at the idea that Caroline was the daughter of someone with Lady to her name. The introductions, which followed shortly on the heels of Mrs. Dutton's announcement, proved that Caroline was likely the closest person to a title in the room.

She began to sense, as she patiently answered an elderly Mrs. Smythe's questions about Hampshire, that perhaps the obligation was not all on her side in the matter of this invitation. The Duttons could not be called social climbers for seeking to patronize a nearly friendless governess, but she did have a distinction in this company.

Nor was her situation unknown, she was startled to find. "You are looking for a governess post, I hear," Mrs. Smythe said with a sharp, assessing stare. "I may have something for you before long, my dear. My son, who is in a very good way of business at Bristol, has four young daughters, and I believe he was thinking of replacing the woman he employs. So hard for a widower to keep good help." A matchmaking light appeared in the lady's eye, and Caroline repressed a shudder.

"Thank you for your concern, ma'am," she had time to say before Desideria, weary of doing the pretty before the older generation, bore Caroline off to the friends she had been talking with earlier.

Among the young people the conversation was all of how many couples the room could be made to hold if they got up a dance later. Caroline took a good look at the young men available as partners. They all seemed young enough to be at school, though many of them spoke of being engaged in various professions. Almost at once she remembered that she had never danced in her life since she was in the schoolroom herself, except on the rare occasions when she had shown the rudiments of the art to some one of her little charges. She instantly offered her services at the instrument.

"You dear thing, I knew you would be so good," Desideria cried with an affectionate smile. "Miss Percival must play divinely," she announced to the others, "for she teaches little ones how to do it, you know."

Caroline's next smile was weaker than before, but she did manage it.

With no further ado, Desideria set the project in train. She bounced across the room to ask permission of her mother, who was all for anything that would amuse the young people, and then set the footmen to moving furniture. They calculated that five couples could take the floor without hazard to the spectators or the Hepplewhite.

Caroline stood among the buzzing young ladies for a while. There were more ladies than gentlemen, and talk now turned upon ways to avoid standing up with another woman, which Caroline gathered was both a usual resort among this set's private parties, and a horror assiduously to be avoided.

"And Desideria told me two new men were to be here, but that was a shameful take-in. I see no sign of any but the same bores," one young lady said, sighing. "I shall simply expire if I get to dance with no one better than Mr. Hempel."

The man in question, a gangling youth with long hair in defiance of the fashion, was just setting up as a clerk with his father's bank. He was certainly not a prize, the others agreed. But he did happen to be the most attractive of the four young men present who could be coerced into dancing, unless one resorted to someone's father.

Caroline soon tired of this line of conversation. Not only that, she felt unbearably mature, for even the young women who looked her age seemed strangely juvenile. She moved to the pianoforte, where she was pleased as well as relieved to see a good selection of music for dancing scattered atop the instrument. She was talented enough at reading music by sight, but she had few pieces by memory.

She was strumming an old favorite of hers softly, by way of preparation, as the dancers formed their set. Then the drawing-room doors opened again, and an audible female sigh ran round the room as two men paused on the threshold.

Caroline looked up from her music and was properly amazed. Mr. Constant and Lord Marchton! Here!

The butler's announcement of the names—especially the viscount's—had a devastating effect upon all the guests. Even those who had been dozing or deeply engrossed in gossip were suddenly awake and interested. A dozen dresses were surreptitiously adjusted, fans poised coquettishly, and cheeks pinched into pinkness as Desideria, in her glory, swept up to the two gentlemen.

Caroline's station was excellent for observation. Mr. Constant was scrupulously polite, and one could tell nothing of his real attitude from his expression, but his younger brother had not yet learned such address and was visibly ill at ease in a roomful of merchants. Marchton's limp gaze traveled over the young ladies with some pleasure however; many of these were pretty, and Desideria must be a stunner in any company.

Miss Dutton first took the gentlemen to her mother, then began to introduce them around the room with a ceremony that had been noticeably lacking in Caroline's case—and for which Caroline was most grateful. She would have hated to attract the sort of notice the two brothers were exciting.

Lord Marchton's title secured him the top honor in this company. Caroline noticed he was being fawned over to a much greater degree than his more attractive brother. But despite this deference to rank, it was Guy Constant whose looks and manners drew most of the surreptitious stares. His tall and well-proportioned frame was set off by the most elegant of dark evening clothes, in contrast to his brother's loud waistcoat and too-high cravat. Constant was also the handsomest man in the room, whereas Lord Marchton, with the "lord" removed from his name, would have been barely passable.

Caroline smiled, telling herself that Constant could have held his own at a gathering of dashing officers and royals. Then she wondered uneasily why she was feeling a sort of proprietary pride at his appearance.

Desideria was apparently informing her newest guests that a dance was about to begin, for Lord Marchton bowed before her and was awarded by a fair, gloved hand immediately clamped down on his arm. Caroline lowered her eyes to hide a grin, then busied herself once more with the music, trying to pick out the best country dance. Mr. Constant was bound to see her sooner or later, but she resolved not to wait in fear of that moment. They had parted on rather good terms, as she remembered, and she had no need to be afraid of him any longer.

Miss Dutton and Lord Marchton were top couple as Caroline struck up a spirited boulanger. She noticed, out of the corner of her eye, that Mr. Constant had disappointed every young lady present and was returning to the side of his hostess.

After the first dance Caroline chose a reel, enjoying the freedom of not being told what to play. The dancers, five couples thanks to Lord Marchton, seemed to be having a very good time, bouncing about with great spirit and vivacity. Caroline grew wistful as she played the next piece, a round dance. Would she ever in her life have the pleasure of a dance? She had no desire to do so this evening, but would she ever dance with a partner the way the thing was meant to be done? She had no doubt that she would be teaching the five positions to unruly children until the day her creaking limbs made such exertion impossible . . .

"May I dance with you when one of the other ladies favors us with a performance?"

Caroline's fingers shook as the last notes of the round died away. "Good evening, Mr. Constant," she said in her calmest voice, smiling at the gentleman who had so uncannily addressed her with nearly her own thoughts. "I'm surprised to see you here tonight."

"The reverse is not true," he replied, returning her smile. "I accepted this invitation solely because I was told you would be here."

"Indeed?" Caroline fought back her confusion, trying for an offhand manner. "I seldom go out."

"Oh, yes, poor Miss Percival can hardly ever get about," came another voice and Desideria Dutton hurried up to the pianoforte, trailed by her latest partner, Mr. Fields. Lord Marchton, the prize of the assembly, had

had to be handed down the line to another deserving maiden after two dances. "She must sit by her mother every evening, you know, and poor Lady Percival is sadly crippled. And then Miss Percival won't be long among us, Mr. Constant. She is to go as a governess, you know."

"He does know," Caroline said, amazed at her self-styled friend's frankness. Desideria had already told everyone else in the room at least twice that Caroline was a governess. "We met at a house where I was teaching."

"Oh, that's right. I believe I did hear something of the kind," Desideria said with an airy trill of laughter. "Shall I tell all my friends that you are going to be naughty, Mr. Constant?" Dropping the subject of Caroline—much to that young woman's relief—she turned a brilliant smile on the tall gentleman who stood by the pianoforte. "Don't you mean to dance at all?"

"I was at this moment asking Miss Percival if I might have the pleasure whenever she is free of her duties here. Surely you mean for another young lady to play, or possibly one of the matrons. Miss Percival ought to get as much pleasure as possible from her rare evening out."

"I do agree," Desideria said after only one moment's hesitation. "Caroline has been a dear to oblige us so long. That is an excellent notion, Mr. Constant, about getting one of the old ladies to take over. I believe Mama's friend Mrs. Banks can play. Excuse me." And she went off across the room upon her business, followed by her silent swain.

"I suppose it's too much to hope for, that Mrs. Banks will play a waltz?" Constant murmured, leaning over Caroline's seat. "Have they really been making you play the whole time?"

"Why, this is nothing. I volunteered," Caroline said in surprise. That was pity in his eyes, and a stern light that told her he was ready to spring to her defense. "I believe there is nothing unusual in one of the older ladies playing while the young people dance."

"Older ladies?" One side of his mouth curved upward.

Caroline was uncomfortable with her reaction to the sensuality of that mouth; she remembered how she had dwelt upon it, unprovoked, on the very day of their meeting as her coach sped toward Bath. "I'm sorry to disillusion you in any way, Mr. Constant, but I am four-and-twenty—hardly a schoolroom miss."

"I see." He nodded, and Caroline somehow knew he was not being altogether serious in his sober reaction.

At this point a bony matron, all sharp elbows and flying lace cap-ribbons, bustled up to the pianoforte to relieve Caroline. "Oh, this is beyond anything odd," said the lady, who Caroline supposed was Mrs. Banks. "I am never asked to play. Is there music here, my dear? Ah, this is excellent. At least—do you think they have anything a bit simpler, Miss Percival?"

Caroline leafed through the music until she came upon a book of easy tunes copied out in large notes—perhaps a book from Desideria's childhood. "Will this do, ma'am? I must tell you, if you are uncomfortable I would be delighted to go on playing."

"Oh, no, my poor girl. You have done your duty twice over, and as dear Miss Dutton says, you never have the chance to go out and enjoy yourself. You must dance now."

With these kindly words Caroline was waved away. Mr. Constant walked by her side, guiding her toward the set.

The shaky notes of "Once I Loved a Maiden Faire" eventually rang out, and Caroline realized, with some surprise, that the moment of her first ball was upon her. She had managed to draw her gloves back on after leaving the instrument, and now she took Constant's offered hand with some trepidation for the first turn.

She was soon smiling. Among the group there were no expert dancers, with the possible exceptions of Lord Marchton and Miss Dutton, and she did not feel awkward. Mama's white muslin dress didn't seem at all the wrong thing to be wearing, though Caroline had feared, on the way to the party, that the gown's year of origin would be somehow emblazoned upon her back.

Mr. Constant was a delightful partner, and if she had not wondered uneasily why he was being so kind to her, she would have enjoyed herself thoroughly. When the music ended she was surprised to find that Constant stood ready to claim her for the next, though the young bank clerk, Mr. Hempel, also solicited the honor.

"Not yet, my dear fellow," Constant said with a smile, keeping his hold on Caroline's arm. "Isn't it the rule in situations such as this for partners to stay together for two dances?"

Hempel was quick to bow to such a *tonnish* older man's superior knowledge and turned back to his previous partner with every appearance of renewed duty.

There was a little time to wait for that second dance, as Mrs. Banks scattered music all over the pianoforte and the surrounding floor and accepted the help of two or three young ladies, her daughters, in assisting her. "This is most kind of you, sir," Caroline said, smiling at Constant, "but you need not stay by me. I know the other ladies are all most eager to dance with you."

He leaned close to her ear. "Don't you want to save me from that? I thought we cried friends at our last meeting."

"So we did," replied Caroline, "but I believed your kind offer to convey my message to little Harriet would quite cancel any obligation you might feel. I must tell you, sir, it isn't necessary to hang upon my sleeve at parties as well." She laughed lightly, hoping to give the impression that parties were an everyday occurrence to her.

"My dear, you need someone to defend you here. I'm not quite pleased at your hostesses' patronizing tone, which the other guests seem to have picked up as well."

"Oh." Caroline paused to consider this. It was rather lowering that he had noticed anything of the sort. "Perhaps it's not quite comfortable, but what else could one in my situation expect? They *are* doing me a great kindness to ask me here, and I think it's rather sweet that they are so pleased with themselves. Perhaps they don't perform much charity in this way."

"Miss Percival," Constant said with a keen look, "you are either a marvel of angelic forgiveness or you're being satirical."

"Neither one," Caroline answered at once. "I'm simply myself. If you must know, the Duttons have even suggested they might do something about finding me a post. They're being useful as well as friendly, and on such short acquaintance."

"Ah! I didn't quite understand the connection. A short acquaintance, you say?"

Caroline's eyes danced; she was getting over being mystified by this friendship with the Duttons and was only amused. "If you must know," she said softly, first having glanced about to make sure no one was near, "Mrs. Dutton recognized Mama from somewhere, but my mother still can't think where she met the woman."

Constant nodded. "There has been more than one occasion of a genteel lady being imposed upon in a like manner by a social climber."

Laughing, Caroline said, "I vow, you have the most suspicious nature, sir! My mother is hardly in the position to be imposed upon. She has no influence, no wealth, not even much in the way of health."

"But she has a title, and they are now free to bandy it about Bath if they wish to. They can also say they've performed this and that service for you, a baronet's daughter."

She looked into his eyes. "Do you really harbor such a cynical view of the world around you?"

He hesitated. "I suppose I do." Looking over Caroline's shoulder, he added, "I fear your good nature is about to be tried, ma'am. I will try to minimize any damages."

"Well, brother." Lord Marchton strolled up to Constant's side. "I insist you present me to this beauty."

"We've met," Caroline said. She couldn't help smiling as she saw Marchton's face change from amiable vacuousness to shock to a knowing leer, all in the space of a moment. She cast a grateful look at Constant, trying to thank him in advance for any service he might be able to do her.

"I say," Marchton said loudly, "it's the governess. Did you sneak in here, my dear?"

"No need to shout, sir, everyone here knows I was a governess," Caroline said smoothly. "I was given my *congé*, you know, at the Brangleys'."

Marchton nodded, still with that predatory look in his eye. "Nothing wonderful to find you here in any case. A lot of merchants and upstarts, nothing above a governess's touch."

"Thank you very much," Caroline said, torn between outrage and amusement.

"Evan, you have no need to insult the company in the same breath as you malign the young lady," Constant put in. He looked and sounded appalled.

"Wondered why you accepted this invitation, brother. Miss Dutton is a dasher, of course, I understand you there, but to sit with her friends for a whole evening seems a bit much when a simple visit to the jeweler's would settle the question much quicker. But now I see you're playing a double game. You knew, didn't you, Guy, that this Miss . . . er . . . Something would be here." With an offhand gesture, he indicated Caroline.

"Percival," supplied Caroline, wondering, as she had more than once, at the sort of world where a man could ruin a woman's livelihood without even catching her name. She felt her bosom swelling, too, with anger on Desideria's account. If she did not mistake the matter, Lord Marchton had just suggested that Constant's motive in coming to the Duttons' party had been a campaign to make the girl his mistress.

"Percival. Thank you," Lord Marchton said with a pleasant nod, ignoring his brother, who was seething more visibly with each passing moment. "I have to thank Guy. He must have heard you were to be here and knew it would amuse me."

"Evan," came Constant's voice, heavy with displeasure, "I warn you to stop now, before you are unlucky."

"Unlucky? D'you mean at cards, old man? Not fair, you know, to hint to the lady that I'm not plump in the pocket."

"I merely meant you might consider it unlucky to be planted a facer by your own brother in a lady's drawing room," Constant said with a pleasant but meaningful smile.

Caroline found herself near giggles and was glad when Mrs. Banks finally chose another piece to her satisfaction and began playing it. Constant took her hand at once and led her away from his brother. As for Lord Marchton, he was seized upon by an eager female and joined the set himself, mercifully not right beside them.

After this dance Mrs. Dutton summoned everyone to supper in an adjoining room, and over quantities of white soup and mince pies—the latter a gesture to the approaching holiday—the dancers recouped their strength while the older members of the company seemed to resent the interruption of their card games. There was some merriment over a kissing bough placed on the central chandelier of the dining room. Lord Marchton was the first to pluck off a berry after accosting his younger hostess to a chorus of wild giggles from all her most intimate friends.

Caroline had walked into the room alone, making sure she stayed far away from the mistletoe. She was glad of something to eat. But her feelings varied between pleasure and nervousness when she found Mr. Constant determined to be her supper partner.

"I cannot understand you, sir," she said finally, accepting a loaded plate from his hands.

"But we speak the same language," he returned with a laugh.

"I mean . . . " Caroline hesitated, not knowing whether she ought to say what was in her heart. Still all too present in her mind was that sarcastic Mr. Constant of London and the Pump Room. "You are so kind to me now," she finished, knowing this to be an inadequate explanation, but ignorant of how else to phrase what she felt.

He gave her a rueful look. "I don't consider myself in the business of being kind. I'm a selfish soul, Miss Percival. If I'm kind to you, it's doubtless in my own best interest."

"What could you possibly have to gain?" she asked with a laugh.

"Why, a charming companion."

This was very pretty, and Caroline decided to take it at face value. She smiled at him.

"What eyes you have indeed," he said softly.

She might have said the same thing to him. His gray eyes were the most penetrating, the keenest she had ever seen. But she looked away in confusion, not knowing if a compliment to a man would be considered too bold. Men could evidently say anything to a woman without being taken seriously; witness Lord Marchton!

She looked at him again. "I do hope you can write that letter to the Brangleys' butler soon, for Harriet's sake," she said, as a way of returning the conversation to a less personal level.

"Harriet?" He appeared to be totally at a loss.

"Your ward." Caroline held back a disillusioned sigh. Constant was treating her with extreme politeness tonight; he was even flirting a little, making her feel more womanly than she ever had. But he was far from perfect. He didn't even care that his little charge was living a lonely and joyless life.

Constant seemed to understand something of what she was feeling. "You condemn me for a heartless guardian."

"I suppose I do," Caroline said with a half smile.

"My dear, I know much less about little, er, Harriet than you do. Perhaps you can tell me more about her. But for tonight, let us enjoy this gathering for its own sake. I believe only frivolous topics are to be discussed at parties."

"You are doubtless right, sir." Caroline couldn't help brightening. She was indeed being pompous and condemning to bring up his shortcomings at a party; she could sense that, and she was glad he seemed to forgive her so easily. And his words allowed her to think that he planned to see her again. Such a joyful hammering took place in her breast at this notion that she was immediately on her guard.

She must be extremely careful not to think much too highly of Harriet's guardian. She had never been taken in by a handsome face and had no plans to start.

6

CAROLINE gave herself little leisure to dwell on her first party and all its ramifications. She discussed the evening with her mother, of course, but she omitted all references to Mr. Constant and Lord Marchton. Since she had both danced and eaten supper with Constant, this entailed quite a bit of equivocation. In truth, she was so confused over her encounter with the man that she didn't want to deal with the probing sorts of questions any mother worth her salt would ask.

One thing Guy Constant had said did stick in Caroline's mind. He had come to the Duttons' party solely on her account. Could that really be true?

The very next morning she composed a note with her Christmas message to Harriet and sent it to Constant's hotel with her thanks. She had been too shy to do so before, but now she got the business out of the way. She told herself the matter was over. Desideria and Mrs. Dutton had been very sweet to invite her to a party, but Caroline would definitely not be fluttering about the social scene in future and would be most unlikely to meet Mr. Constant again—unless, indeed, she were to come upon him in the street. Thus the danger that threatened her from his charm was easily avoided.

Having told herself she could only meet Constant by accident, in the street, she found herself looking about her with an extra interest whenever she went out. No Mr. Constant was to be seen; but then, she went out only to young ladies' seminaries and the shops, hardly places frequented by fashionable gentlemen.

When Caroline came home one day, after disappointing interviews at three more seminaries, she found her mother half fainting on the sofa, clutching her vinaigrette in limp hands and being fed Constantia wine by a solicitous Mrs. Binberry.

"Good God!" cried Caroline, rushing forward. "What is it, Mama? Bad news? You . . . you haven't injured yourself, have you?"

"Are you well enough to speak of it, ma'am?" Binberry asked, hovering about her mistress with a worried expression.

"Yes." Lady Percival closed her eyes and opened them, pressed her hands to her temples, and finally looked at Caroline. "Oh, my dear girl, this is the most extraordinary thing. I've just had a visit from a solicitor. I vow, you must have passed him in the corridor; he can't have left five minutes ago."

"I may have," Caroline said carefully, thinking wild thoughts about everything from outstanding debts of her father's, to the Brangleys somehow having decided to persecute the Percival ladies for some spiteful reason. "Oh, Mama, what did this dreadful man say to you?" She knelt by the sofa and took her mother's cold hands.

"He wasn't at all a dreadful man, as you will hear. It's simply this." Lady Percival's expression was still dazed, but she managed a smile. She took a deep breath, then another. "We're rich, my love. Mr. Pennyfeather came to tell me of a legacy from my great-aunt Lucretia, who died seven years ago. It seems there was some difficulty with the paperwork that delayed my inheritance; at any rate, now I'm to have a competence of—what did he say, Binberry?"

"One thousand a year, ma'am," Binberry said in awed tones.

"And there is a thousand for each of the years since the will was read, which I may draw upon without injuring the capital," Lady Percival added, her hand on her heart.

Caroline sat back on her heels and stared. "This is

surely all a hum," she said without thinking. "Did you ask for the man's identification, Mama? Someone could have been playing a cruel joke."

Lady Percival let out a long, shuddering breath. "I regret to say I was as mistrustful as you, my dear, and demanded to see all the documentation as well as Mr. Pennyfeather's own papers. He was most obliging, wasn't he, Binberry?"

"Indeed, ma'am. And most respectful," answered Binberry, herself sounding more deferential than had been her habit of late. She shot a look of disapproval at Caroline.

"Did he leave anything here, Mama?" Caroline asked as she carefully studied both her mother and Binberry for signs of madness.

"Oh, yes. The papers are over on the table by the window. There is a copy of my aunt's will, an accounting of the interest the money has drawn in the seven years since her death—it's invested in the funds, you see—and a draft on the Bath and Somersetshire Bank."

"A draft?" Caroline crossed at once to the window and picked up the papers, her hand lingering on the draft. It was made out to her mother in the amount of five hundred pounds.

"Those dear solicitors thought I might wish for a little something for my immediate needs," Lady Percival said with a sigh. "Wasn't that thoughtful of them?"

"Most thoughtful." As Caroline read the papers over and over, she was astonished to find her hand was shaking. This had to be a mistake. She did remember hearing of an Aunt Lucretia, but she didn't recall any tales of the lady's great riches. Yet she had been hardly more than a child at the time of Lucretia's death; why should anyone have discussed such matters with her?

"And now, my dear," Lady Percival said, leaning back upon the sofa, "the only question in my mind is where we shall live."

"Do you mean to move house, Mama?" Caroline was alarmed. "Perhaps we had better wait a little, to see if this is all some unhappy error. Perhaps we'd do well to live as if nothing had happened."

"Caroline," Lady Percival said with a stern look at her daughter, "you will not adopt a miserly attitude, I hope."

"Miserly! I hope not too, Mama. This is simply happening so fast . . . "

"I know, dear. But there's no reason one in my state of health need spend a minute more than necessary in these dreadful, dreary old rooms. I intend to go out first thing in the morning to look over small houses in the better streets. Mr. Pennyfeather promised to send a reliable agent to me."

"Oh. Small houses. Well, I suppose . . . "

"And then there's the matter of clothes," Lady Percival went on, beginning to be quite animated after another convulsive gulp of her wine. "My dear Caroline, do you know how long it's been since I ordered something new? And I'll finally have the opportunity to dress you as you ought to be dressed. And Binberry, you shall assist me in the hiring of a staff. You'll be housekeeper again. Think of that."

Mrs. Binberry beamed all over her face.

"Oh, dear." Caroline sat down on the floor again, there being no seat near enough for her suddenly weak knees. She laughed until the tears streamed down her face.

"What is the matter, my dear?"

"For some ridiculous reason, I'm thinking of the Duttons," Caroline said, grinning. "I fancy they like us as we are—poor gentlefolk glad of their patronage."

"Oh, bother the Duttons," Lady Percival said in irritation. "We shall be polite to them, of course, but I see no reason we should cultivate people of so little refinement."

"Mama," Caroline cautioned, returned to seriousness in an instant, "we must guard against pride at all costs."

"Pride? I have none left after so many years of privation," replied her mother. "But you must allow me, dear, to give all three of us a Christmas we won't forget."

* * *

The next few days whirled by in a dazzling confusion of houses, dresses, and fawning tradesmen. To her daughter's relief, Lady Percival did indeed take a house smaller than most she had been shown. An establishment for two ladies did not need to be uncomfortably large. Size, though, was its only modest feature.

Caroline found herself, by the end of the week, ensconced in a comfortable bedroom in the fashionable Crescent, the most exclusive neighborhood in Bath. The chamber was larger than both Mama's rooms in Westgate Buildings. From her bed she could look in astonishment at a wardrobe full of new dresses. Outside her window the December morning was breaking, foggy and cold. Belowstairs, she knew that Mrs. Binberry was also waking in a comfortable bed and putting on a new gown.

It was Caroline's first night in the soft, roomy tester bed, yet she hadn't slept as well as she had on the hard cot in Westgate Buildings. She was still harboring the notion that everything—the bed with its warm coverings, even her new nightrail and the soft slippers beside the bed—would vanish during the night like fairy gold.

But morning was here, and so was everything else. Caroline kept staring at the wardrobe and the dresses. More outfits were due in the next few days; her mother had insisted on getting her such useless fripperies as ball gowns and even a riding habit, though she hadn't sat a horse in twelve years.

It occurred to her that she had only to ask, and Mama would supply her with a horse. Caroline was shaking her head in disbelief as she got out of bed and made up the fire. She hadn't been poking at it long before she remembered she should have rung for one of the new maids to do this very chore.

Belatedly she did ring and get back into bed so that she might play the proper young lady, wondering as she burrowed back under the covers how she could broach the subject of economy to Mama. Her ladyship might be the heiress to riches, but she would soon run through her income if the activities of the past few days continued unchecked.

Caroline was quite certain that her mother would be insulted if one were to suggest retrenching in any way; and there was really no need other than Caroline's unsettling feeling that something was not quite right about this sudden change of fortune.

But perhaps there was no cause for worry. The expenses of the past days would not be repeated, after all. They wouldn't need another house, or more clothes or servants. Mama hadn't even insisted on a carriage once Caroline pointed out that chairs would always be more convenient in the hilly town of Bath.

A maid came in, carrying a tray of early tea and muffins. Another maid appeared with cans of hot water. Soon the drapes had been drawn and the fire made up to even greater warmth than Caroline's ministrations had caused. She was left alone in more luxury than she had known since her childhood.

If only the Brangleys' could see her now! Caroline swung her legs out of bed after she had finished her tea. She washed and dressed herself, ringing for a maid only when it came time to do up the back buttons of her crimson merino gown.

"Oh, this shade of red is lovely with your hair, madam," gushed the young servant, fumbling with the buttons. Like all the staff, she had heard the story of the sudden riches of her new mistresses and understood all their opulence was as new and exciting to them as to her. "Shall you leave it loose this morning? Such pretty curls."

"No, I'll tie it back with a ribbon," Caroline said vaguely, going to look into the mirror above her dressing table. A modish stranger stared back at her.

Little Sukey presented a velvet ribbon in the same shade as Miss's dress, and Caroline tied back her hair, letting several brown waves escape to frame her face. Who was this lady in the rich gown? Crimson, of all things! Caroline was so used to dressing in grays and browns that she had balked at the bright color, but Mama had counseled festive shades in honor of the season and their new way of life, and the modiste had said much the same, citing the becoming effect of this particular hue of crimson on Miss Percival's complexion.

"Perhaps a sprig of holly just here." Caroline touched the white frills which filled in the square neck of the gown.

"Oh, lovely, ma'am. Quite the thing for the season. The Christmas greens will be arriving today, so Cook says, and I can pluck off a sprig to bring to you as easy as anything."

"I was only joking," Caroline demurred with a smile. "I feel quite festive enough as it is."

In that strangely celebratory mood, tempered only a little by the lingering feeling that the morning dress, not to mention the house, would at any moment crumble to dust at her feet, Caroline proceeded to her mother's room on the ground floor.

Lady Percival, an early riser, was breakfasting in bed and reading the papers. A Worcester breakfast set in blue and white reposed on a silver tray by her bedside. She wore a lacy cap and lacier dressing gown. A newly hired nurse hovered about her, rivaled in obsequiousness by a superior-looking abigail. A sparkling new Bath chair stood ready in a corner.

"My dear, you look beautiful in that frock. Aren't you glad I insisted on red?" Lady Percival greeted her daughter, holding out her arms.

Caroline kissed her mother's cheek and gave her a hug. "You look very pretty yourself, Mama. You rested well? I was afraid all the exertions of the past days would knock you up."

"Oh, never say so, Caroline. This bed is so very comfortable I can scarcely credit the change. I believe my condition is improving already; a sad comment on the state of things for poor people, but most convenient nevertheless. Caroline, do remind me to send a large draft to the Charity Hospital today. We mustn't forget others in our good fortune."

"You're so very kind, Mama." Caroline was touched, but more than ever convinced that their good fortune was ephemeral. Knowing Mama, she would give away half her income and not even realize she had done so.

"And now." Lady Percival motioned to the servants to leave the room, then indicated that Caroline should sit on a chair near the bed. "What shall be our first order of business? Shall we simply wait for people to call on us?"

"Do you think your health would permit much of a social life, Mama?" Caroline asked gently, fingering a delicate, ivory-handled spoon from the breakfast tray.

"Yes," was the decided answer. "I cannot pay calls myself, of course, but what is to prevent me from sitting in my own drawing room? Heavens, it is only two rooms away from this one; this snug house is indeed arranged most conveniently. And if I am sitting in the drawing room, why need I be alone?"

Why, indeed? Caroline hoped that it would not be because no one did call on them. For the first time she wondered about her mother's social standing; the few times they had been to the Pump Room together, Lady Percival had seemed to see no one she knew. Or was that only because her former acquaintances had dropped her?

"And I mean to go to the theater and the concert," Lady Percival continued. "I believe many people are carried to both places in chairs; all one needs is a couple of stout footmen to carry one up the stairs, and another to carry cushions and things, and we have those now."

"Why don't we send one of the footmen out for tickets?" Caroline suggested, liking this scheme. She had never been to the theater or a concert. "I believe we should wait a few days, though. You might not think you're tired, Mama, but I would make sure you're not doing too much. Is the doctor coming today?"

"Yes, at noon. I have every hope a talk with him will convince us both that I'm not about to embark on a foolish whirl of activity."

The doctor, when he did come, assured both Lady Percival and her daughter that, provided his patient got plenty of rest and took care not to neglect her visits to the warm baths, she might do what she liked. "Chance has unhappily made you an invalid, dear lady," he intoned in professional solemnity, "but I see from your bright eye and blooming cheek that you will not let your spirit languish in melancholy gloom. And for that, you are to be commended. The happiness of the patient is often the surest route to robust health."

Caroline followed this poetic medical man out into the hall. "Doctor, my mother's bright eye and blooming cheek notwithstanding, I believe she could easily overdo this round of frivolity she means to embark upon."

Dr. Knowles looked surprised and not at all pleased. "My dear Miss Percival, it is the Christmas season, and for the first time in all the years I've known her, your mother plans to celebrate. Would you deny her a little pleasure?"

"Certainly, if being quiet would save her from a painful illness in the new year." Caroline was exasperated; at every turn she was being made to feel an absolute spoilsport, and all she wished to do was see that Mama didn't run through her money and ruin her remaining health in the process. Yet Mrs. Binberry had frowned when Caroline suggested the Percivals did not require so grand a house as this one in the Crescent; Mama bristled when asked not to embark upon such a social whirl as she had not seen in years; and now even the doctor was chiding Caroline.

"Miss Percival, you need have no fear of that. Your mother does not have the use of her legs; indeed, I cannot hold out much hope of her ever recovering that. And it is that very circumstance which will keep her as quiet as you could wish."

Caroline did not agree; she could imagine her mother's procession of chair and footmen appearing everywhere from gaming hells to dress balls. "If she overtires herself, is she not in danger of a decline, or a fever, or something of the sort?"

Dr. Knowles smiled, at last, in understanding. "I see you're a careful daughter. Her ladyship is lucky to be so blessed. Will it satisfy you, Miss Percival, if I go back in to see your mother and instill in her a horror of dissipation?"

"Yes," Caroline said, returning his smile. "I truly don't wish to spoil her amusement, sir. She deserves much more than she will be able to get, I'm certain. But I don't wish to lose her to ill health, either."

Whatever words Dr. Knowles chose to convey to her ladyship the idea that too much of a good thing would be bad for her, they must have worked. Caroline wasn't present at the interview, for fear of being recognized as its instigator, but when she and her mother sat down to dinner, Lady Percival was much calmer and did not have quite so many grand schemes. She looked over the cards that had been left that day and seemed quite thoughtful.

"My word," she said, glancing up from this task, "perhaps we ought to have been at home today. I recognize so few of these names, I'm curious to put faces to them. Here are the Duttons, of course, but there are so many others."

"Neighbors, I suppose," Caroline said. "We couldn't receive, Mama, what with the doctor and your trip to the baths."

Lady Percival ruffled through the cards. "Yes, I believe these must be neighbors. I confess I'm pleased to think so many distinguished names live in our immediate vicinity. Well, I mean to be at home tomorrow. Do you know, Caroline, I have half a fear that all these callers are people I really did once know but can't recall—like Mrs. Dutton. Do you suppose illness and misfortune could have so addled my wits?"

"No. I believe Mrs. Dutton met you once, in passing, and is presuming upon what only she chooses to remember as an acquaintance. Harmless enough. She seemed so pleased the other night to tell people I was Lady Percival's daughter. Until two gentlemen arrived, I was the closest thing to a title in her drawing room."

"Heavens! I didn't know you were being used in such a manner, dear, and I can't say I approve. Don't worry, it won't happen again. I wager our callers tomorrow will be of a different stamp."

"I wish I could be with you, Mama."

"What? Why can't you?" Lady Percival's eyes widened in curiosity.

"I have an appointment at a school," Caroline murmured into her plate.

"Caroline! Never tell me you're still looking for work as a teacher."

Caroline adopted a soothing tone. "Now, Mama, it is only that I made the engagement before I knew anything of Aunt Lucretia's legacy. I can't very well not appear."

"Nothing easier than to send a servant with your regrets," Lady Percival said with a wave of her hand.

Caroline admired the imperiousness of the gesture; her mother might never have spent twelve years in poverty. "I don't choose to do that, Mama," she said quietly. "I'm not very trusting, you see. Should anything happen—should this turn out to be some happy dream—I intend to have a way to earn my living."

"And if nothing happens? If the solicitors are not telling lies, and if my eyes are not deceiving me when I look at my new bank balance? Then what will you do? Embarrass me by earning your bread when I am quite able to take care of you?"

"I suppose not, Mama," Caroline said, suddenly very ashamed of herself. "I'm sorry I've become such a cynic. But may I keep the appointment? I swear I'll be by your side all the next day."

"Very well," Lady Percival said as though conferring a great boon. "I wish everyone I meet to know my lovely and *dutiful* daughter."

When Caroline came in from her much-maligned appointment with Mrs. Deschamps, headmistress of a most impressive school in Henrietta Street, she was still dazzled by the alteration in every facet of her life wrought by a change in funds.

The Miss Percival of a week before, genteel but shabby, had met with nothing but refusal from at least seven ladies' seminaries. At each one her abilities had been doubted and her references scrutinized as though they were certainly forgeries before her services were declined with varying degrees of curtness.

Today Caroline had seen the other side of the coin. Mrs. Deschamps had taken but a cursory look at the references her visitor produced from a costly new reticule. The headmistress asked only a few rudimentary questions about proficiencies, and then she offered Caroline a post.

Mrs. Deschamps had offered a post to a very well-dressed young woman accompanied by a footman, Caroline knew in her heart. Why, such a young person as she had looked today stood in no need of a position as a teacher, and so Mrs. Deschamps should have realized. But the woman had been completely taken in by a well-cut pelisse and a striking bonnet. Her school was exclusive and fashionable, yes, but she surely couldn't expect every applicant for a teaching position to be richly dressed.

Caroline felt she had hit on some important information; perhaps she ought to write a book of advice for would-be governesses and teachers, urging them to eschew the traditional quiet garb.

She also suspected that the very fact that she had not been desperate for today's position had made her more attractive to the headmistress. Absently handing her outdoor things to the servant who stood ready to take them, Caroline walked into the drawing room still preoccupied by these thoughts and found her mother in conversation with a lady.

"Dear Caroline." Lady Percival was beaming, and she held out her hand. "Do let me make you known to Lady

Lambert, who is our neighbor. We have also discovered she is a connection of the Staffords whom we knew in Hampshire."

Caroline approached and made her curtsy to a little woman in elegant garb. Lady Lambert appeared to be about Lady Percival's age, and Caroline did not doubt that she had once been a great beauty. She was still delightfully pretty, with speaking gray eyes, dimples, and dark hair suspiciously untouched by gray.

"I am delighted to meet you, my dear." Lady Lambert gave a merry smile. "Do you know, I am almost as new to the Crescent as you and your mother. I opened my house but last week."

"Oh?" Caroline sat down, quite ready to be pleased with the acquaintance. Lady Lambert seemed friendly, refined, and certainly not at all encroaching.

"I haven't spent much time of late years in Bath— though I was a proper Bath miss once upon a time, having attended school here—and I'm reacquainting myself with the city and its inhabitants." Lady Lambert had a tinkling laugh, and it rang out charmingly.

"Caroline, this is the most fortuitous thing," Lady Percival said, smiling at her new friend. "Her ladyship has offered to take you about with her as a favor to me."

"Why, how kind of you, ma'am." Caroline was astonished at such civility on short acquaintance. The offer was not only kind, but daunting. Being taken about at Caroline's age might be a little ridiculous.

"There is to be a Christmas ball at the Upper Rooms, my dear, and I am to shepherd another young lady," Lady Lambert was explaining. "If you would go with us as well, what a merry party we should be."

"You are too good, my lady! But I'm much past the age of coming out, you know," Caroline felt bound to admit, "and I never did. I'm not quite certain if I should know how to go on."

"Oh, what does that matter?" Lady Lambert, who reminded Caroline rather of a bright-eyed bird, fluttered her hands at Miss Percival's words. "You are well-bred and have pleasing manners. Your mama has told me all about your governessing days—a shame, I call it, that our first families should ever be brought to such a pass!—and she and I agree that you mustn't be allowed to distance yourself from the world now because of your profession in the past."

Caroline nodded, unable to think of a thing to say.

Lady Lambert rose and took Lady Percival's hands. "Now I must go, my dear, but I'm so delighted to have met you and your charming daughter. I'll see both of you tonight."

"Tonight?" asked Caroline when Lady Lambert had gone on her way in a cloud of scent and fur.

"We are going to the play with Lady Lambert and her sons, and she also hopes to be joined by that young lady she is taking to the ball with you. Oh, Caroline, this has been the most wonderful day."

"Did anyone but Lady Lambert call?" Caroline asked curiously.

"The Duttons, of course. Miss Dutton was desolated at your absence. She seemed to wish to talk over her party with you. But there were a few others. One of my old schoolfellows, and a relation of your papa's, and one of our old neighbors from Westgate Buildings."

"How news does travel, to be sure."

"Caroline, you aren't becoming cynical again, are you? I know very well that most of these people are interested in me only because of my new fortune. Except the Duttons, of course, who are interested because of my title. But you shan't spoil my pleasure in this delightful turn of events."

"I don't wish to spoil your pleasure, Mama," Caroline said. "Now what shall we wear to the theater?"

In spite of herself she was wondering if Mr. Constant would be attending the play this evening; and, if so, what he would think on seeing her in the company of people of fashion. She was certain the Lambert sons would be unexceptionable young men.

She had not seen Constant since the Duttons' party.

The busy events of the past week had by no means driven him from her mind, but she had not the leisure to think of him incessantly.

Now, for the first time, she realized that when next she met Mr. Constant they would be on more equal terms. How would it change things between them now that she was not the pitiable, poor governess? She hoped she would have the chance to find out.

"My dear, you are woolgathering," Lady Percival admonished. "Please pay attention. Now, once again: what do you say to the blue crepe for you and the purple moiré for me?"

"The blue crepe—the one with the odd sleeves? Is that my most becoming costume?" Caroline asked with a degree of interest her mother had not noticed before.

"For theater-going, certainly," said Lady Percival with a shrewd look. "I must say I'm looking forward to this evening. Do you expect to meet anyone in particular, dear?"

"I? I hardly know a soul in Bath," Caroline said, blushing deeply.

"I see," returned her ladyship with one of those looks by which mothers seem to penetrate to the very soul. "The blue crepe it is."

7

CAROLINE could scarcely wait for her visit to the Theater Royal that evening, and she knew her mother was thrilled. They had both spent too many years without amusement of any sort. Lady Percival had of course seen plays aplenty before her accident, and her anticipation was for the spectacle and the conversation with Lady Lambert rather than anything else, but Caroline had a different view. A great reader, she knew all the English comedies and dramas, and she had wished all her life to see a professional theatrical performance. This night's offering was to be *Twelfth Night*, and Caroline read the play thrice over before the afternoon was gone.

"My dear," said Lady Percival, shaking her head as Caroline read some striking passages aloud to her for the second time, "we will be the only people in Bath actually to have studied what we're going to see."

"I suppose it's the governess in me," Caroline said with a twinkle in her eye. "I never got as far as Shakespeare with any of my charges, and now you, dear Mama, are a captive audience." She crossed the room to the pianoforte and looked through the new music; she thought she had seen a musical setting of "O, Mistress Mine," one of the songs from the play, in a collection she had recently bought. She found it and began to sing, accompanying herself softly to compensate for a voice she knew was less than perfect in tone and quality.

"Oh, Caroline," said Lady Percival when her daughter had finished the song, "I know you'll delight in the great theaters of London. Covent Garden! Drury Lane! Only think."

"London?" Caroline looked at her mother in concern. "Surely you weren't planning such a long journey, Mama."

"Oh, merely a little visit someday—not a season, to be sure, you have impressed upon me that you would never sit still for a season—but a visit to attend the theaters, shop for some really modish clothes, and perhaps have one of my friends take you about to one or two tiny balls, you know the sort of thing."

Caroline didn't have the heart to cast doubts on such a modest plan, nor did she want to. Except for the part about being taken about socially, the scheme had much to recommend it to her, provided her mother could stand the trip. She resolved to ask the doctor about travel when he made his next visit; and she had to smile at her mother's notions of subtlety. "Tiny balls," indeed!

Time crept by until they left for the performance, and then it began to fly once the Percival party arrived at the theater in Beaufort Square. They made quite a stately procession, what with the two liveried footmen necessary to convey Lady Percival's chair up and down the stairs. She was by no means the only such invalid in attendance. Both ladies looked around with shining eyes (in Caroline's case sparked by a bit of particular interest) at the holiday crowds. No matter where she went, she found herself searching for Guy Constant. He might not be astonished to see her out at the theater, but he would be surprised to find her anywhere except in the Duttons' train. She hoped he would be pleased to hear of Lady Percival's good fortune.

She need not have bothered searching the crowds. When she and her mother entered Lady Lambert's box, they found their new friend sitting down with none other than Guy Constant. The pair looked quite cozy, and Caroline experienced an irrational surge of jealousy at the thought of Constant in the toils of such a charming older woman.

Precisely how irrational, she was soon to find. "My dears!" Lady Lambert held out her hands and stood up to greet them. "I'm so delighted to make you known to my elder son."

Constant had also risen on their entrance; now he bowed, first over Lady Percival's hand, then her daughter's. "This young lady and I have met, Mother," he said with a special smile. "In fact, Miss Percival and I are old friends."

Caroline was aware of her mother's sharp eyes on her; and Lady Lambert did not look unintrigued. However Caroline did not explain how she and Constant had met or tell of their encounters in Bath. Neither did he. She was grateful that Constant made no allusion to her change in circumstances; indeed, she couldn't even say he looked surprised. Well, he probably was not. Lady Lambert would have mentioned the name of the ladies who were joining her party, and he would have heard they were new neighbors. He must have assumed some change in the Percivals' circumstances if they had moved from Westgate Buildings.

"Your ladyship must have been married so young." Caroline came out with these words before she could stop herself. She was looking back and forth from Lady Lambert to Constant and tracing a resemblance indeed, but she would have taken them for brother and sister. This impression, she believed, was based on Constant's air of maturity and his mother's girlish manner rather than the youthfulness of her ladyship's looks.

She was soon thanking Providence that she had not put this last thought into words. As it stood, she could have said nothing more calculated to put herself in her hostess's good graces. Lady Lambert preened and looked extremely pleased. "Ah, yes, when I married Mr. Constant I was barely out of the schoolroom. Let me think: was I even out of it?"

"We must all agree you look too young to have a son of my venerable age," Constant said. "And you certainly don't act like the mother of a middle-aged man."

"Middle-aged! You must not be ridiculous, young man," put in Lady Percival with a mischievous smile.

Caroline listened to the exchange of compliments with half an ear, still sorting out the relationship between her mother's new friend and Mr. Constant. Lady Lambert, of course, had married again. More than once, for if Constant was her son, and the younger Lord Marchton was his brother, they could not be related on the father's side. "But this must mean your ladyship's other son . . . " Caroline hesitated to speak the hated name of Lord Marchton. It didn't seem possible that this pleasant woman could have so forgotten herself as to have such an offspring.

"Ah, yes, perhaps you have met my younger son, Lord Marchton." Lady Lambert beamed in motherly fondness. "My second marriage. Evan should be bringing Lady Georgiana Stapleton into the box in the next moments. Dear Georgiana is the daughter of the Duke of Davonleigh, you know. She had to stop out in the corridor to greet one of her father's old friends, and—ah! Here they are."

Velvet curtains pushed aside, and there stood Lord Marchton, in sleek evening clothes and an even flashier waistcoat than he had worn to the Duttons' party. By his side was a bored-looking young woman of about Caroline's age.

Lady Georgiana was elegant, tall, and graceful. Caroline got the impression that the young woman was too well-bred for conventional beauty; yet she was attractive, with mild green eyes and flaxen hair, and she dressed with a simplicity that could only be bought from the first modistes. Caroline looked into the other girl's eyes, thought she interpreted exasperation with Lord Marchton, and liked her instantly. She had never before met the daughter of a duke—or indeed, any relations of such a noble personage—and wondered uneasily how Lady Georgiana would like to find out she was to be seated in a theater box with a former governess.

Lady Georgiana headed at once for Lady Lambert and

greeted her affectionately. The elder lady proceeded to introduce Lady Percival and Caroline.

"I knew your mother, Lady Georgiana, years ago at school in Kensington," Lady Percival said.

Lady Georgiana and Caroline's mother began an earnest discussion while Caroline looked on in silence, knowing she should not be so astonished at Mama's connections. How easy it had been to forget, in the years of governessing, that her family was anything but obscure. Now she remembered that her mother was the last surviving representative of the junior branch of a very ancient family. Lady Lambert joined in with Lady Percival and the duke's daughter as Georgiana shyly brought forth some amusing tale her mother had told her of Miss Towers' Kensington school.

Caroline was impressed, but she had no chance to meditate further on her change in circumstances. Lord Marchton's prominent eyes had boggled on recognizing her, and, after only a slight pause to gather his forces, he approached her chair. A familiar, sly smile appeared on his narrow face.

"What, you here?" he began, leaning down and giving her a good-humored wink. "You are a persistent little thing, upon my word." He put his hand on Caroline's upper arm and had time to caress the area between her long glove and her sleeve before she could twitch away from him.

"Well, brother." Constant had been greeting some friends in an adjoining box, but he was suddenly at Caroline's other elbow. "Let's see if you can save the situation all by yourself by not saying something unforgivable."

The male voices had attracted the attention of Lady Georgiana, and now she turned curiously, leaving the older ladies to their talk.

"I say," Marchton exclaimed, "you don't mean she's followed *you* here, Guy? What use would that be? Everyone knows you don't keep a mistress."

Caroline spread the fingers of one hand across her

reddening face. Miraculously her mother and Lady Lambert were so engrossed in their chat that they appeared not to have heard the exchange, but she felt any possibility of friendship with Lady Georgiana Stapleton receding by the moment.

With a great effort she smiled pleasantly at the other girl. They had barely been introduced, but she felt obliged to set the situation straight. "You must forgive Lord Marchton's confusion, ma'am, but he met me first when I was working as a governess for a family of merchants; then he saw me at Bath, living in modest circumstances with my mother; and now he doesn't yet know that my mother and I are Lady Lambert's new neighbors."

Lady Georgiana smiled with friendly interest. She looked enthusiastic, not merely polite as she had when talking to the two older ladies. "Indeed?"

Caroline could see Constant looking at the lady with approval and was amazed to feel a little pang of envy.

"But m'mother lives in the Crescent," Marchton said, looking utterly at sea. "I live with her, dash it all. Nice place, the Crescent."

Caroline could not pretend to misunderstand him. "My own mother has had a change of fortune recently, my lord."

Constant gave Caroline an inscrutable look and said, "Most pleased we are to hear it, ma'am, and to welcome you as my mother's neighbors."

"What a fine thing, indeed," Lady Georgiana put in. "One doesn't often hear of good fortune, only bad, and how pleasant, especially at this time of the year."

Caroline smiled. "It was rather a seasonal stroke of luck, was it not?"

Lord Marchton's confusion was still evident. "But to show up in m'mother's box—I understand anyone can get into a party such as the one we saw this filly at t'other night, but—"

"Evan, come with me." And Guy Constant took his

brother by the arm and firmly escorted him from the box.

Caroline and Lady Georgiana quickly moved on to talk of other things. By the time the play began they were well on the way to an amicable understanding. Long past schoolroom age, they were each a bit embarrassed at the prospect of being displayed at the upcoming holiday ball in the Upper Rooms. Lady Georgiana brought this concern forward hesitantly; she considered herself, at five-and-twenty, past the age for dancing, but her papa insisted on her accepting Lady Lambert's kindness. Caroline was glad to talk over her own qualms. Having established such a bond, they were soon happily discussing quite different subjects. Caroline's teaching experience was of consuming interest to Georgiana, who was trying to open a school in one of her father's villages.

When Constant came back into the box—alone—Caroline looked down into the stalls and observed Lord Marchton walking about there in an idle fashion, as many other young men were doing. He looked disgruntled. Constant caught her eye and winked at her. Then he sat down beside her and whispered, "Don't worry over my brother, Miss Percival. I've finally managed to hammer into his head that you're not following him around."

"Have you really, sir?" She gave him a grateful look as she whispered back.

"One can but hope." And, settling in with an air of great accomplishment, he folded his arms and directed his keen gray eyes away from Caroline and onto the stage just as someone on it declaimed in a booming voice, "If music be the food of love, play on."

Caroline was surprised to find that she was no longer so interested in the play as she had been before Constant sat down; yet concentration on something kept her at the edge of her chair for the rest of the evening.

She woke up next morning with an idea that had come to her out of the blue sometime during the night: the most logical idea she had ever had, and one she was amazed she had not thought of before. Still in her dressing gown, she hurried to her mother's room to propose it.

"Why, what a delightful project," Lady Percival said, laying aside the morning *Post* to smile at her daughter. "I should like such a plan above all things. It would give me a new interest in life."

"But, Mama, you must remember that this would mean no work for you. I would engage to take all the trouble on myself. Oh, I do so hope it will work out."

"Dash off a note to Mr. Constant at once, child, and ask him to call on us. One of the footmen can carry it down the street." Lady Percival surveyed her daughter carefully. "Would you rather be alone with him to explain yourself?"

"Perhaps that would be a good idea," Caroline said, lowering her gaze to the brilliantly colored carpet.

"Perhaps it would," her mother remarked in a speculative tone.

As usual, Caroline breakfasted in Lady Percival's room. Then she dressed in her finest morning gown and went to sit in the drawing room over her needlework while Lady Percival diplomatically remained in her chamber on some pretext. Glancing into a mirror, Caroline wondered if she was too obviously dressed up for a special visitor. She had given up trying to convince herself that she was not attracted to Constant, but she was not at all eager to impart the news to him.

Her thoughts ran in a familiar, self-effacing manner that she deplored, but could not seem to stop. The night before she had seen Constant in the company of Lady Georgiana Stapleton, the daughter of a duke, evidently a young woman of whom his mother greatly approved. He had not seemed particular in his attentions to Lady Georgiana, true, and the lady had shown no signs of attraction to him, but who was to say how the situation stood? In great families, Caroline knew, marriage was a matter of form rather than inclination.

Thoroughly depressed, she rose from her chair, meaning to run up to her room and change to a plainer gown, something which would state clearly that she had no interest in any man, when the door opened and Baxter, the butler, announced Mr. Constant.

Caroline moved forward, hand outstretched. "Mr. Constant, I'm so glad to see you. Shall I have Baxter bring some refreshment?"

She was gratified when he agreed. The butler went off to do her bidding, closing the door behind him.

Constant gave her a penetrating look as he took her hand. "I confess I was surprised to get your note, Miss Percival. You have something particular to say to me?"

He was quoting the words of her letter. Caroline flushed, eager to get on with the subject at hand, yet not at all sure of the outcome. What if he became angry, took her idea as a criticism? She could not endure that.

"Yes, I do," she answered him in little more than a whisper. Now that the moment to use it was at hand, she felt all her courage deserting her.

"My dear, you are in no sort of difficulty, are you?" His words were gentle, caring; Caroline couldn't help contrasting his attitude now with the scorn he had once shown her.

"No, no difficulty at all," she answered, leading the way to some chairs.

"Am I to see your charming mother this morning?" Constant asked as he sat down.

Caroline understood the hint. He was surprised that she would receive him alone; he might even be chiding her. "No, Mama and I agreed that I should speak to you alone. Oh, sir, I suppose there is nothing for it but to begin."

Constant was staring at her in astonishment when the door opened again, admitting Baxter with a tray of sherry and biscuits.

Grateful for the interruption, Caroline served her guest and spoke not another word until he was balancing a diminutive glass of sherry and a plate with some biscuits on it—Caroline thought a man must need more than one.

Constant detested biscuits. Women were fiends for forcing food on one, he thought, gamely swallowing an almond-flavored wafer. He noticed that she took nothing herself. She was probably too nervous to eat, for her fidgeting was growing worse. What the devil could she have to tell him? Some trouble with Evan, Constant assumed, and steeled himself to soothe her if his rapscallion brother had propositioned her again.

"It's about Harriet," she said with a little tremor in her voice.

"Harriet?" he asked pleasantly, sipping the sherry so that he might put down the glass. "And who is she?"

Caroline's eyes flashed. "Your ward."

"Oh. Harriet. Of course." The memory came back to him, and along with it the uncomfortable knowledge dawned that she had asked more than once before about that child. Now what had been the reason? Ah, yes. He was pleased to have done the task Caroline had set him. "I did write the child a letter, and sent her your love, the very day after the Duttons' party when I received your message. Under cover to the Brangleys' butler, as you suggested." He had indeed. At the time he had pictured the six-year-old girl's dismay at receiving a letter from a person she had never seen, but Miss Percival's request had made him follow through and send the child a rather ponderous letter of Christmas greeting and not much else.

"Thank you." Caroline's voice sounded a little cold, and he realized he had made a mistake by letting his unknown ward slip his mind again.

"Was that why you wanted to see me? To ask if I'd sent the message to young Harriet?" he asked after a silence in which she twisted her hands in her lap and stared at them.

"No." She looked up, and he was struck as he so often was by the beautiful blue depths of her eyes.

Before he could make her the flowery compliment

suddenly at his lips, she took a deep breath and plunged into her tale. "Sir, as I'm certain you've guessed, my circumstances are no longer as straitened as they were when we met. My mother has come into some money, and I now have the means—that is, my mother is the one with the means, and naturally I have asked her, and she has agreed to my plan—oh sir, may I have Harriet?"

"Have Harriet?" He stared at her. "What on earth do you mean, Miss Percival?"

Caroline gave him a sunny smile. "I would be so happy, so very grateful if you would let her live with my mother and me instead of the Brangleys. She isn't happy there—indeed, she has been miserable—and I'm so fond of the child."

"You want the child to live with you?" His voice registered disbelief. "This is what use you'd make of your new fortune? You're no connection of the little girl's—there is no reason for you to bother your head—"

"I think she would be happier here than at the Brangleys'," Caroline interrupted him, her voice firm. She gave him a pleading look. "My mother is so pleased with the idea, too. She says it will give her a new interest in life, and I dare say having a little child about the place will keep her amused long after the novelty of society has worn off. And if it didn't work out to your satisfaction, you might easily find a school here in Bath for Harriet. I would engage to help you there; I've made quite a study of schools myself."

He couldn't get over the strange sense of disbelief. "My dear Miss Percival, the child is well enough provided for. You can't seriously be thinking—that is, you take too much upon yourself. You are a young lady having her first taste of society; why would you wish to take on such a burden?"

"I love her," was Caroline's instant answer. "Perhaps love is always a little mad. You mustn't think I would meddle where I don't belong if I didn't have a strong attachment to Harriet—to Miss Deauville, and a strong interest in her welfare. I would be a sort of aunt or god-mother. Will you think it over, sir?"

"I don't have to," he said, looking at her steadily. "I'll write the Brangleys at once, then go to fetch the child. You must understand that if she's reluctant to leave them after all, if you've misread the situation, I won't engage to bring her."

"Naturally not." But Caroline was confident; she knew that Harriet would be thrilled to escape from the prison of her life with her cousins. She wondered why Mr. Constant was reacting so strangely; surely it could make little difference to him where the child lived, and Harriet would add so much to her life and her mother's.

He rose. "You must remember, Miss Percival, this charge is such a heavy one that no young woman should take it on lightly. What if you meet a young man who doesn't fancy the idea of a ready-made family? Have you thought of that?"

"I'm certain no man worthy of being cared for would balk at my wish to help a little girl." Caroline said with a blush.

He nodded. "You are a lady of firm principles, ma'am."

"Thank you." Caroline was a bit confused by such a comment, but she was too happy at the outcome of the interview to quibble. "Now, when shall we leave? Do you think we might have her here by Christmas? You will have to write to the Brangleys at Croydon, you know, for they will be visiting that relation of Mrs. Brangley's, and if it happens they've taken Harriet with them this year—"

"We?" He frowned. "Surely you weren't thinking of going with me to fetch the child, ma'am."

"Well, of course I must go," she replied, speaking quickly. "Harriet hasn't even met you, and she might be frightened to be swept away on a journey to an unknown place without even a familiar face to comfort her. She is such a sensitive child. Of course I would prefer not to

see the Brangleys should they still be in Town, but I
thought I could be waiting in the coach . . .

"Miss Percival, pleasant though the prospect sounds,
you and I can't possibly travel together." Constant's
brow, which had been drawn up in such a forbidding expression, relaxed, and he smiled at her. "You haven't
thought this through. Your reputation."

"Oh. That." It was true. Caroline hadn't even considered that a woman of her years, a governess by profession until so very lately, could be thought to have an
ordinary thing like a reputation. Surely that was a luxury
only a lady could afford. She remembered, with a little
start, that she was now what the world called a lady.
"But I might bring a maid," she suggested without much
conviction.

In the back of her mind, she realized, had been a
pretty picture of herself and Constant traveling to London together—she and he talking in the coach on the
way and growing closer; she watching, with an affectionate eye, while Constant and the little girl captivated
each other on the return journey. She had been overly romantic, she could see that now.

"I think it best not," Constant said, taking her hand.
He kissed it, and Caroline shivered.

He seemed to notice; he dropped her hand rather suddenly, leaving Caroline to wish she could explain to him
that her reaction had proceeded from excitement, not
disgust. While she puzzled over how to convey this, he
continued to talk, and Caroline felt he was trying to save
her further embarrassment. "I'll endeavor not to frighten
the little girl out of her wits. And I believe you're right
about it being wise for you not to confront the Brangleys
on this issue. I'll simply tell them I've found another situation for Harriet and leave it at that. If they have no affection for the child, it can only mean improvement in
their domestic arrangements to be rid of her."

Caroline looked at him in gratitude. "I know you're
right, sir, and I do thank you—and my mother will thank

you also—for making this possible. How soon can you return?"

He laughed at her eagerness. "Oh, you see me dropping everything and speeding off on the road to Town, do you?"

She could tell by his amused tone of voice that he was teasing her; though this kind of flirtatious byplay was new to her, she determined to join in. "Well, yes," she said, giving him a confident smile such as a beauty might give a lovestruck swain who longed to do her bidding.

"I am naturally at your command," he said, shaking his head as though he mocked his own weakness.

Caroline was astonished at her new power and instantly thought better of her teasing. "I don't really mean you to drop everything, sir. You have engagements, and you are staying with your mother, who must depend upon you for much of her domestic comfort since her other son—that is . . . " Her words trailed away; she had come too close to insulting his brother.

"I've often heard it said in Town that there is no engagement in Bath worth keeping," said Constant. "I'm sure I'll regret any trip that takes me from your side, Miss Percival, but if I go at your command I must simply bear it and hope for greater reward when I return."

Caroline let a laugh escape her; she was out of her element and had to let him know it. "I scarcely know what to make of this, sir. Extravagance is all the thing in flattery, I know, but do remember that I'm not used to it."

"Do you consider what I say to you flattery?" he asked, a disturbed expression passing across his face.

Smiling, she answered, "Well, no. Until quite recently in our acquaintance, sir, I would have called much of it insults."

"Touché, ma'am." He lifted her hand to his lips and kissed it for the second time. This time there was no startled reaction from Caroline, and he held her fingers for an experimental moment. She did not draw them away.

They looked at each other, a wondering sort of look on Constant's side; he thought he saw the same emotion in Caroline's eyes.

He broke the suddenly awkward silence. "I'll be off now to prepare. I think, if you really want little Harriet with you by Christmas, that I'd better travel now and trust to personal explanations rather than letters. One never knows about the weather."

"Sir, you're being so kind about this, I scarcely know what to say but thank you. I do so hope it works out."

"So do I, Miss Percival," said Constant, "so do I."

He went away still wondering what in heaven's name a young single lady wanted with a child—a child who was no blood relation and whose only recommendation was that she was presently unhappy.

He hoped Miss Percival would not repent her kind decision.

8

NOT MANY days later, a traveling coach and four drew up in front of the Percivals' house in the Crescent. A small figure came dashing out the instant the footman let down the steps. The tiny passenger was dressed in a shabby, outgrown pelisse, scuffed half-boots and an ornate bonnet a bit too large for her. She raced to the door and stood on tiptoe to reach the knocker.

A gentleman who had been riding beside the coach dismounted, tossed his reins to one of the outriders, and followed the child up the steps while a maidservant laden with bandboxes made her way out of the carriage and brought up the rear of the procession.

The door was just opening to them when a feminine voice cried from the street, "Harriet! And Mr. Constant. Oh, what a delightful surprise."

Caroline had been out early to the shops and was just making her way home, followed by the footman who always dogged her steps these days by her mother's order. Baxter, the butler, was beginning to voice his first words of greeting and query when Harriet streaked back down the steps and into Caroline's arms.

"Miss Percival! Miss Percival! My guardian came for me, and he wasn't a monster at all. Here he is, in fact, and he bought me this new bonnet and a doll and took me right away from my cousins' house and said he would bring me to you, and so he did. Oh, isn't he splendid?" After which torrent of words, Harriet pulled back from Caroline's embrace and directed a worshipful stare up the steps at Mr. Constant.

"Splendid indeed," Caroline said, smiling at the gentleman.

He smiled back and shrugged. "My ward is easily impressed."

Caroline didn't think so, but she chose not to embarrass him in front of the servants and the little girl by the praise she knew he must deserve. Instead, she ushered everyone into the house. The servant girl who had come with them proved to be a nursemaid newly hired in London. She was sent with Baxter belowstairs for refreshment, after which someone was to show her to the newly fitted-up nursery. The coach and Mr. Constant's horse were spirited away to their stable.

Lady Percival was sitting in the drawing room over some of the fine lacework she now occupied herself with rather than mending. She looked up with a delighted smile. "Why, Caroline, I thought you went out to match some thread, and here you are with Harriet instead. For I know you must be Harriet, child." She held out her hand, and the little girl trotted up to the sofa where the lady was reclining and stood beside her, smiling shyly.

"I did bring the thread, too," Caroline said with a laugh. "Mama, as you've guessed, this is Miss Harriet Deauville. Harriet, this is my mother, Lady Percival."

"But you must call me Aunt Elinor," Caroline's mother said, patting Harriet's cheek.

The child looked about her with wide eyes from under the ponderous new hat, smiled brilliantly at Caroline and her guardian as well as her new "aunt," and burst into tears.

"Oh, dear." Caroline was beside Harriet in an instant. "I believe the journey has tired you out, my sweet. Would you like to go up to the nursery and see your new bed? I've had such fun in decorating a room for you; but I do think it important that the bed be tried as soon as possible so we'll know whether we have to change it."

"Oh, yes," Harriet said in a wavery little voice. "I'd be glad to help."

Caroline led the child out of the room. When she returned a short time later, having helped Harriet out of her things and tucked her up with her new doll into the fluffy comforters of a small white bed, she found her mother and Mr. Constant being confidential over glasses of wine and slices of iced walnut cake.

Lady Percival looked up. Her blue eyes were flashing. "Caroline, my dear. I've been having such an interesting discussion with Mr. Constant, and I believe he should repeat everything to you. Really, the heartlessness of those people. It quite makes me want to shake them. And to think my dear daughter worked for them, was at their mercy! It passes all bearing."

Caroline sat down near the others and looked expectantly at Mr. Constant.

He seemed to have grown handsomer in the last week; was this the exhilaration of the journey, or was he simply more charming in her eyes because he had brought Harriet so quickly in true knight-errant fashion? Or had she been missing him more on his own account than she cared to admit? She looked down, embarrassed at where her thoughts were wandering, and found herself concentrating on his muscular thighs, encased in buckskin.

This was no help at all. She raised her glance again and felt the need to say something to break the spell his presence was casting on her. "I do thank you for bringing Harriet, sir. You must not get the wrong impression because she cried; I believe she's quite happy to be here."

"I don't doubt it," Constant said, rather gruffly, Caroline thought. "As I was but a moment ago explaining to your mother, I took Harriet away from the Brangleys as soon as I got to town. That is, I would have taken her from them had she been with them." He frowned darkly. "I found her in their house in Upper Wimpole Street, virtually alone."

"Alone?" Caroline's mouth dropped open in disbelief.

"As you had told me, the Brangleys were gone on a Christmas visit. The house was shut up; the butler I had written to was not there. I saw my letter unopened on a table. Nobody was there but a deaf old housekeeper—"

"Mrs. Stephens," Caroline remembered with a nod. "Kind enough, I suppose, but she can't hear a thing. What about the rest of the staff?"

"If I interpreted correctly the shouting match I had with Mrs. Stephens when I finally managed to get into the house and make her understand I was no burglar, the rest of the household had been given a holiday for economy's sake," Constant said, his mouth grim. "The Brangleys simply left Harriet with that deaf old woman. I found the child in a chamber near the attics, cowering under the bed. She had heard me get in and thought I was come to murder her."

"My old room," Caroline said softly. "Oh, the poor little thing."

"She is a very engaging child," Constant said with a cough. "And most attached to you, Miss Percival. When I told her I was there to take her to you, she simply put her hand in mine and asked if we might go now. Reminded me of how you insisted that I go to London and find her at once." He paused. "I thank God I really was her guardian and not some blackguard who meant her ill."

"Mr. Constant has been telling me how dreadfully he feels for not being more careful about Harriet's living arrangements," Lady Percival put in with a keen look at her daughter. "Did you see that old rag of a pelisse she had on? It was her best."

Caroline had known, of course, that the Brangleys dressed Harriet in their daughter Amanda's castoffs. In the past she had mentally chastised the child's cruel guardian many a time for not making sure her needs were met. "He is not to blame," she said at once, negating with ease every former opinion she had held about Constant's heartlessness. He had come through for her and Harriet at last, and everything else seemed a long time ago. "What can a man know of children, especially girl children?"

"Vindicated by one of my sterner judges," Constant said with a rueful laugh. "You won't talk me out of my self-loathing, ma'am, no matter how hard you try. In only one matter do I absolve myself: I've been providing a liberal dress allowance for Harriet, and it's plain the Brangleys have been pocketing it. But now I hope we can make up to the little girl for all she's gone through. Abandoned in an empty house! I couldn't believe my eyes. And she had a very calm tale to tell of the situation. Mrs. Brangley, it seems, told her she would have a much better time by herself, and Harriet agreed."

"She probably was having a better time on her own than she would have being pulled every which way by her cousins," Caroline said thoughtfully. Having no companions but the Brangley children had been an evil; yet there were other dangers. The child mustn't become isolated. "Mama, we must make the acquaintance of some people who have little children. Harriet will need playmates."

"Don't worry, my dear, we shall do everything in time. First, though, we must give the child a perfect Christmas. I've had Cook make a large plum pudding, and we are having Lady Lambert and Lord Marchton—and you, Mr. Constant, if you will be free—for dinner on Christmas day, and then there is lovely singing at the Abbey that the child would enjoy, and perhaps we can contrive a children's party by Twelfth Night . . ."

"Oh, Mama." Caroline gave her mother a hug. "You're certainly entering into the spirit. You haven't been an aunt ten minutes, and I know you've never been a fairy godmother."

"Too bad a little girl can't go to the ball at the rooms," Lady Percival said with a sigh. "How she would enjoy seeing all the gowns. Well, she will see yours, and perhaps Lady Georgiana will come here beforehand and show herself to Harriet, too. But the dear child would have so loved seeing the dancing. You enjoyed peeking down the staircase whenever we had a ball at Willowdown. Do you remember, my dear?"

Caroline exchanged a merry glance with Constant. "You see, sir, Harriet's being here is no trouble at all. The only trouble will be to restrain my mother from spoiling the child."

Constant grinned. "I do find myself less inclined than formerly to beg you ladies to reconsider taking such a step as having Harriet here to live. But I stand by my first thoughts. If this should prove too much for you, Lady Percival, Miss Percival, simply say the word. There are many fine schools right here in Bath, and as for the holidays, my own mother would be more than delighted to take the child."

"Oh, sir, you must not deprive us," Lady Percival cried, looking stricken. "She is but just arrived. Your mother has a claim, to be sure, but can Harriet not stay with us for the present?"

"I didn't mean to imply . . ." Constant hesitated. He didn't believe his mother would be thrilled by the prospect of playing hostess to a nursery child, yet he wouldn't have saddled the Percival ladies with such a charge, either, and they seemed quite eager for it. He wondered if Lady Lambert would take a maternal turn on meeting Harriet; stranger things had happened, and his mother was at relative leisure. Her dearest project, making up to the Duke of Davonleigh, had not yet materialized since the duke wouldn't have the goodness to appear and be charmed. "I promised Miss Percival the pleasure of Harriet's company, and I intend to stand by my word."

Caroline smiled brightly, and he felt himself well rewarded for any small trouble he had been put to. "And so it is really all arranged with the Brangleys, sir? I'm so glad."

Here was the only flaw in an otherwise perfectly executed plan. "As I told you, I saw no reason to wait for permission to remove the child from her predicament. I got their address in Croydon from the housekeeper and fired off a letter to them. In any case, I am Harriet's guardian, and she must go where I say. The Brangleys will be surprised I've bothered to take her, that's all."

"And no doubt relieved," Caroline added, shaking her head. "We do thank you so much, sir, for bringing her here." She smiled tremulously. "Harriet was right. You're not a monster at all, you know."

He grinned back. "I did feel somehow shrunk in stature when Harriet told me I was not."

Constant noticed there were tears in Miss Percival's eyes as he took his leave. Even Lady Percival, who had not had a prior attachment to the child, was looking a little weepy.

As he strode down the pavement to his mother's residence, he was feeling a bit sentimental himself. He had bought the little girl that absurd hat and an expensive doll, but that had been mere masculine fussing, a lack of knowledge of what a child would really like. Now that he had seen her ensconced in the Percival house he felt he had finally done something useful for Harriet, and there was a spring in his step.

Harriet slept deeply, ate ravenously, and chattered nonstop for the next couple of days as she adjusted to her new home. Soon she was running up and down the corridors, examining all the rooms, and making herself extremely useful in fetching and carrying for Lady Percival. Caroline took Harriet on walks about the streets of Bath, into parks and gardens all battened down for winter, and into the shops to order new clothes.

Constant insisted on paying for Harriet's needs, Caroline insisted back, Lady Percival and Lady Lambert threw in their own directions, and it finally fell out that all of them were contributing to give the child everything she might require. Harriet's cheerful and pragmatic temperament was all that saved her from becoming immediately spoiled under such a weight of attention.

She did not so much walk through the days as dance. Caroline rejoiced in the little girl's company and was satisfied that she had done the right thing in asking for her.

On the night of the Christmas ball in the Upper

Rooms, Harriet perched on a high stool in Caroline's bedroom to watch Lady Percival's dresser turn the young lady into a fairy princess. Such, at least, was Harriet's opinion once Caroline was dressed in her new ball gown.

Caroline had never had such a thing as a ball gown before, and she also was inclined to look at herself with the eyes of a wondering child. Who was that creature in the mirror? She must not be Caroline Percival at all, for Caroline Percival could surely not look so very much like a modish lady accustomed to the social scene. Well, if she were not herself, she would not have to worry.

Such extravagant thoughts were flying through her mind as she descended the stairs in a cloud of white and silver—much too young! she had objected, but been overruled by Mama and the modiste—to show herself to her mother and wait for Lady Georgiana and Lady Lambert. Harriet scampered at her heels.

"Oh, you are magnificent," Lady Percival cried, clasping her hands as Caroline entered the drawing room.

"A fairy princess," Harriet said for something like the tenth time, hopping from one foot to the other.

"Two unbiased opinions, I'm sure." Caroline responded with a nervous laugh, having caught yet another glimpse of that finely turned-out stranger in the glass above the mantel shelf. Dressing had been fun with Harriet there to exclaim and make much of her, but now she would rather take the costume off and spend the evening at home. How was she to go to a public assembly when she hadn't been to one in all her four-and-twenty years? This was such a sudden pitchforking into society. Surely it was a mistake.

Her only comfort was that Georgiana had evinced a similar reluctance—in her case, not because she had never been to a ball, but because she had been to too many. When the duke's daughter and Lady Lambert arrived to collect Caroline and kindly show themselves to Harriet, Georgiana did indeed look nervous, though her cool green gown gave her an aura of calm from a distance. Lady Lambert was the epitome of voluptuous, mature loveliness in opal satin and a superfluity of diamonds.

"From Lord Richards. My third," she said to Lady Percival, touching her fine necklace. "All his family jewels were unentailed. I made a very good bargain there, my dear."

"Indeed. And had you any children of that marriage?" asked her friend.

"No, only jewels," Lady Lambert said with a sigh. "Now, isn't my son's ward the most engaging little creature, speaking of children? Her mother was a lovely young woman, quite took the town by storm in her come-out year, and Harriet is the image of her. We'll have our hands full, presenting her in a dozen years' time."

Caroline heard this and was touched in a strange way by Lady Lambert's blithe assumption that the families would still be acquainted when it came time for Harriet's come-out.

She was further gratified when Mr. Constant arrived to escort the ladies. Unfortunately, he was accompanied by his brother. Lord Marchton cast a bored eye over both Caroline and Georgiana and, holding back a yawn, drawled out something about the pleasure of accompanying them.

Constant stepped up to Caroline as soon as the bustle of greeting was over and he had tossed Harriet up into the air three times as was his new custom. "Miss Percival, will you permit me to beg the second two dances of you?" He spoke over Harriet's shoulder, for he still held the little girl in his arms.

"The second two? Of course, sir." Caroline was pleased to be asked at all, but wondered a little about the first two dances. Of course, he must have asked Lady Georgiana, as all the rules of precedence and hospitality would dictate. He would ask both the girls under his mother's wing, and he couldn't put second the claims of a duke's daughter.

Constant smiled almost as though he could guess her thoughts. "Do you know, only the rules of the assembly prevent me asking you to dance with me all the evening, Miss Percival."

Caroline was confused into an excited reassurance of his regard.

She felt some alarm when Marchton, who had been talking with the older ladies, next approached her. She noticed that his mother pushed him forward. He asked for the first pair of dances.

She had been taught enough to know that she had to accept him unless she could come up with a compelling reason, and she had none to give. "Thank you, my lord," she said with a bow.

"Yes, I thank you as well—an honor and all that." He surveyed her through a quizzing glass which magnified one watery eye to an alarming size; he was looking puzzled, as he always did now when she saw Caroline.

She could almost understand him. "My lord," she added in a confidential tone, "you don't have to dance with me. I realize your mother told you to ask, but I know you're rather confused by me, and I wish you to know you must not feel obligated."

He looked startled, and the quizzing glass dropped to dangle by its ribbon. "I assure you, madam, I find you a most charming girl, most charming. Pleasure to give you a dance." He put on an intimate smile. "If I understand a bit more about you than these others—Mother and Guy and the rest—then perhaps we can find a way to keep what I know under my hat. Not sure yet exactly what rig you're running, you and the woman you live with, but if you're nice to me . . ."

Caroline was thoroughly disgusted. The woman she lived with? Was he implying that she and Mama were hardened adventuresses masquerading as mother and daughter? "My lord, there is nothing about me to know, and what little there is, your mother and brother have heard. I would appreciate, too, if you didn't insult my mother. I think it would be better if we didn't dance after all." She turned from him, her cheeks suddenly flaming.

Constant had been watching from across the room as Harriet told him about her day; now he excused himself to the little girl and strolled over. "Evan, are you making a pest of yourself again? Miss Percival does not look amused."

"It's nothing, Mr. Constant," Caroline said with a desperate look. "Lord Marchton has every right to suspect me of 'running a rig,' as I think he expressed it. I claim a corresponding right not to dance with someone who thinks me an adventuress."

"So that's how it is," Marchton said with a familiar leer at Caroline and his brother. "Heard my brother's richer than I, and going for bigger game? I'll get to the bottom of it, don't worry. Sharper than I look."

"I'll get to the bottom of you, young scamp," Constant retorted in a low voice. "Let's not cause a scene in front of the ladies, if you please."

"Cause a scene? No such thing." Marchton looked indignant. "You know, Guy, she's pulled the wool over your eyes. Got you to steal that child for her, even. That mite belongs with the vulgar people you visited in town—the Brangtons."

"Brangleys. And Miss Deauville is my ward," Constant interrupted. "Evan, I don't know how your brain gets onto these obscure byways, but I expect you to say nothing further in disparagement of Miss Percival. I'd hate to call out my own brother."

Lord Marchton snorted and folded his arms. "Impossible, Guy. I outrank you. 'Tis I who do the calling out, and I don't chose to muddy my honor in such a way. Fighting a brother, indeed. I'm sure it's not in the Code."

Constant rolled his eyes, and Caroline, not wanting to hear more, walked across the room to Lady Georgiana and Harriet, who were being confidential in a corner.

Harriet looked up with shining eyes. "Caroline, the lady says I can go to her house and ride her pony. She has lots of ponies, she says."

Georgiana smiled. "Yes, and I have a very dear old pony I haven't ridden since my legs got too long. He would love to meet Harriet."

"His name is Stubby," Harriet put in.

Georgiana looked keenly at Caroline. "Why is Lord Marchton looking so fierce? Wouldn't you dance with him either?"

"You mean you refused him?" Caroline asked with interest. Perhaps saying no to disreputable young men wouldn't be so difficult as she had thought.

With a sigh Georgiana replied, "His mother had him ask me for the first two dances, and he did, in front of everyone in the room last time I was visiting Lady Lambert. I had to say yes; there was no polite way out. He then added that he would try not to make me feel large and awkward, since I'm slightly taller than he. At which point I told him it would be better if neither of us had to endure such an aesthetic nightmare." Lady Georgiana inclined her head in acknowledgment of Caroline's appreciative giggle. "Then Mr. Constant, who had been listening, asked me to dance himself, saving me from embarrassment before a roomful of people, and incidentally making his brother look like an ass. I don't want you to think"—and here Georgiana favored Caroline with a penetrating look—"that I'm trying to rival you. Mr. Constant was merely being polite."

"Oh, but Lady Georgiana, there is nothing between Mr. Constant and me," Caroline said, horrified at the relief surging through her. For though she had told herself he had considered Georgiana first out of some sense of duty, she hadn't really believed it.

Georgiana gave an arch smile, and Caroline felt thoroughly exposed.

At this point Lady Lambert began herding movements. "Come, my dears, we don't want to be late to the rooms. That is, we are late already, but we don't want to dally longer. The Assembly lasts only until eleven."

Caroline shivered and exchanged a glance with Lady

Georgiana. It was a long time until eleven. Did Lady Lambert plan on staying for the whole thing?

Harriet and Lady Percival gave the party an affectionate send-off, and soon, too soon for Caroline's taste, she and the other ladies were extracting their delicate skirts from sedan chairs and walking into the Upper Rooms in Bennett Street.

The Octagon Room and the chambers beyond it were all hung with Christmas green and brightly lit. Through the doorway to the ballroom, they could see and hear the opening minuet just coming to a close. Caroline was charmed with the setting, yet daunted by the other players in the drama about to unfold. Everyone in the room, almost without exception, seemed to own a fashionable hardness which she did not. She had the unsettling feeling that at any moment she would be identified as an interloper and ejected from the room by one of the many liveried retainers.

Before she could meditate further on the discomfort of not belonging, Desideria Dutton was beside her. Mrs. Dutton was nowhere in sight. "You dear thing, you look divine," cried Desideria in a high, carrying voice. "How delightful to see you. *And* your party." Desideria put her lips close to Caroline's ear. "Isn't that the daughter of the Duke of Davonleigh? I should love to meet her."

Caroline held back a sigh. She had considered these social dilemmas, expected them, but to be faced with one immediately on entering the rooms seemed unfair. Lady Georgiana was standing close to her, had probably heard Desideria's loud whisper, and Caroline felt she had no option but to turn, smile, and present Miss Dutton. Desideria's curtsy almost sank her through the floor, it was so deep and reverent.

However, instead of backing away in an excess of awe, Desideria then proceeded to attach herself to Caroline's group. Soon she had been introduced to Lady Lambert and was renewing her acquaintance with Mr. Constant and Lord Marchton, reminding them with a loud giggle of the night they had attended her mama's little party.

"Don't worry," Lady Georgiana said into Caroline's ear. "This happens all the time."

Caroline liked Georgiana all the better for understanding; she smiled in answer.

In truth Desideria's presence had its uses, for she took care of the problem of where to bestow Lord Marchton. She prodded him into asking her for the next dance almost before he could blink. As he took the floor with Miss Dutton, she triumphant, he dazed, Lady Georgiana walked away on Guy Constant's arm. Caroline and Lady Lambert found chairs.

Caroline was glad enough to sit down and take in the scene. She told herself she would have been much too nervous to dance at once on coming into the room. She kept her gaze fixed on Constant and Lady Georgiana, who were top couple in the country dance just forming. Was this an accident, or did everyone at the assembly know who Lady Georgiana was and grant her precedence? There probably wasn't another duke's daughter in the room.

How would it be to be so well known? Caroline was turning to Lady Lambert to debate this point when she noticed a couple promenading down the corridor between chairs and dancers. The woman, a substantial creature with bright gold hair, leaned upon the arm of a small, wiry man with sharp eyes. As Caroline watched in horror, the pair stopped before another vulgar-looking couple at some distance from Caroline and seemed to renew a close acquaintance.

"My child, you look as though a goose walked over your grave," Lady Lambert said, patting Caroline's hand. "Don't worry; you'll be dancing as soon as some of these shy young men stop eyeing you from afar and make their way over here. Ought I to summon someone? I know young Farnsworth over the way . . ."

"Ma'am," Caroline said, "I see some people—it's

dreadful, but I've just seen the Brangleys, the people Harriet was staying with in London. My old employers."

"Those wretches?" Lady Lambert had heard the story of the Brangleys' ill treatment of little Harriet. She looked about, the jewels in her ears and hair flashing. "Point them out to me, my dear, and I will give them my most haughty stare. I suppose what all my friends have been saying is true—anyone can get into the assembly nowadays, and I should not have brought you girls here."

"What could they be doing in Bath?" Caroline wondered aloud, a thousand worries flashing through her mind. "I wish . . . ma'am, I wish I might go home and make certain Harriet is all right."

"What? Harriet? My dearest creature, you've but just arrived. And if these Brangburys, or whatever they call themselves, are here at the ball they can hardly be making mischief for little Harriet."

"I suppose you're right," Caroline said, keeping her eyes on the Brangleys. Mrs. Brangley was in a dreadful gown that blended sky blue satin and gold spangles; she looked right at Caroline once and didn't seem to know her. Caroline felt a measure of safety; of course the Brangleys would not expect to see their old governess here. She was probably as safe from their censure as she would have been if she were invisible.

Not that Mr. Brangley, whom Caroline thought of as a downtrodden soul, would chastise her. Caroline had seen little of him in her time in his employ, but she didn't think he was nearly so bad as his wife. If Harriet had been miserable in his home, it had been because he was ignorant of his domestic arrangements like many another male.

She toyed with the idea of presenting herself to their notice if only to see the shock on their faces. A governess dressed up and attending a ball!

Her worries beguiled her until the two dances were over. Desideria bounced up, followed by a languid Lord Marchton. "Dear Lady Lambert, dearest Caroline, I must go back to my mother, but I simply had to ask you to join us for tea."

"If we are able, dear," Lady Lambert said in a non-committal tone.

Desideria was undaunted. "You must try very hard. Mama will be delighted. Lord Marchton, do let me introduce you to that young lady just over the way, Selina Smith. She'll be pea green with envy." And, giggling, Desideria went off, leading Lord Marchton.

Caroline noticed the young man's bemusement and thought he deserved it. Then she saw that Mr. Constant and Lady Georgiana were approaching and forgot all about the younger brother in her rapt contemplation of the elder. Lady Georgiana placed herself in the seat they had saved for her, and Constant bowed before Caroline. "Well, Miss Percival? Will you redeem your promise?"

She rose and accepted his arm, a little nervous. Now that the moment was upon her, would she acquit herself well at a public assembly?

As they walked toward the dancers, Caroline felt other worries overcoming any excitement about the dancing. She sighed. Well, she might come to another ball, some-day, and this one, alive with Christmas gaiety, would be well lost if she could but set her mind at rest. "Mr. Constant," she said in a low voice, "may I ask you to take me home?"

He looked at her in astonishment. "Take you home? Are you ill?"

"No, but I'm most anxious—I know I'm being fool-ish, but I've seen the Brangleys here, and I can't get over the feeling that they mean some mischief to Harriet. I wish to go home and see if she's safe."

"The Brangleys? Here? They were supposed to be in Croydon. Point them out to me, my dear." Constant looked concerned, serious.

Caroline was satisfied that he did not think her silly. She searched about the room for that dreadful dress of Mrs. Brangley's but could glimpse nary a spangle.

Maybe she had imagined seeing the couple . . . "I can't find them, but I know they were here."

Constant looked into her eyes. "I can see you're worried—for no reason, I hope." He smiled and laid his hand on hers where it rested in the crook of his arm. "What do you say to going back to your house very quickly? Then you may grant me the next two dances when we return to the ball. We won't even have to alarm my mother by telling her we're leaving; we'll simply make haste and go."

"Oh, sir, that's the best solution possible. I do hope to allay my fears quickly, and if we could come back to the ball, my own mother would be so happy—that is, I suppose I would, too, but my mother is the one who wanted to hear all about this assembly."

"You are either too modest or too shy, Miss Percival," he said. "I had planned for this to be an evening of great pleasure for you." He paused as though sensing he had said too much. "And I'm sure half a dozen other gentlemen have the same design."

He escorted her quickly out the ballroom door and into the busy entry. Caroline stood by the fireplace while he sought her cloak. People were passing in and out all the time, and she kept looking for the Brangleys. Had she truly imagined seeing them? By the time Constant arrived and placed her wrap over her shoulders, she was half convinced she was dragging him on a fool's errand.

"What if the Brangleys are here, for whatever unaccountable reason?" she said, half to herself, as she and Constant emerged into a torchlit winter night. "Anybody may come to Bath. How could they know where Harriet is staying even if they know she's in the city?"

"My dear, don't apologize for your worry over the child. It does you credit. And if the Brangleys are here by pure hazard, and we find no threatening message at your house or my mother's, I'll have had the pleasure of a companionable walk with you."

"Oh, yes, let's walk." The night was blessedly dry, and

walking sounded much faster than the complex business of finding a chair.

"I'm glad the thought of impropriety is not crossing your mind," Constant said. She could see his keen, questioning look in the light of the moon now they had walked away from the rooms and were heading downhill to the Crescent.

"You're right; I should have remembered." Caroline was stricken; why couldn't she keep in mind the correct manners for a young woman of her station? Someone like Lady Georgiana would never forget the proper thing. "But," she had to add, "naturally there can be no question of impropriety between you and me, sir."

"Naturally not," he said after a moment of silence.

They walked quickly then, saying nothing further, both in a hurry to set Caroline's mind at rest. Soon they arrived in the Crescent. The Percival house was dark, for over an hour had passed since the ball-goers had set out. Caroline knew her mother had been planning an early night and was not surprised to find no lights burning save a lamp in the entryway, meant for her own convenience when she arrived home.

Constant waited at the bottom of the stairs while Caroline dashed up to look in on Harriet.

She noticed that the child's door was left ajar, as it never was; yet for all her forebodings, she was still shocked to look into the little white bed and find that Harriet was gone.

9

IN HER short life Harriet had grown accustomed to sudden changes. First there was the change from having a mama and papa to having no one; then the change from a neighbor's house to her own particular purgatory at the Brangleys'; then the few sweet days of happiness with Caroline and Aunt Elinor. Through it all, grown people had appeared and told Harriet what she was to do and where she was to go. She was used to it.

This occasion was no different. She had just been put to bed when Nurse Binnie tiptoed into the nursery and told Harriet to get up at once, for they were going on a journey. In no time Harriet was dressed and ready, her things had been packed, and Nurse carried them down along with cases of her own. Harriet was cautioned to go quietly because Lady Percival was sleeping and must not be disturbed; and when she asked why she couldn't leave in the morning, so as to be able to say good-bye to both the Percivals, Nurse simply said that they wanted Harriet gone before they woke.

This was familiar ground to Harriet; Mrs. Brangley had always been wanting her gone no matter what time of day it was, and that lady had made a practice of not saying good-bye to her small cousin, whatever the occasion.

Harriet tried to hold back her tears as she left the house where she had been so happy, for she knew Caroline and Aunt Elinor would not like to think of her crying.

What she could not understand was why, having been

so kind, they wished her to leave. But she had never known the reason she had had to leave places before, and she did not think to ask questions this time, especially since Nurse was so unexpectedly cross. Harriet sighed as she was bundled into a dark coach waiting on the pavement a little way down the street. She had probably done something naughty, something she couldn't remember, and her misbehavior was the reason behind this mysterious departure.

"I shall never have a premonition again," Caroline said bitterly, twisting a handkerchief in her lap. The handkerchief was the beautiful new one that matched her white and silver gown, she noticed as though she were looking on the scene from afar. She had much admired the silver lace edging it. She would mend that new tear someday.

"Now, now, my dear, this could not have been foretold," Lady Percival said in a soothing voice. Nightcap askew, she had been wheeled in her Bath chair into the drawing room to join the young people. "I simply cannot believe Harriet was stolen away so quietly that I didn't hear. And who could have done it?"

"More to the point, why?" Constant was grim as he paced back and forth. He and Caroline had roused the house, set all the servants to look into every corner, called the child's name a hundred times before coming to an inescapable conclusion: Harriet had left the premises. Her nurse was missing, too; and whether both had been spirited away or whether the nurse had taken Harriet remained a mystery. Nobody in the house had a reason to dislike Nurse Binns, but nobody really knew her as yet. At least, Harriet's friends concluded, the child was likely not alone. Not that a companion who meant her harm would do her much good . . .

"Tomorrow is Christmas Eve," Caroline said. "I did want her to have a lovely Christmas. Now she'll be frightened, scared."

"We'll have her back by Christmas," Constant said,

stopping in his perambulations to stare piercingly at Caroline. "I'm going now to set my servants to picking up the trail. A six-year-old child, alone or with a companion, is no common traveler, especially at night."

"They probably locked the poor little thing in a box," Lady Percival said, drying a tear. She was a great reader of Gothic novels and the more sensational newspapers.

"Mama!" Caroline was horrified.

"Well, my dear, I don't like to dwell on the worst possibilities, but one does hear of dreadful things happening nowadays—"

"I can't think of it," Caroline said resolutely. "She must be under the care of Nurse Binns, she simply must. Whoever took her had some regard for her comfort, whether it was the nurse or someone else. I really do think the Brangleys had something to do with it, for it's simply too great a coincidence for them to suddenly appear in Bath the very night Harriet goes missing. Mr. Constant, can we not return to the ball and question them?"

"Why not? I'll return for you in fifteen minutes, when I've set my own people to search. I have yet to claim those dances, Miss Percival." And Constant hurried out of the room.

"You didn't even get to dance? What a pity." Lady Percival shook her head at her daughter. "And you look so lovely. Little Harriet was in raptures over seeing you and the others in ball dress. I simply can't believe—oh, Caroline, do you think we can really get her back?"

"We must, Mama," Caroline said, lifting her shoulders in determination. "She will need us more than ever now."

Constant returned before the quarter-hour was up, and he and Caroline walked quickly back to the Upper Rooms, quiet comrades in worry. As they entered the ballroom Lady Lambert rushed up to them.

"My dears, I knew you hadn't really left the room together. But I'm afraid some of the old cats in the place are quite ready to make much of your absence, so if you please, Caroline, do think quickly of some story about a torn hem or a faint. Now I must go back to dear General Fontaine. Only think, the man managed to smuggle all his fortune out of France in the nineties. No title, though. Come with me, Caroline, and remember, act ill—or as though you just repaired your dress—something." Lady Lambert's smile was conspiratorial, and she actually winked.

Caroline was somewhat dazzled by the torrent of words. Through her fear for Harriet she was just able to grasp the fact that Constant's mother seemed to think her son and Caroline had been carrying on a flirtation or worse. And she didn't seem to mind!

"Ma'am, Mr. Constant and I must walk about the room looking for that couple I pointed out to you earlier—the Brangleys."

"That dreadful gown with all the spangles." Lady Lambert nodded seriously. "I saw it not five minutes ago. There! Just going into the card room."

Caroline looked; she was too late to see anything but the smallest swish of sky blue satin disappearing into the chamber in question. But she made her excuses to Lady Lambert and headed across the room, closely followed by Constant.

The Brangleys were indeed in the card room; Mrs. Brangley was standing behind her husband's chair as he sat down to whist. Constant murmured in Caroline's ear, "Leave this to me," and stepped up to the table, leaving Caroline stationed near the door.

"Mrs. Brangley," Constant said loudly.

The woman gave a start and turned toward him in surprise. Her wide smile seemed to fill her face. "Why, dear Mr. Constant. Look, Arthur, it is Mr. Constant. We little expected to see you here."

"Did you not?" Constant's voice was calm as he acknowledged Mr. Brangley with a nod. "I distinctly remember telling you in my letter that I could be reached in Bath at present. You do remember the letter? In it I explained that I was taking little Miss Deauville away from your house."

"Miss Deauville? Oh, you mean dear, sweet Harriet." Mrs. Brangley simpered in an almost ghastly manner, Caroline thought. "As a matter of fact, we were going to call on you in the morning, Mr. Constant. I'm certain you meant very well, dear sir, but we simply can't part with Harriet, you see. My Amanda is much too fond of her."

"Ah, your Amanda. Isn't she a small hellion in petticoats who tried to drown Harriet in the Serpentine last summer?"

Mrs. Brangley's eyes bulged. "Who told you such lies?"

Constant shrugged and smiled.

Caroline had told him that story, of course. She shrank farther back against the wall, her old dread of her employers returning full force as she imagined Mrs. Brangley lashing out at her. That she was no longer in their power seemed beside the point; she supposed it took longer than a matter of weeks genuinely to change from a browbeaten servant to an independent woman. She felt her ball gown enveloping her not as a becoming garment, but as a disguise.

"You were coming to see me tomorrow?" Constant was saying. "Then I confess I'm at a loss—how did you think you could remedy the situation by removing Harriet from her new home tonight?"

"Removing her?" Mrs. Brangley looked incredulous, and even her mostly oblivious husband looked up from his cards at the shrill sound of his wife's voice.

"Forgive me," Constant said, "I must have made a mistake."

Caroline couldn't believe that he was quitting the field when that awful woman was evidently hiding something. Mrs. Brangley wouldn't balk at falsehoods. Didn't she claim her family had to have Harriet back for affection's sake? What Caroline couldn't fathom was why they should really want the child. All fears of her late employers forgotten, she stepped forward, rigid with contempt.

"Where is she?" She snapped out the words and was just able to stop herself from shaking her fist in Mrs. Brangley's face.

"Young woman, this is a private conversation between me and this gentleman," Mrs. Brangley stated grandly. Then she looked closer at Caroline, gaze sweeping over gown and hair as well as face. "Why, you look vaguely familiar. Have me met, madam? Do you perhaps have a lowborn relation in straitened circumstances who works as a governess?"

"No," Caroline said. "I am Caroline Percival, ma'am."

"Why, so you are." Mrs. Brangley stared in evident fascination. "How on earth do you come to be at a ball in Bath? And in stolen finery, no less."

Caroline was nearly beside herself with fury. "Never mind. It's none of your affair, ma'am, how I come by my garments or how I choose to spend my time. What is important is that you tell us at once where Harriet is. You can't have thought how frightened she would be; she is such an insecure child—"

"What in the world?" Mrs. Brangley turned to Constant. "Do you know this young person, sir? Can you do me the greatest favor and remove her from my presence? She is a wanton creature I once employed, and naturally I don't wish to speak to her now she's become deranged."

Constant ignored Mrs. Brangley. "I think the woman is telling the truth. She knows nothing," he said to Caroline, speaking low. Then, as her eyes widened with disbelief, he added, "I've been watching her face and her husband's. They are genuinely surprised at the idea of Harriet's being gone. They didn't know you were in Bath, so they wouldn't have been likely to trace Harriet to your house. We must look elsewhere for our villain."

"Mr. Constant," Mrs. Brangley said, glaring at Caroline, "that governess person is still here."

"Your pardon, madam. Sorry to have troubled you,"

Constant said. Taking Caroline by the elbow, he headed back into the ballroom.

"Guy, they must know where Harriet is. You can't mean to leave without prying her whereabouts from them." Caroline noticed, once the words were out of her mouth, that she had called him by his Christian name. In private she had started to try out the sound of that name on her tongue, but she had never called him anything but Mr. Constant in public.

"No, I don't think they know a thing," Constant responded. If he noticed Caroline's lapse in formality, he gave no sign. "Now, my dear, shall we go back to your house once more? Let's say good night to mother before we leave. I say, if that's General Fontaine with her, he's older than her usual pick. Must have done his fighting a half century ago."

Caroline was not distracted by his attempt to lighten the mood, but she appreciated it. "Thank you, sir, you are very good, but I wouldn't notice tonight if the general were a hundred. We must set out at once and look for Harriet. And I would have someone search the town and the Brangleys' hotel."

"It's been done," Constant said, and Caroline was reminded of the quarter hour he had left her with her mother earlier. She also remembered how powerful he must be to set all things in motion with so little trouble. "What do you mean, 'we'?" he continued. "You surely can't be thinking of journeying out to look for the child."

"If you go, I go," Caroline stated. "Propriety means nothing to me, sir. I must get to her as soon as I can and show her that some adults are trustworthy; that she can count on both you and me."

"You are a stubborn young woman, but one whose fortitude I must admire," Constant said, taking her hand. "Well, shall we be off? My men ought to have some information for us by now. Perhaps we can take out my curricle and catch up with the abductors. Do you have something warm for driving in an open carriage in December?"

She had a new Witchoura cloak. She nodded and hurried in the direction of Lady Lambert and Lady Georgiana, anxious to get the business of leavetaking over as soon as possible.

"Someday," Constant said near her ear as he accompanied her through the crowd, "I will see that lovely ball gown of yours put to better use than in walking quickly across a room."

Caroline had to smile at his sally, but she was already thinking ahead to how fast she could remove the delicate gown and hurry into her warmest walking dress.

Harriet was finding the journey to be quite an adventure. Nurse told her they were going Bristol way, and as the post chaise hurried through the night, one of the wheels plunged into a large hole in the road. Harriet thought the bouncing sensation was quite delightful, but Nurse hit her head on a heavy toilet case and lay motionless in the vehicle.

Harriet sat very still for a while. The coach was listing to one side. Nurse was breathing; Harriet had learned from the Brangley children's experiments with hapless animals that all would be well, eventually, so long as the subject breathed. Outside she could hear colorful language coming from the postillions, who were trying to quiet the horses. They would probably right the carriage in a moment, and she would be sent to travel with someone else—someone who was awake.

Eventually Harriet felt the unusual sensation of the chaise coming to rights again. She waited for someone to open the door, and, when no one did, she opened it herself and peeked out.

The postillions were arguing some point in the ditch not far from Harriet. She didn't think they looked nice, either one of them, especially when the coach tilted again and they began to speak in angry words she had never heard before. She wouldn't stay with them; she would be better off walking back to the Percivals' in Bath. She jumped down from the coach, slipped past the

men and began to stride along the road, thinking wistful
thoughts about muffins, and a warm bed, and all sorts of
things she couldn't have at the moment.

She thought she walked for a very long time. Her feet,
though in sturdy new half-boots, were sore from the
rocks in the road.

"Hey, there, what's this?" bellowed a strange, deep
voice. Harriet looked in the direction of the sound—it
was a full moon, and she could see quite clearly—and
beheld a dark, scowling face peering out of the window
of a massive coach that had halted just beside her. At
least it was something like a face. Despite the bright
moonlight, all she could really make out were a jutting
nose and heavy, beetling brows.

Not knowing what else to do, she curtsied as Miss
Percival had taught her and said, "How do you do, sir?"

The sort-of-a-face stared in astonishment; the whites of
the man's eyes shone in the moonlight. Harriet thought
he looked very nice, but it was so odd that there didn't
seem to be much to him besides nose and eyes. From
within his carriage came growls and muffled snarls, then
a chorus of loud barks. Harriet's head tilted in interest.

"Quiet, there, you hellbound curs, I'm talking to the
lady. How do *I* do?" The man scowled again, so far as
Harriet could tell. "I'm not the one five years old, gadding
about the king's highway looking for the bogeyman."

Harriet gasped, and for the first time she looked
around at the night as though it could be less than
friendly.

"You come up with me and my Fellows," the man
said. "Who are you, and where do you come from?"

"Harriet Deauville, sir, and I come from—well, I was
in Bath this evening, so I think I come from there. I'm
six years old," Harriet said.

"Your pardon, madam, for misreading your age," the
stranger said. The door to the coach opened, and a large
hand reached out. "Grab on, little one. We'll have you
back in Bath in no time. This team of mine does twenty
miles an hour, day or night."

Harriet did not think she would mention that she had been heading away from Bath at the last. Bath was where the Percivals were, and though they had wished her to leave, they would certainly not mind if she stayed another day until they could arrange things better. She would like to sleep in her bed again and say a proper good-bye to Caroline and Aunt Elinor. She spared not a passing thought for Binnie, the nurse, unconscious in the ditched carriage.

When she jumped into the coach, she was immediately surrounded by furry bodies and large, seeking tongues. She giggled uncontrollably as four huge dogs nosed at her.

"Here." The strange man untied her bonnet. "What the Fellows want is an ear, missy. Once you give it them, they'll leave you be."

The man was right. All the dogs licked Harriet's ears, and then they settled down, one on either side of her on the carriage squabs, one beside the man opposite, one on the floor. They were very big dogs. The one on the floor occasionally licked Harriet's foot in its tiny half-boot, and the ones on the seat with her snuggled up close.

Harriet knew she ought to look at the man, ask him who he was. He had asked her, and so it must be the polite thing to do. But the warm fur of her new companions made her sleepier than ever, and so did the gentle rocking of the carriage. Before long she was nodding.

"Child!" The man shook her awake from a half-dream involving large dogs and a country field. "What is your father's name? I will take you to him."

"Papa's name?" Harriet answered from the depth of her memory. "His name is Harry Deauville." She thought she ought to mention that Papa was dead, but perhaps he was not, since she was being taken to him . . .

She fell asleep.

With a strange sense of unreality, Caroline found herself settling into Constant's curricle. She had on her warmest gown, for the night had turned bitterly cold, and her gloved hands were buried in a fur muff. She was well wrapped in her cloak lined with matching fur, and Constant tucked a carriage robe around her besides.

"I'll take good care of her, Lady Percival," he called softly, out of regard for the neighbors, who might not be sympathetic to all these frantic comings and goings in the dead of night.

Her ladyship had been wheeled to the front door of her house, and she raised a hand to the pair in leavetaking.

Constant proceeded to head the curricle in the direction of the Bristol Road. One of his servants had come back with the news that a likely post chaise had been seen traveling in that direction at about the time in question.

"Mama took the danger to my reputation remarkably well, considering that she won't let me out of her sight without a footman now she's come into money," Caroline remarked, for lack of something more clever to say.

"Remarkable, indeed," responded Constant, tooling the ribbons as expertly as Caroline had known he would.

She gave him a sharp look, thinking she caught something odd in his tone, but he was looking at the road and she couldn't see his expression.

Though the moon was up, clouds were gathering in the cold sky above, and Caroline shivered under her many coverings, hoping that Harriet, wherever she was, was not only safe but warm. They had brought along extra wraps for the child.

"Cold?" Constant transferred the reins to one hand and encircled Caroline with his arm.

She went rigid with shock, knowing she should pull back in a true missish manner, yet hating to end this unsettling experience. Again she sneaked a look up at him. Was he only trying to keep her warm? She would be mortified to read something more intimate into a purely friendly wish for her comfort.

Suddenly their eyes met. Constant said softly, "You've guessed it, Miss Percival, I'm using the sharp weather for purely selfish motives. May I call you Caroline?"

"Yes." She kept looking into his eyes, surprised at her own bravery. She supposed there were some advantages to not being a schoolroom miss; she was more than ready for whatever was coming.

Unfortunately, what was coming was another carriage, barreling at them from the opposite direction and appropriating most of the roadway. Caroline held her breath as Constant averted disaster with a masterful handling of his pair.

"Well—Caroline—that clumsy driver neatly took the wind out of my sails. I was about to kiss you. Did you guess that?"

"Yes." She spoke the word softly.

"Then there's nothing for it. We must simply lose a few minutes' time." Constant pulled the carriage up at the side of the road, circled both his arms around Caroline, and brought his lips down on hers.

Caroline had been kissed before, by men whom she had longed to injure with the nearest blunt instrument for taking such unwanted liberties. As a governess she was always being trapped and assaulted by mischievous gentlemen; Lord Marchton's try at her had been no isolated incident. Kissing was not an activity she had ever enjoyed. She didn't think she was a prude; she simply felt that such an experience as a kiss should take place in a more emotional mood than anger on her part, boredom on the man's. In the back of her mind, though, had been the fear that no kiss would be anything worth having; that she *was* somehow unnaturally cold as more than one molester had accused her.

Now she found her fears were groundless. Constant's kiss was gentle at first, tender; then it became something much more. Eventually he dragged his lips from hers and kissed her throat, her cheek, the lobe of her ear; Caroline matched him, stealing one arm around his neck. Their lips met again, this time with no hesitation, and they kissed deeply, the passion coming as a true shock to Caroline, yet the most pleasant one she had ever experienced.

"We'd better be on our way," Constant said after much too short a time. "We have a task before us. I had to do that, Caroline; I won't apologize."

"I won't ask you to," Caroline said, rearranging her little fur hat, which had become somewhat dislodged in the last moments.

She said nothing further—she was unable to think of anything—and Constant gave her a quizzical look as he set the restive pair in motion.

"And so much for the proprieties," he finally said with a short laugh when they were moving again.

She managed to return that laugh with one of her own, trying for the touch of sophistication that must be expected in one of her years. "Best to get that out of the way, as you said."

"Get it out of the way?" In the moonlight she could see his puzzled face. "Did I say that?"

"Something very like it." Caroline shrugged, wishing she had kept silent. She felt, somehow, that they had both ruined a lovely moment with chattering.

She made up for her loquacity with silence, and he, too, said nothing further. The freezing air cooled Caroline's cheeks as the curricle rolled on through the night countryside, past barren winter fields and the dark houses of the occasional hamlet. Once Constant halted his equipage at an inn where there were signs of life; but nobody in the place had seen a little girl, nor had any coach but Constant's stopped in the last few hours.

Caroline had finally stopped thinking of the kiss, and had her mind entirely on Harriet, when she saw something dark and not right in the road ahead. She pointed.

"A ditched chaise." Constant steered his horses to the side and came to a stop behind the vehicle. "We'd better see if we can be of help."

"Of course." Caroline hated to lose more time, but naturally the poor travelers must be in need of assistance. She jumped down from the curricle after Constant, though he told her to remain in her seat.

"I may be needed," she insisted, marching up to the carriage as he went on to the men who were cutting the traces of a nervous team. She couldn't do much, but she had salts in her reticule and had been told in the past that she had a nice way with sick people. She would hope to put this talent into practice if anyone lay injured.

Caroline peeked through the wildly tilting window nearest her; by standing on tiptoe she could just see in. A woman was lying down, half on the squabs, half on the floor.

"Ma'am?" Caroline called. "Are you all right?"

The woman moaned loudly and turned over, falling completely onto the chaise floor in the process. Caroline ran around the back of the chaise, and, noticing the door was ajar, managed to get herself into the vehicle with the woman. She sat down on one of the squabs and felt in her reticule for the salts, which she held to the other's nose.

The victim came awake with a squeak, drawing back in surprise.

By her dress she was a servant. Caroline looked closely at the female, struggling to see the features, for she was almost certain something about the person was familiar.

"Who are you?" she asked, returning the salts to her reticule.

"Martha Binns, ma'am," responded the other, rubbing her forehead. "My word, what happened?"

"Binns? Binnie!" Harriet's nurse! Caroline took the woman by the shoulders. "Where is Harriet, girl? Do you hear me? Where is she?"

"Why, here in the chaise," Binnie said in surprise. Still dazed, she began to poke about, feeling the squabs, even lifting a rug. "She were here a moment ago."

"How long have you been unconscious—no, of course you wouldn't know." Caroline knew she should stop to question Binnie about what exactly was going forward, but her first priority was Harriet. Leaving the woman without another word, she got out of the coach carefully, as it was still askew, and began to call the little girl's name, wandering into the middle of the quiet road to see if any small shadows were moving on the road ahead or behind.

This attracted the attention of Constant, who had been helping the men with the horses. "Caroline! What are you doing?" He rushed up to her and caught her arm.

"Harriet's nurse is in the coach, and she expected Harriet to be with her," Caroline told him. "Harriet must have got out when the coach was ditched. Did the men see her? Oh, please, we must find out how long the carriage has been stopped. To think of her out here, in the night—it's intolerable." She pulled away and continued to call out Harriet's name, walking.

Constant's reaction was instant. He rushed back to the chaise and yelled questions at the men; then he spoke to the nursemaid inside. Caroline could hear his voice as she kept calling for Harriet; he was controlled, yet a note of suppressed rage was evident in his tones.

He joined her within five minutes. "They've been stopped for under half an hour. The men are hirelings from the Pelican in Bath. As for that fool of a nursemaid, she says some gentleman she had never seen before paid her well to convey the child to Bristol. From the description she gives, he could be anyone. A plump, middle-aged fellow. They were to rendezvous at a tavern there, the Llandoger Trow. I mean to go there and discover what sort of fiend would kidnap an innocent child."

"But we can't leave this area," Caroline cried. "Harriet must be here somewhere. We simply must find her. She could freeze in this weather."

The moon had gone into hiding some time ago. As though on cue, the first snowflakes dropped out of the leaden night sky.

Constant heard the note of hysteria in Caroline's voice and held her close for a moment, simply held her and let his strength flow through her. She leaned against him for a precious moment, shocked by the sense of communion.

Then they broke apart, and Guy organized his forces quickly. The men and horses were to go to the nearest village, about a mile east, and obtain help for their chaise. The maid could go with them or wait in the carriage; he didn't care. He would go to that village and also the next one west down the road, where he would get up search parties. Then he meant to go to Bristol and find out if the kidnapper was waiting at the rendezvous. Caroline let him tell her this, but through it all she was busily walking up the road and down, calling, "Harriet! Please come out. You're safe now. It's Caroline. Harriet!"

So certain was she that such a little child had to be nearby, though Harriet might have wandered off anytime during the last half hour, that she simply refused to leave. The snow was falling faster now, and before many hours had passed dawn would be breaking on the morning of Christmas Eve, but this was certainly no incentive for Caroline to get to shelter.

"That poor little girl is out in this, don't you understand?" she cried with tears in her eyes when Constant urged her to come with him to the nearest settlement.

"I do, my dear, I do. If we get every able-bodied native of these parts searching the area, we'll find her much faster than if we simply stood here and called her. We must do the most efficient thing, mustn't we?"

"How can you be so logical?" Caroline demanded. "Don't you care at all?"

"I care too much to let you catch your death while endeavoring to see she doesn't catch hers," he said, drawing her into his arms. "Come, Caroline. We've done all we can here. We'll find her before she's harmed; mark my words."

"Oh, Guy," Caroline said miserably, "she could be harmed already."

"We'll have to start praying for a Christmas miracle, then, won't we?" Constant returned. His expression was grim as he led Caroline back to the snow-covered curricle.

10

"'ERE, NOW, MUM, don't you worrit yourself," said kindly Mrs. Dumfrey, pouring a cup of tea and setting it firmly before Caroline. "Get some warm into you. You're froze to the bone."

Motherly talk of how cold she was gave Caroline no comfort; she only set to worrying harder over Harriet's condition. Almost against her will, her fingers closed around the teacup. She sipped, coughed in surprise, and sipped again.

"Just a bit of Christmas cheer to warm you," Mrs. Dumfrey explained with a benign smile. "I'm betting a lady like yourself, mum, would have refused, but best you have a little drop of the creature. 'Twill relax you."

"I don't want to relax," Caroline said, but she kept sipping. Outside the window of the inn's kitchen, where she sat at Mrs. Dumfrey's table, the snow was beginning to blow. Day had broken, thank goodness, but the men and boys of the village would be having a difficult time in their search.

"My man knows every inch of this country, and so does every soul who's gone out to search," Mrs. Dumfrey said. She smiled on seeing Caroline's look of hope. "There, there, if the little girl is out in this neighborhood, she'll be found. The men knows all the places she could hide, all the holes she could fall into, all of that."

Caroline shuddered.

She was about to reach for a bit of bread from the platter on the table when Constant appeared in the doorway, in the act of putting on his greatcoat. "Well, my dear, I'm off to Bristol."

"But I'm coming with you."

"You are not." Constant had been very firm on this issue, undeterred by the fact that Caroline had never agreed with him. "You're chilled and exhausted; besides, you'll be needed here when they find Harriet."

"But Mrs. Dumfrey has promised to keep her safe, and there's that wretched nursemaid. At least Harriet knows her." Caroline cast a look of loathing to the chimney corner, where Martha Binns was hunched over a mug of warm ale, her rabbity features wrapped in gloom. "I want to help you deal with the monster who kidnapped the poor child. Oh, if only we knew why. I still can't believe the Brangleys aren't somehow concerned."

"I'm Harriet's guardian. Better to let me deal with the man, whoever he is," Constant said. "And I don't wish to involve you. We don't know the rules to this game as yet." He put an arm about Caroline, and Mrs. Dumfrey immediately smiled in understanding.

Unlike any other couple in their situation, Caroline and Guy hadn't lied about their circumstances. In the confusion and hurry to get a search party out into the snow after Harriet, they hadn't had time to concoct some story about being brother and sister or man and wife. They had simply presented themselves as what they were: friends concerned for a child's safety. Now Mrs. Dumfrey was apparently embroidering upon their simple tale.

Constant observed this, grinned at the landlady, and planted a kiss on Caroline's forehead. He followed this by a gentle one on her mouth. From the corner, Binnie signed enviously.

Caroline's cheeks were already red from the dubious spirits Mrs. Dumfrey had put into her tea, and so she was not put to the trouble of blushing. She did feel warmer than she had a moment before. "Will you come back as soon as you can?" she asked. "And what shall we do about communicating with my mother? Mrs. Dumfrey says the mail coach has already gone by."

"Yes, it's a night mail in these parts," Mrs. Dumfrey put in, still regarding the possible lovers with close attention.

"Your mother will have to trust us until we can get a message through," Constant said. "She knows we're sensible, mature individuals without an impetuous bone in our bodies; and if she has any questions of propriety in her mind, she will be glad later on to hear that we spent most of this adventure in separate locales. Mrs. Dumfrey"—he turned to the hovering woman—"I wish you would get Miss Percival to lie down and rest while I'm gone."

"Aye, sir, I'll see she does that," the landlady replied cheerfully. "Now, mum, you be going up to bed. I'll ring for Bertha." She clanged a large bell as she spoke. "I'll be a-making of some good beef tea for the little one; bound to be cold and hungry when she comes in, and I won't stuff her full of mince pies and marchpane, even if it is Christmas."

Caroline nodded, feeling defeated and suddenly very tired.

"Good work, Mrs. Dumfrey," remarked Constant, helping Caroline to rise. "Our cause is aided by the fact that Miss Percival is dead on her feet, but we'll use whatever methods we must. Now, I'm off." He kissed Caroline once more and went out the kitchen door, letting in a flurry of snow.

"The weather,'" moaned Caroline. "He won't even get through to Bristol."

"To be sure he will, ma'am. My man said 'twill come to nothing, this snowfall."

"And is Mr. Dumfrey an expert on the weather?" Caroline asked, summoning up a weak smile.

"Not he, but his bones is; the rheumatism always tells him with a surety what the weather's to be. And he says a little fall, then good weather to melt it off before the freezing rain sets in."

"He can tell about freezing rain in the future?" Caroline asked, curious despite her fatigue.

"Nay, mum, that's naught but him looking on the black side of things," Mrs. Dumfrey said. She bustled about the kitchen as she talked; Caroline was comforted by the mere sight of her.

She swayed as she stood at the table and was about to sit back down when the servant girl, Bertha, arrived to help her to a bedroom.

The inn was an ancient one with uneven floors and unexpected stairs, darkly paneled, hung with Christmas holly and ivy. Caroline would have been charmed by the hostel's picturesque qualities had she not been so worried. She was indeed capitvated by the folk she had met. From Mrs. Dumfrey, who seemed to run the village as well as the inn, to little Bertha, smiling so shyly as she showed Caroline all the conveniences of the bedroom and then helped her out of her woolen gown, they were all delightful people. Was it only the holiday spirit that made everybody so eager to help, or were they truly an extremely kind set of individuals?

Caroline might have debated this point with herself for a long time if she hadn't fallen asleep as soon as her head hit the goosedown pillow of an ancient cabinet bed.

Constant had halfway expected disappointment at journey's end.

All the way to Bristol, a jaunt of some seven miles from the village where he had left Caroline, he had taken great pleasure at thought of the meeting between himself and Harriet's prospective abductor. Oh, he was looking forward to it. He only hoped the fellow would be of suitable age and rank for calling out; but failing that, fisticuffs would certainly be in order.

Wrathful thoughts and pleasurable ones chased each other through his mind. He had kissed Caroline; finally, after weeks of wanting to, he had broken the physical barriers and got his arms around her. It felt good; their intimacy was natural, right.

He realized that he had wanted to be close to her since the first time of seeing her in the Brangleys' house. No one had been more surprised than himself. He had never so much as looked at a governess in his life, and if she hadn't raised her eyes to him, those incredible, defiant blue eyes, he wouldn't have looked at this one.

Plans for further opportunities to kiss Caroline were busying him as he drove into the bustling morning streets of Bristol. The spire of Saint Mary Redcliffe soared above the busy holiday scene. The snow had mercifully stopped some time ago; only a few icy flakes were blowing about above the River Avon, just enough to remind one it was winter near the seacoast.

Constant inquired of the first person he saw the way to the Llandoger Trow; he was directed to King Street near the harbor. When he arrived, he walked quickly into the old half-timbered inn, pausing only to throw his reins to a young street urchin with a few words of instruction for the benefit of the horses.

"There is a man here awaiting a nursemaid and a little child," he said to the innkeeper with an unmistakable air of authority.

Evidently the landlord was not in the business of hiding people's dark motives or taking bribes from villains. He pointed the way to the private parlor the gentleman awaiting the child had hired, and where he was sitting now.

Constant strode into the low-beamed room, blood in his eye; and when he found himself facing a small, round, jolly-looking fellow in late middle age, a man he had never seen before and who looked a cross between a clergyman and a country squire, he stopped short, disconcerted.

"You are waiting for the child Harriet Deauville?" Constant demanded, recovering himself.

The little man had been sitting in an armchair near a crackling fire. He blinked, then got to his feet and bowed. "Yes, sir, I have that charge. I am only the agent for the little girl's guardian, you know. Do you come from him?"

"Guardian?" Constant was careful not to betray his anger. Perhaps the fellow would reveal himself.

The man seemed to have no reason not to do so. "Yes. A Mr. Guy Constant. I act as his representative. Permit me to introduce myself. I am Demetrius Hyde, solicitor. You see, sir, little Miss Deauville has been spirited away from her proper caretakers and placed in the charge of some loose women in Bath. We're paying her nursemaid to bring her here, where we will see to it she is conveyed safely back to Mr. Constant."

"I see."

"And whom do I have the pleasure of addressing?" Mr. Hyde asked, apple cheeks rounding in a broad smile.

"My name is Constant."

The other man gave a start. "A relation? Have you come to take Mr. Guy Constant's part in this?"

"You might say so. Mr. Hyde, would it interest you to know that there's been an accident, that Miss Deauville has disappeared somewhere between here and Bath?"

"What?" Demetrius Hyde's eyebrows flew up. "But I paid that nursemaid to bring her here in safety. I'll see to it that an action is brought against the flighty girl, do you hear?"

Guy certainly did hear; Mr. Hyde's voice had risen by several notes during his impassioned speech. Guy looked in spurious pity at the choleric little man and shook his head in what he must hope would pass for regret. "And now I suppose you'll have to tell the person who hired you, Mr. Guy Constant, that the plan has failed. Where would you find my relation? I'd be glad to convey the message to him myself."

Mr. Hyde nodded; his part in this was over, and Guy wouldn't have been surprised if, his fee paid, the solicitor would not prefer being supplanted in the role of bearer of bad news. Hyde searched his pockets, coat, and waistcoat several times before coming up with a card. This he placed into Constant's hands.

Guy was not too shocked to find that the card was his own, and that on it was scribbled—in clumsy capitals of the sort to foil handwriting experts—his own direction in Bath.

Caroline awoke after a few fitful hours of rest and found the world a less threatening place. It was full daylight, as it had not been when she had lain down. The snow had fined to almost nothing, and the wind had stopped. But when she rushed downstairs to Mrs. Dumfrey's kitchen, she could see at once that Harriet had not been found.

Several men were dripping and steaming before the fire, gulping down warm ale and sandwiches. Mrs. Dumfrey was busy at the hearth, stirring soup, and the small maid, Bertha, trotted to and fro, serving food and drink.

Caroline recognized the men as some of the searchers. "Nothing," she said, her shoulders sagging as she paused just inside the kitchen door.

"No sign of the mite, Miss," one of the men corroborated, shaking his head. "Been up hill and down dale for miles around and questioned every cottage on and off the road."

"Did no one hear or see anything strange during the night?" Caroline asked, wondering if she, as a stranger, might be able to interpret some untoward occurrence in a way the village men could not.

"Naught but a barking of dogs, mum," another man informed her, taking a pull on his mug. "Strange dogs, old Nancy says. She be the one lives on the road, down near where the coach went into 'er ditch. But old Nan ain't never been one to hear right."

"Dogs!" Caroline couldn't have imagined anything to alarm her more. The very idea of great, vicious beasts cornering Harriet was heart-stopping.

"Not a sign of trouble down that way," said the man, meeting Caroline's eye. She nodded, understanding the things he hadn't said about blood, and signs of a struggle, and torn fabrics.

"Now what I think," spoke up Mrs. Dumfrey, casting a disgusted look at the last speaker, "is if there's no sign of the little dear, then someone gave her a lift to the next village. It ain't impossible, for she'd likely keep to the road. Wouldn't know any of the footpaths, a child like that, a stranger here." She smiled reassuringly at Caroline. "I've sent my Jem, I have, second oldest boy, to ask at the settlements nearest on either side of us. Could be the young missy is holed up in some cottage, being cosseted by a good wife, and never knowing there's anyone worried about her."

"Oh, I do hope so," Caroline said, and sank down onto a kitchen stool.

The next hours brought more of the men who had been searching, none of whom had found a trace of the little girl or heard any word; the Dumfreys' Jem, who had ridden the cob to several of the nearby villages and found no suggestion that Harriet had been to any of them; and a friendly squire, the local magistrate, who promised to marshal even more forces to seek the missing child.

Caroline received this gentleman in the inn's one parlor, a happy-looking, chintz-trimmed place hung with Christmas. Squire Donaldson patted the young lady's hand, downed two mince pies and a mug of mulled wine, and spoke at last of the people he would set to searching and the various avenues he would take to find the child.

"I can do things these good people can't," said the squire, a hearty, middle-aged man. "I'm ordering searches of every place, hovel or manor, in the country round about. Meanwhile talk runs on quicker feet than we can; no secrets in this part of the country, if I do say so myself. A convenience, gossip is, in rooting out wrong 'uns. If someone's got the child, I'll know about it, mark my words, by morning."

Christmas morning! Caroline's heart sank as she remembered the special day she and her mother had planned for Harriet.

Though she couldn't summon up much enthusiasm, she thanked the good man for his efforts. She did feel satisfied, at last, that she had left no stone unturned. And before long she might expect Guy back from Bristol, with the answer to the mystery of who had been so blackhearted as to steal a child from her bed.

Binnie, the erstwhile nurse, had spent the day in skulking or cowering about the inn, not attempting to run off into the snow by any means, for she was a town-bred creature to whom the surrounding countryside was more terrifying than the green-cheese surface of the moon. Caroline had no idea what to do with the girl. There was no getting any information from her; the man she described as having hired her couldn't have had less in common with the only person Caroline could with reason suspect, Mr. Brangley. Caroline's former employer was distinctively thin and small, and Martha Binns described the one who had hired her as a man of more than ordinary girth. Somehow, Caroline did not think the girl was lying.

Martha Binns had taken all her own luggage with her in the ditched carriage and, while she might have counted on caring for Harriet in the next little while, she had certainly had no plans to come back to Lady Percival's in the Crescent. The modest traps had been brought to the inn.

"Well, Binns," Caroline said, coming upon the frightened nursemaid in the corridor at some time during the interminable morning, "I suppose you would as soon go back to London, am I not right?"

"To London? Oh, ma'am, you ain't sending me to Newgate?" Tears started out of Binns's eyes, and she looked as absolutely woebegone as only a person without much of a chin can manage.

Caroline shook her head. "I leave it to Mr. Constant to determine whether you ought to be prosecuted, but I think that, once Harriet is found *safe*, he might decide to be lenient. He is the one who hired you, and he must be the one to decide your fate."

As for Caroline, she was inclined to mercy, though she scarcely knew why. It was the holiday season, of course; that was part of it. Also operating was Caroline's personal knowledge of what servitude was like. The temptation of money—money to live on, to build dreams on—was a powerful lure to those who had known nothing but hardship. Through Binns was much to be blamed for violating the trust Harriet's guardian had placed in her, Caroline didn't think the girl was black at heart. According to Binnie's own testimony, she had merely been transferring the child from one place of safety to another. She had been told, besides, that the little girl's proper guardians were desperate to have her back. Also on her side, Mr. Constant was a stranger who had hired her in a hurry in Town to help remove a child from a house; that was all she knew.

"If only you could tell us more about who paid you to do this," Caroline said to Binns, feeling desolate. "That rotund man was acting for another, you say?"

"I do say, ma'am." Binns had been questioned at least a dozen times on this issue, and she stood firm in her story. At least, if she was telling tales, she was not the sort of liar whose stories came rolling easily off the tongue. Caroline had to give her some credit.

"I know I've asked you many's the time," Caroline said, "but I'm so desperate to find Harriet that I really don't know what else to do."

"Oh, the poor little creature," Binns sniffled into a much-used handkerchief. "I was never so shocked, ma'am, as when you woke me and I found her gone. I . . . I never wished her harm, Miss Percival. Never."

"I believe you," Caroline said, patting the girl's shoulder. Leaving Binns to return to the kitchen, Caroline went to pace up and down the small private parlor, wondering if she would ever be tranquil again.

The short day had long since turned to night, and she was doing her best to wear a trench in the ancient oak floorboards when the door to the parlor opened and Constant entered, looking tired, cold, and dispirited.

Caroline rushed to him and took his hands. "Oh, Guy, what happened?"

He touched her face gently. "I didn't find out much, my dear. The person waiting for Harriet and Binns in Bristol was a solicitor—a solicitor who was the very image of Binns's description. He was acting for Harriet's guardian, so he claimed."

Caroline drew back. "But how could that be?"

"Someone presented himself as me, that's how. I spent much time in Bristol looking over the solicitor's correspondence on the matter. That's why I've been so long." Constant sighed, sinking down into a settle near the fire. Caroline sat beside him, searching his face for any sign of hope. There was none.

"Who was the person who hired the solicitor? Surely you must have got a description."

"The devil I did! The whole transaction was done by letter. Here is the story: this Mr. Hyde, the solicitor, received letters from the spurious Constant all containing some faradiddle about how Harriet had been removed from his—my—care by some sort of wiles and placed in the keeping of . . . I'm afraid the term was loose women in Bath. I had Hyde show me the letters once I had convinced him he'd been misled, that I was the real Guy Constant. I didn't recognize the writing, which is not saying much, for handwriting can be disguised, either that or someone else can do it for you. I happened to have a sample by me of my correspondence with Brangley; it wasn't his hand. The most disconcerting thing, though, is that Hyde has been writing to the spurious Constant at my own address in Bath. One of my mother's servants, I must suppose, has been intercepting letters."

"Oh, what a tangle." Caroline sighed. "And what was this person—this solicitor—going to do with Harriet when she arrived in Bristol?"

"He had orders to wait until Mr. Constant collected her."

"In other words," Caroline said slowly, "we know no more than we did before."

"Ah, but we shall know a great deal as soon as I interrogate my mother's household. We should go back to Bath now, Caroline. You know that, don't you?"

"Leave here before Harriet is found?" Caroline was horrorstruck.

"My love, if she is found hereabouts, we have the next thing to a doting mother in Mrs. Dumfrey. Surely you would agree that she's qualified to care for the child until we can return to fetch her?"

"I can think of no one more suitable than Mrs. Dumfrey," Caroline had to admit, remembering that earlier she had been willing to leave Harriet to Mrs. Dumfrey's care in order to free herself to go to Bristol and face the kidnapper.

"And I've spoken to Squire Donaldson," Constant continued. "I'm satisfied that everything that can be done to find her, will be done. The snow is even beginning to melt, which should make it easier—forgive me. I shouldn't have mentioned that."

Caroline had been doing too much solitary thinking to pretend not to understand him, or to be offended at his suggestion of something she had already thought of herself. If the snow melted, it would be easier for the searchers to come upon a small body. "I continue to hope, but we must be prepared for anything," she said with a catch in her voice. "Oh, Guy."

She burst into tears and found herself being held against his superfine coat, so near that the buttons were digging into her chest. They clung together for a moment while Caroline gave way to her sorrow. She looked up at Guy and was astonished to see a suspicious moisture at the corner of his eye. Timidly she reached up a finger to wipe it away.

"I'm fond of her too, you know," he said gruffly. "And I swear to you, Caroline, we'll find her."

Caroline pressed up against him again, finding his strength somehow more real than she had a moment before. Now she felt, in a strange way, as though he could take comfort from her power as well as she could from his.

"Do you know," she said, bringing her idea forward slowly, "you may call this feminine intuition if you will, but as the day has passed with no word of Harriet, I've come to feel that she can't be here. That she must have been taken somewhere else."

"That thought has crossed my mind," Constant said. "She's very little, but she isn't a foolish child. She'd try to find help if she could. And if she couldn't—well, they have searched all the byways where she could be."

Caroline nodded, again imagining the dear little creature lying by the wayside. She couldn't make such a terrifying picture come clear and interpreted this as a sign of hope.

"Now let's see about getting back to Bath," Guy said in a brisker tone, dropping a kiss on Caroline's forehead. "We won't arrive until late tonight, but I don't think we should stay here longer. There's nothing for either one of us to do here, and I'd like to get you safe at home before that freezing rain the landlord talks of materializes."

"What about Martha Binns?" Caroline asked as she stood up and straightened her gown—much less embarrassed in the aftermath of their latest embrace than she would have expected to be.

"Who?" Guy was drawing on his driving gloves.

"The nursemaid. What shall you do with her?"

He thought about it, frowning and narrowing his eyes while the tight gloves went on finger by finger. "I'm tempted to drown her in the nearest stream, of course," he said at last. "But I've interviewed her, and I'm satisfied she meant no real harm. However Harriet was taken from the chaise last night, the nurse had nothing to do with it. I've told her she may go on her way." He cast an inquiring look at Caroline, as though thinking she might disapprove of his decision.

She was silent.

"The other choice," he went on, "is to hand her over

to a magistrate and prosecute her. As she was only some-one's instrument, and as she's in such a menial position that, to her, following orders is no different from one set of people to another, I'm inclined not to place blame for this entire incident on the girl." He paused and half smiled. "Though it is tempting."

Caroline felt a rush a relief—quite irrational relief, for Martha Binns was definitely guilty of something, though they did not yet know what. "My thought exactly," she said. "She wasn't in a position to make the best choice. I don't want to make her an example; I'd rather punish the people who were behind this dreadful scheme in the first place."

"Oh, believe me when I say I'm saving my anger for the proper object, and that my wrath is considerable," Guy said with a dark look in the direction of the fire. "Well, my love, I see you've brought your outdoor things down here." Caroline's cloak and hat were hang-ing on a peg just inside the door. "Shall we go?"

Caroline felt a little tremor go through her. Selfish to be thinking of her own concerns at such a moment, when they were so worried over Harriet, but he had called her his love for the second time. As she allowed him to help her on with her things, she was filled despite her fears with a new serenity she had not thought she would ever feel: a peace that had to do with knowing, at last, where she belonged.

11

THE DRIVE back to Bath was pleasure and pain to Caroline. She gloried in Guy's presence, yet couldn't really enjoy it because of their troubles.

Harriet's danger masked the new discovery but couldn't stifle it. Caroline hardly knew by what process she had come to the conclusion that Guy loved her, for she could not call it rational thought. But she sensed him beside her, thinking as she did about their relations with each other. Audacious of her to believe such a man could harbor real affection for her; yet the emotion was right with them in the curricle. She would swear to it.

They were quiet; there wasn't much to say, for they could hardly chat blithely about the social scene, nor did it seem the occasion to get to know each other better by a discussion of views and interests. They had one common interest, Harriet, and for the moment there was no more to say, no more conjectures to make. Caroline knew Guy must have leaped to the worst conclusions even as she had; but she could not speak them aloud and give them an added dimension of reality. Neither, she suspected, could he.

As they approached the town, Caroline began to think about her mother, who had been waiting with virtually no news for about twenty-four hours. She spoke words her mother would have said, echoing Guy's reassurance of the night before.

"It's Christmas. We can hope for a miracle on Christmas, surely?"

Guy smiled at her and tightened his arm; it had been

about her shoulders for most of the drive. "We are certainly not so lacking in imagination that we can't do that."

Without even thinking about it, Caroline reached up and kissed him on the cheek. Her lips moved to his almost of their own volition.

The fact that one of them was the driver of a moving vehicle was all that kept the moment from getting out of hand. "Merry Christmas, Caroline," Guy said with a touch of regret, turning his eyes back to the task at hand just in time to ease the horses over a rut in the road.

"Merry Christmas, Guy," she returned, wondering what had come over her. At this time last night she had never touched any man of her own free will. Now she didn't seem able to keep her hands off the person she had thought of as Mr. Constant up until about the time she had started, recklessly, to kiss him at every turn. The sudden change was most confusing.

In the Crescent, Lady Percival was waiting up. She had received the message Caroline had managed to send by a coachman traveling to Bath earlier in the day; but that note had only concerned Caroline's location in case of further emergency. Now her ladyship had to be told the whole story of Harriet's disappearance from the post chaise that had been sent to convey her to Bristol; the duplicity of the nursemaid Binns; the awful news that no trace of Harriet could be found.

Caroline reached out to clasp her mother's hand. "I somehow can't give up hope yet, Mama."

"Then I shall not either," Lady Percival said with a tired smile.

Caroline knew that her mother's health would suffer if she wasn't put to bed at once, and she rose to wheel the Bath chair into the nearby bedroom.

"Mr. Constant," Lady Percival said as she gave in with a sigh to her daughter's insistence, "will you bring your family to dinner tomorrow as planned, or will you prefer not to go out?"

"We all love Harriet," Constant said. "Best if we are all together tomorrow, don't you think?"

"Oh, yes, my thoughts exactly. It won't be a happy celebration as I once wished for, but we will have another festive dinner for Harriet when she returns."

"That's a fine idea, Mama," Caroline said, suddenly near tears and eager to hide them. "If you'll excuse me, Mr. Constant, I'll return in a moment to say good night."

Lady Percival had a sharp look for her daughter, the first such look she had given since Caroline and Constant had come in. Caroline remembered, all at once, that she and the gentleman had been most improperly alone, though not always together, since they had left Bath the night before.

The dresser and nurse were waiting in the bedroom, and so Lady Percival had no chance to say anything about Caroline's situation if she had wanted to. Caroline planned to explain on the first likely occasion that there had naturally been no irregularities during the hurried journey.

She was trying to think what words she would use to convey this exaggerated message of innocence and moral rectitude when she arrived back in the drawing room and was immediately clasped in a pair of strong arms. Taken by surprise, she found herself kissing Guy more deeply than she ever had before.

"Mistletoe," he muttered, gesturing above their heads to where some enterprising servant had hung a beribboned cluster of the plant. He reached up to pluck one of the berries and pocketed it. "I know now why this bush was sacred to the ancients." He kissed her again. "There's nothing like a ready-made excuse for this type of behavior."

Caroline restrained herself on the point of telling him he needed no excuse to take a liberty with her, knowing such a statement would be much too bold, not trusting their new intimacy far enough for words.

"Good night, my dear," said Guy, pulling her to him

for one last embrace. "I can't trust myself if I stay longer."

"You have a point," Caroline said in a daze. "My scruples would be no help at all. Good night, Guy."

He touched her face, gave her a searching look, and left her.

She would have gone to sleep dreaming of him had she not passed by Harriet's door on the way to her bedroom some moments later, after Guy had gone away. Instead of thinking warm thoughts of the guardian, she fell into a strange half-sleep beset with worries about the ward; worries that were beginning to take on the tinge of normality, it seemed she had been plagued by them for so long.

Christmas morning came, heavy with the sound of sleet dashing against the windows. Caroline turned on her pillow one last time in an attempt to banish the nightmare. Someone had stolen Harriet, and she and Guy could not get her back, and that sound was the sound of horses' hooves crunching their way down an icy road . . .

She was suddenly sitting up in bed, shivering beneath her thick flannel nightrail and the pile of comforters. A few disoriented moments passed, and she remembered everything. Dull with disappointment, she got up to make ready for the day.

Lady Percival had wished for some time to attend Christmas services in the Abbey rather than the small chapel nearer home; and the project seemed doubly necessary today. Caroline tried to be cheerful as she encouraged her mother to go on with the visit to the Abbey, despite the bad weather and their uncertainty about Harriet. However, what with the crowds and the dismal wet, the project took some time. The ladies barely arrived home in time to change for dinner, which had been previously set for early in the day to allow for a longer celebration—and for Harriet's pleasure.

When Lady Lambert and her sons arrived, it was to

face a bravely smiling Lady Percival in a festive dinner gown. Caroline, standing beside her mother, was also trying for an air of cheer, and she also wore her best. She had even put a sprig of holly into her hair, but she was fighting back gloom with every breath. Even the cheerfully burning Yule log made her sad; she remembered how she had planned to explain the old custom to Harriet, carefully saving a bit of this log to light next year's.

Constant and his mother put up a brave front, too, but the sadness behind everyone's eyes was evident despite the determined holiday air of the room and all its inhabitants. Caroline couldn't count Lord Marchton in this, because the viscount wore his usual blank, bored air. He seemed totally unaware that anything untoward had occurred. Not that he hadn't been told.

"The brat's gone?" he greeted Caroline cheerfully. "Good riddance, I say. Can't have been a convenience to you to be saddled with an infant."

"Why, you . . . how dare you, you unfeeling monster," was Caroline's instant rejoinder. "Has no one told you we miss the little girl? Besides which, she could be hurt and frightened."

"Oh, to be sure. As you say, ma'am." And he calmly began to maneuver his hostess to the nearest sprig of mistletoe—the same bunch Caroline had kissed his brother under the night before! She couldn't possibly tolerate such an unfeeling sequel to that most meaningful of moments. She pulled away from the viscount in anger, much as she had done at the Brangleys' what seemed like centuries ago when he had cornered her in the schoolroom.

"Still unsocial?" Marchton said with a vapid smile. "It's Christmas, ma'am. Can't turn a fellow down when it's Christmas."

"I most certainly can." Caroline stalked off across the room and pretended to busy herself with adjusting one of the swags of greenery decorating the mantel.

Constant cleared his throat and glared at his brother, while Lady Lambert let forth her tinkling laugh and said,

"You must forgive my dear boy, Miss Percival. Such an impetuous young man. I believe he must take it from his father. Marchton and I had a most tempestuous relationship." She sighed in mournful reminiscence.

"For my part, I'll be glad if a young man's antics can take our minds off poor little Harriet, dear Lord Marchton," Lady Percival said, proving to Caroline that she could be a perfect hostess. "Caroline, won't you go to the instrument and play for us? Something cheerful."

"Oh, yes, my dear, do please oblige us," Lady Lambert said. She had actually taken out a handkerchief and was dabbing at her eyes, whether at thoughts of her departed second husband or of her son's small ward, it was impossible to tell.

Caroline exchanged a glance with Guy and headed to the pianoforte, pleased when he caught her hint and followed her. "Shall I turn your pages, Miss Percival?" He made the request formally, but there was a streak of intimacy under the proper words.

"Thank you." Caroline smiled at him and threw a triumphant look at Lord Marchton, who had been done out of one more attempt at dalliance. Another spray of mistletoe had been hung above the pianoforte by some housemaid with a sense of humor.

Caroline was striking the opening chords of "Here We Come A'Wassailing," hoping to urge the others to sing, when the knocker sounded. She was close to the window and peeked out to see who would be visiting so close to the dinner hour on Christmas Day, but whoever had knocked had already gained entry. How odd; the butler would surely have the wit to deny the family to callers.

Another moment and a sort of scuffling and clicking was heard in the entryway. The drawing room doors opened. Baxter stood on the threshold, looking puzzled, and opened his mouth to speak. And then Harriet ran into the room, followed by four enormous dogs.

With a little cry the child ran straight to Caroline. "Oh, here I am again, ma'am. Do you mind if I stay the night? The carriage was taking me away, but it broke down, and this gentleman brought me back with him." Harriet was having difficulties learning not to point her finger; now she used the gesture to signal a burly stranger who stood in the doorway.

The man was dark, wore a fur-trimmed greatcoat over garments of a most countrified cut and cloth, and had that most unsettling of facial features, a full beard. "So!" he thundered, striding into the room. "There you are, faithless female! So ye're in Bath. And making up to the Duke of Davonleigh after what we've been to one another. Ah, you'll catch cold at that game, my own."

As the others watched in amazement, this extraordinary person walked right up to Lady Lambert and snatched her from her chair, crushing her to his barrel chest with a mix of passion and anger. Meanwhile the dogs were sniffing about the room, their toenails making a pleasant scratching sound on the exposed wood at the edges of the carpet. One of the beasts licked the boots of Constant. Another seemed to find some fault with Lord Marchton, for the huge dog was emitting a low growl as it sat squarely in front of the viscount, blocking all avenues of escape.

"Good heavens," Lady Percival said softly.

Caroline was too busy hugging Harriet to ask questions, but she hoped someone would, and soon. At least the man now assaulting Lady Lambert wasn't a desperate character, though he might look like one. Lady Lambert, if Caroline wasn't mistaken, was enjoying this display.

Lady Percival spoke up. "Sir, if you would but tell us . . ."

The stranger did not loose his hold on Lady Lambert, but he bowed to the other lady. "Pardon, madam, ought to have mentioned. The little girl there is someone I'm taking to her father. Can't find the man, but tomorrow's another day. Didn't think anyone would mind the child coming along."

"But who are *you*, sir?" Lady Percival elaborated.

Lady Lambert turned around in the big man's embrace

at this and said, "This is Lord Effrydd, Elinor. He's a Welshman." The last sentence was evidently meant to excuse all irregularities.

Caroline, with Harriet's little waist safe within the circle of her arm, looked at the dogs. One of them came up to lick Harriet's face, then Caroline's, and submitted to being patted on the head. *Strange dogs barking.* She remembered someone back in the village had heard the sounds on the night Harriet had been lost. These were gigantic, shaggy beasts, like nothing Caroline had ever seen before. Rather like Newfoundlands, or shepherds' dogs, or wolfhounds.

Constant had by now arrived at their side and was hugging Harriet to him. "Are you injured, my dear?" he asked her seriously, kneeling down to look straight into her eyes. "Have you been hurt in any way?"

"Hurt?" Harriet looked truly puzzled. "I've borrowed the most delightful doggies, sir." She pointed to each beast in turn. "This is Rhodri, and Hywel, and Gruffydd—he is the cross one—and Llywelyn. Lord Fred says I can keep one of the puppies next time Bronwen has babies, but for now he let me borrow all the Fellows. Bronwen is the Fellows' mother, you know. She lives in Wales."

Caroline and Constant simply stared.

"She's a bitch," Harriet added helpfully. "That means a lady dog."

"How did this come about? Has she said where she has been all this time?" Constant asked Caroline over the top of Harriet's head.

"No, we haven't had time to do or say much of anything."

At this Guy stood up. "Attention, ladies and gentlemen! We have a mystery here to be solved, and I'd appreciate everyone's help."

The talk in the room died down at once, and Guy was left in a gratifying silence. Lord Effrydd pulled Lady Lambert down to a sofa and snapped his fingers, which brought the dogs to their stomachs in a neat row before the hearth. Lady Percival leaned forward in her Bath chair. Lord Marchton, though he looked bored as ever and tapped back a yawn, made no objections from his manly stance leaning against the mantelpiece.

Guy nodded, gratified. "Now, let's hear the tale. Harriet, my dear," and he leaned down to the child, "what happened to you when you left this house?"

Harriet looked surprised that anyone would ask. Caroline was reminded of how sure children always were that everything passing in their own little realm was of pressing interest to everybody. The child answered in a little, clear voice, "Why, the carriage stopped, sir, and turned crooked, and Nurse was sleeping. So I climbed down and walked along the road, and Lord Fred stopped his coach and asked if I would like to get in."

"Oh, my," Caroline exclaimed before she could stop herself. Harriet would evidently have gone with anyone. What luck, what marvelous luck that it had been a benign character like Lord Effrydd.

"Where did he take you, Harriet?" Constant asked. As Effrydd opened his mouth to answer, Constant held up a hand to let him know the little girl should tell her own story.

Harriet was not at all reluctant. "Why, Lord Fred let me sleep in the carriage, and then he brought me to a big place where there was a bedroom for me to sleep in, and another woman called Nurse to take care of me."

"Saracen's Head," Lord Effrydd put in. "Always put up at the Saracen's Head. And the woman was hired from an agency the instant I got here. She's gone belowstairs with your butler, ma'am." He nodded to Lady Percival.

"And he let me play all day yesterday with the doggies while he looked for people, and now we're here," Harriet finished her tale. She looked round at her adult audience, appeared to reflect a bit, then curtsied.

Lord Marchton took her cue and applauded, which displeased Caroline, but was most gratifying to Harriet.

She beamed at this unexpected approval from the tall young man who had never noticed her before.

"Baron Effrydd, what have you to add to this?" Constant continued the interrogation. "Why didn't you bring the child back where she belonged?"

Harriet looked puzzled.

"Tried to," said Lord Effrydd with a black scowl made especially frightening by his bearded countenance. "The mite told me her father's name, and I've been having the devil of a time locating the fellow. Nobody in Bath's heard of a Harry Deauville. Glad you all know her; she's bound to be sorely missed at home—a taking little chit. I was thinking she'd made a mistake and come from Bristol, not Bath."

"Her father is dead," Caroline said. Turning to Harriet, she added, "Didn't you mention, dear, that your papa is no longer living?"

"He didn't ask me that," Harriet responded at once. The at-sea expression on her face changed as understanding dawned. "Oh. Was Lord Fred looking for *Papa* yesterday? Oh."

"But, Govan, you mustn't keep me in suspense any longer," Lady Lambert put in at this point, fluttering long black lashes at the man by her side. "Why have you come here?"

His scowl deepened. "You can ask that, woman, when you sneaked out of my castle in the dead of night and ran away from me? I came after you, and I've spent all this time picking up your trail."

"I believe that trail must have been cold by the time you started to search," Lady Lambert said with a toss of her head. Nevertheless, she looked pleased. "It's been weeks."

"And what do I find England buzzing with but the news you're setting your cap at the Duke of Davonleigh," Lord Effrydd snapped out. "Read it in one of those London gossip sheets."

"Oh, has such news spread abroad? I didn't even know, living so out of the world as I do, not even taking the London papers," Lady Lambert said with a dimpled smile. "The truth is, dear Govan, I haven't even met his grace of Davonleigh. I befriended his daughter, through an old connection on my mother's side, and I've been taking her about with me. That is all."

"All?" The baron glared.

Lady Lambert seemed to feel compelled to confess everything. "If you must know, I had every hope of creating a nearer interest. But that was before I found that no one ever sees the Duke of Davonleigh. If it weren't for his daughter, I'd believe him to be a myth created expressly to make poor widows act foolishly. I'm out of patience with the man."

"So it's rank you will have, and a baron's not good enough, even one with the blood of the Welsh princes pumping through him," Effrydd said in disgust. "Fie upon you! I'll take this back to the shop." And, reaching into a pocket, he brought forth a vulgarly sized emerald set in a ring.

Lady Lambert gasped, and her eyes took on a special glow. "Dear Govan, you bought that for me? And I believed you didn't care, the way you deserted me at your castle. After taking me away so romantically, you didn't even pay any attention to me."

He tossed the ring up and caught it in his beefy hand. "Want it? You'll have to take what comes with it."

"And that is . . ." Lady Lambert looked avidly at him, as though she expected her suitor to extract from his pocket a matching necklace and tiara.

"My lovestruck self," Lord Effrydd said in a gruff tone.

"Oh, how sweet." Lady Percival spoke up at this point. She and the others had been watching this exchange as though it were taking place on a stage. "How fitting upon Christmas Day. You've found your own true love, Fanny. I'm so happy for you."

"But I haven't said whether I'll do it," Lady Lambert objected with a worried look.

"Sir," said Guy, stepping forward, "there are reinforcements ready to aid your cause with the lady." And he pointed to the ceiling.

"Capital idea, boy," roared the Welsh baron, and he forthwith plucked his love from the sofa and held her under the nearest kissing bough, where he demonstrated a goodly amount of primitive ardor.

"I say, Mother," Lord Marchton said, looking on with approval, "you've caught another one. Dashed fine emerald."

"So." Guy turned to Caroline and her mother while his own mother made a spectacle of herself. "We've established that his lordship, here, found Harriet by accident and brought her home by the same sort of hazard. We still haven't solved the mystery of who took her in the first place; my mother's servants either know nothing, or they're dashed fine actors."

"Well, then," Caroline said in a distracted tone, fascinated by the sight of a female of Lady Lambert's age engaging in such a passionate display before a drawing room of onlookers, "I still believe we should question the Brangleys. They admitted to us already they've come to Bath to get Harriet back." She paused. "Yet they seemed so genuinely surprised she'd gone missing."

"It is a puzzle," Constant agreed. "And today is no day to solve it. I have an idea, but I won't say anything until I'm certain of my facts."

"Do you mean you know who could have done this?" Caroline demanded.

"I have a guess. But without knowledge, with only suspicion, I don't want to slander any human creature, even one with no principles. Let it wait."

Caroline had to honor Guy for his generosity, but she was mightily curious. She gave him a dissatisfied look.

He smiled. "I promise you, first thing in the morning I'll track down the Brangleys and question them further. They are concerned in this somehow. I feel it even as you do. Besides, I must explain to them for good and all that Harriet is to stay with you."

"I am to stay with Caroline?" Harriet piped up. "Truly, sir?"

"Yes." Guy smiled down at the little girl. "And you must never let anyone take you away from her again. If someone should try, you must object."

"Yes, sir." Harriet was thoughtful. "What if it's the Brangleys? They are my cousins."

"Especially the Brangleys," Guy said. "You must tell them your time is engaged to Miss Percival, and you can't accept their kind invitation." He paused. "I'll tell the Brangleys myself that you're not to be taken away."

Harriet clasped her hands in delight.

Caroline thought of Mrs. Brangley's face when she heard such news from the lips of the man she had so wanted to impress and wished she could be there to see it. Perhaps Guy would take her. She looked up to ask him.

All conversation was forestalled, though, as Baxter chose this moment to enter the room, clear his throat loudly, and announce that dinner was on table.

Lady Lambert and Lord Effrydd drew apart, and the company proceeded into the dining room, where the servants had thoughtfully set two more places for the unexpected arrivals. In addition four dishes loaded with meat scraps had been set on the floor near the hearth for the canine visitors.

Since the board was groaning with Christmas delicacies, and such emotions as relief and luck in love had made everyone's appetite sharper, the human diners brought quite as much enthusiasm to the feast as did the Fellows. Harriet added much to the entertainment as she voiced delight in this or that dish, and her round eyes were incredulous when the plum pudding was finally brought in aflame. She had never seen or heard of such a thing before.

"This child," said Lady Percival, as she served Harriet a large helping of the fruity concoction, "has not had enough happiness in her life. Fancy, to have lived six years in the world and never to have seen a plum pudding!"

"It will be such fun to make it up to her, Mama," Caroline said.

"Indeed," put in Constant, "we shall make it our business to remedy these deficiencies in my ward's education."

Harriet was digging through her pudding with enthusiasm, but she paused to give her guardian a look of starry-eyed worship.

The only soul at the dinner table who was anything less than merry was Lord Marchton. Lady Lambert and Lord Effrydd were wrapped up in each other; Caroline and Lady Percival were aglow with happiness and relief at Harriet's return; and Constant alternated between this same relief and a preoccupation with Caroline. Marchton hid his ill-temper for a while in a great attention to the food—for it had to be admitted that Lady Percival employed an excellent cook—but by the time the company joined up again in the drawing room, Caroline could see that he was in a mood of dangerous boredom.

She sighed. She had noticed the viscount's discomfort at dinner, and though he was such an obnoxious young man she had even felt a little guilt over his isolation, but she had hoped a companionable interlude with his brother and Lord Effrydd over the decanter of port would work another Christmas miracle and send him out to the ladies a pattern card of good cheer. Evidently this was not to be.

Well, perhaps he would think he had given enough time to a gathering he could not enjoy and take his leave, or perhaps there was a way he could be amused. Caroline would have meditated further on the problem, but Guy came up and engaged her in conversation, taking all thoughts of his brother right out of her head by the subject he chose to open.

"Do you suppose," he began, sitting down by her, "that we could manage to get under the mistletoe subtly, without anyone else noticing?"

She smiled at him, delighted. "Not unless we can make an excuse to go out into the hall. Mrs Binberry rigged another kissing bough right over the staircase. I heard Baxter grumbling about it."

"By all means let us do so," Constant said, seizing her hand where it lay under a fold of her skirt. He twined her fingers with his own, causing such a thrill to go through Caroline that she wished they could be transported by magic to a private place, whether or not there was a seasonal excuse for kissing.

Despite the frowning figure of Lord Marchton, who had resumed his earlier place by the fire, the scene in the drawing room was one of Christmas cheer. Lord Effrydd was helping Harriet put the dogs through their paces off to one side of the room, farthest from any breakable figurines or vases; Lady Percival and Lady Lambert were talking earnestly; and Caroline smiled at Constant—smiled easily, with a touch of bravado.

"Should we really leave the room? We might pretend it's for some reason. Perhaps to get the things for a Christmas game. Now that Harriet's back, I remember I had plans for things like snapdragon and hunt the slipper. Although I don't know whether we should attempt a bullet pudding; we did it when I was a little girl at home, but I remember it as so untidy." She took a deep breath; she knew that she was rambling, nervous. Never had she done anything so brazen as to initiate a scene of passion.

"What in heaven's name is a bullet pudding?" asked Constant, looking at her in such a knowing way that she knew he could interpret her hesitation.

She was grateful that he did not tease her outright. "Well, it involves a pile of flour in a dish, and you put a bullet at the peak of the pile, and then everyone cuts into the 'pudding.' The one who is cutting when the bullet falls has to find it with his teeth."

He laughed. "That's where the untidy part comes in."

She nodded. "Yes, and it was often quite amusing. Even if all in the room were good sports, and playing the game, it would inevitably be one of the stuffier grown people who would have to find the bullet—not any of the children, who would have been glad for the opportunity of messing about."

"Perhaps that game is not prudent in this company," Constant said with twinkling eyes. "Though I should like to see it. At any rate, let us make some excuse. I'm finding myself most eager for a moment alone with you."

She stared at him, finding it still so strange for a man to express such a wish for her company—here in her home, where it was not her lowly status as governess tempting him to dalliance.

A flurry of noise outside in the hall drew their attention before they could say anything further, and Baxter opened the double doors with a flourish. "Mrs. Dutton and Miss Dutton," he said loudly. "And the Taylors."

All conversation stopped, and Mrs. Dutton and her daughter, decked out in their finest, surged into the room, followed by three people Caroline vaguely remembered meeting at the Duttons' party: an older woman, a young lady, and a young man. "Dear Lady Percival!" cried Mrs. Dutton. "We were on our way home from the jolliest party, and I happened to think you were probably having a dull Christmas of it, so confined as you must be, and my friends and I would stop to cheer you. But I see you have company. How fine, to be sure."

"Why, how kind of you to call, Mrs. Dutton," Lady Percival said. Caroline could see her mother was fighting to control her amazement that Mrs. Dutton had burst in upon her on Christmas Day, dragging people Lady Percival had never met before. She did this admirably, sinking all natural feelings under a placid lake of politeness. "Let us have the introductions, by all means. Caroline"—here Lady Percival signaled to her own daughter—"why don't you ring for the tea tray?"

Caroline moved to do so, and Constant followed her. "On the bright side," he murmured into her ear, "these visitors might prove such a distraction that I can kiss you in this very room and arouse no comment."

She shook her head, fearful that someone might have heard his remark though he had uttered it in such a low voice. "Sir, why do you keep talking of kissing? You'll put me quite out of countenance."

"I didn't think it appropriate to talk of anything more intimate at this stage of our acquaintance," he answered with an innocent expression that neatly finished her composure and set her laughing.

12

To Caroline's chagrin the sudden influx of relative strangers into the drawing room did not mean more privacy for her and Constant. He was called away by Miss Dutton, who wished to tell him a killing anecdote about having seen him in his curricle on such and such a day and not having got his attention. Caroline saw that he was lost to her and busied herself with hostess duties. She ordered tea and coffee, cautioning Baxter to bring a generous supply of small mince pies, preserved ginger, and Mrs. Binberry's special Christmas cake.

Tea was a merry affair. Caroline had to admit it: the Duttons and the Taylors, not to mention Lord Effrydd's dogs, lent a spirit to the day in the form of liveliness and noise that hadn't been there before, yet seemed most appropriate under the circumstances. Young Mr. Taylor set himself to entertaining Harriet. Desideria tried to monopolize both Lord Marchton and Mr. Constant, quite leaving out her plain little friend Miss Taylor, while Mrs. Dutton and her equally voluble companion, Mrs. Taylor, kept up a running flow of mostly good-natured gossip. Miss Taylor evidently liked dogs, and she amused herself caressing the largest of the animals.

In the midst of all this Caroline slipped from the room to get her mother's new silk shawl, thinking with an unworthy little pang of how she might earlier have made just such an excuse in order to meet Constant on the stairway, under the kissing bough. These thoughts in her mind, she was doubly displeased when, on coming out of her mother's room with the large square of flowered silk over her arm, she ran right into Lord Marchton.

His plain face was wearing the rakish look she associated with it; and she knew he had been steadily drinking brandy instead of tea and coffee for the last little while. "Have you lost your way, sir?" She spoke with a pleasant, impersonal nod of her head. "You were probably about to take your leave. This noisy party is doubtless a bore to someone like you."

"I was looking for you," he said, backing her up against the wall of the corridor with a no-nonsense attitude. "I say it ain't sporting of my brother to take up all you time. I'm the one who noticed you in the first place. Something is due to me."

"I have no idea what you're talking about, sir," Caroline said. She tried to remain calm as panic rose in her. She would hate to scream and cause a scene, but she was prepared to do so before she would let him touch her.

"Oh, come now, Miss Percival." Lord Marchton gave a knowing leer. "My own brother's got you in his keeping, and I say I'm owed a few favors for bringing you to his notice. Blood's thicker than water."

"And neither is as thick as you, sir. Have you run mad?" Caroline felt anger boiling just beneath the surface. She would probably give way to temper and do him an injury if he didn't desist, but she tried to remember that in his inebriated state he was likely to do her harm, especially if she tried something so tame as the kick to his shin she had used on him before. He was damnably strong, she remembered from his last assault. "I am not in your brother's keeping," she said in a reasonable, calm tone.

"Oh, ain't you?" The words were taunting, disbelieving.

"No, I'm not. As you ought to remember by now, I live here with my mother. And before you make any more of your insinuating remarks, she really is my mother, and we are not a pair of adventuresses." Caroline glared and tried to step past him.

"Oh, so he's been franking for you out of the goodness of his heart? Your pardon, madam." Marchton made her a mock bow but did not move enough so that she could slip away.

"Franking for me? Have your wits gone begging, my lord?"

He shrugged, folding his arms and grinning. "None of my business, you must think; p'rhaps you didn't know I was clever enough to find out. Merely came upon the information when I was leafing through my brother's papers t'other day."

"You were going through your brother's papers? That's surely the most despicable thing I've ever heard." Caroline took her chance to step away from him and march down the hall. What he had said was surely nonsense. Constant had insisted on paying for Harriet's keep, of course, but that was as yet an unsettled matter. Could Marchton have seen some paper concerning those arrangements? That had to be the case.

"Guy's never been a one to throw good money after bad. Don't even do much gaming," Marchton was saying. He followed her, keeping up easily with his long stride, and clapped his arm around her waist. "When I found he'd been paying your way, I knew there was something to it. Stood to reason he must be getting a fair return for his blunt. Won't even pay *my* bills, devil take it, and I'm his own brother. So he'd never pay yours without a fair incentive." He winked.

"You're mad." Caroline struggled to get out of his hold.

He did not let go. He was indeed as strong as she remembered, despite his rather wispy look. "I know old Guy must mean for me to share in his expensive little fling—brothers, and all."

"Will you stop saying that?" Caroline had kept walking in self-defense. Now she stopped just at the head of the stairs and turned to him, glaring into his leering face as she fiercely shook free of his grasp. "I have indeed come into money, but it's not what you think. My mother has recently received an inheritance, if you must know . . ." Her words trailed away as a horrifying thought struck her. The inheritance, which she had always looked on in suspicion! What if . . .

"Oh, an inheritance." Lord Marchton winked at her again. "Your *mother*, who happens to be in a Bath chair. Quite an effective cover for a bawd. Not many Cyprians travel with a lady in a Bath chair. Clever, ain't you."

"It can't be true." Caroline raced down the stairs. She ignored his continued insults to her mother and herself; she could deal with those at any time. But this! That Constant had been footing the bills for their establishment was surely only another example of Lord Marchton's overactive imagination.

She had to ask Guy, though. Before she entered the drawing room she stood before the door, breathing deeply. A glance up told her that Lord Marchton was ambling down the stairs, quite unconcerned, whistling a tune. She slipped into the drawing room and closed the door in his lordship's face, nearly nipping his long nose in the process.

Within, the young ladies had got up a game of blind man's bluff for Harriet, and the four dogs were milling about in the resultant excitement, tails fanning the room's human occupants. Constant was leaning on the pianoforte, an amused look on his face as he watched Desideria flail about, blindfolded, with exaggerated caution. Caroline went directly to him.

He saw her, and a smile lit his face. The difference between that smile and the indulgent look he had worn for the ladies' game was so striking that Caroline fell back a pace. Then, taking courage from this proof that there was no deceit in their relationship, that this was a man who truly cared for her on some level, she took another deep breath and opened her mouth to speak.

"One moment," he said, drawing her forward. Caroline had just time to remember that mistletoe was hung above the pianoforte before his lips met hers in a quick but fervent kiss. "You see?" He let her go. "No one even noticed."

"I did." Caroline felt inexplicably more flustered by that nearly chaste Christmas kiss than she had by any of their others in the past day or two.

He smiled again—a slow, lazy smile that thrilled her.

She cleared her throat. "Guy, I must talk to you. Lord Marchton has made the most amazing statement, and I need you to deny it—that is, I am sure you'll deny it." She glanced around. All others in the room were still making merry, the young ladies with Harriet, the older women in a conversational knot save for Lady Lambert, who was close by the side of her bearded gallant on a sofa, admiring the look of the large emerald on her diminutive hand. Young Taylor had dared to speak to the grand Lord Marchton, who was evidently deigning with appropriate hauteur to listen to the callow youth's chatter.

"What has Evan said to you now?" Guy asked, his gray eyes full of concern.

"It's quite a wild statement, I'm sure. He must have made it up out of whole cloth. He mentioned going through your papers."

"He did, did he? Young puppy!" Guy cast a murderous look at his brother.

"He might have found something relating to Harriet's trust."

"He might indeed! How did you know what I suspected? Surely he isn't enough of a fool to have bragged about it to you."

Caroline stared at him, unable to fathom what he could be talking about.

"Caroline, I'll be honest with you though at the cost of family loyalty. More than once I've found my papers disarranged, and Evan the only person who could have been in the room at the time. Dash it all, I've all but caught him in the act a time or two. He must have come across the documents my man of business sent me, confirming my suspicions that the Brangleys are making free with Harriet's money. That's why they wanted her back, to use her as a shield; and I suspect Evan of trying his hand at blackmailing them. I've had inquiries made, and I think he might even be the one who had Harriet taken away, perhaps to hand her over to the Brangleys for a sum of money. My plaguey brother is outrunning the constable, and he's proven in the past that he's nothing if not resourceful when it comes to dishonest schemes."

Caroline had nothing to say to this. She simply groped for the nearest chair and sat down.

"I've shocked you badly," Guy said, kneeling by her side. "Do you need anything? Some brandy?"

Recovering, Caroline shook her head. "I'm sorry; no, I'm not vaporish. I don't need anything. I'm simply floored." She looked across the room to Lord Marchton. He was laughing at the moment with Mr. Taylor—a rather braying laugh. He was totally unconcerned that he had but moments before tried to seduce his hostess's daughter. Was there no end to his vagaries? "Could your brother really have been the one to have had Harriet kidnapped? Could he really be so unthinking, so cruel?"

"I see nothing remarkable in that possibility; Evan is singularly lacking in character. I can see, too, that the plan would just suit his streak of deviousness. As for the practical side, nothing easier than for him to use my seal and write letters passing himself off as me. My card was given to the lawyer in Bristol, you know."

"Oh." Caroline remembered this detail. "Yes. And that would explain how the man could have been corresponding with someone at your address in Bath."

He nodded grimly. "Never cast stones at a servant until you've examined your own family. Not a word of this, though, Caroline. I mean to get my facts in order before confronting my brother. And aside from a stern warning and a lot of threats against any further mischief with my ward, I don't think there's much I can do to him."

"He says you're franking us. My mother and me," Caroline said, quite suddenly.

Guy say back on his heels and looked at her. "He says *what*?"

"That you are paying for my mother's household; that's what he implied. More than implied." Caroline was sure now that Lord Marchton was lying or had made some false leap in logic while he was ransacking his brother's desk. Such a villainous young man wouldn't care whether what he said to a mere governess was truth or not.

"I'm sorry you had to find out this way," Guy said with a deep sigh.

"What?" Caroline stared into his eyes and read the most amazing thing: that on this issue his brother had not been romancing. "Oh, you can't mean it."

"Caroline, let me explain. I'd wanted to wait, but now is as good a time as any."

"How could you?" She looked around at the richly appointed room in dismay. He had paid for everything in it, and Mama was so happy, so secure in her new independence. It had been false fortune after all. "And what possible explanation could there be but something along the lines your brother already told me?"

"Wait."

But Caroline had stood and was rushing away across the room. She paused by her mother's chair for an instant, whispered something into Lady Percival's ear, and ran off.

"My daughter is feeling a bit ill," Constant heard her ladyship say to the females sitting with her.

He straightened his shoulders, wanting to rush up the stairs and invade Caroline's chamber. But those would not be the tactics of a gentleman. She was obviously so overset that only privacy would serve. He would wait— but not for long.

Boxing Day dawned much as had Christmas Day, to the tune of heavy, cold rain beating down on the rooftops of Bath. Guy spent the morning at his desk, going over papers and listening to the information of one of his agents who had been out all Christmas Day asking questions and tracking down this or that lead.

When Lord Marchton strolled into the room, Constant's man was just leaving and bowed only slightly to the young lord when they passed in the doorway.

"Who was that fellow?" Evan asked with his usual cheerful, vapid smile. "Could use a lesson in manners. Looks a bit familiar, but not at all respectful."

"Perhaps what he's recently learned has taken away the inborn reverence he must of course harbor for any member of the peerage," Guy remarked dryly.

Evan shrugged, obviously not recognizing the satire. "Well, Guy, let's be off on some errand of pleasure, what do you say? Mother's no use; she and the Welsh fellow are in the drawing room, billing and cooing, and she's told me to be on hand today. Lady Georgiana's coming to luncheon, which will be cold thanks to this dashed servants' holiday. That makes two aggravations. I must get out instead. A good gallop in the hills sounds the perfect solution."

"In this rain?" asked his brother in a deceptively mild tone.

"A little rain? What's that to us?"

Evan had his dandyish qualities, Guy reflected, looking out at the driving deluge, but a care for his feathers was not one of them. He had ever been one for riding out in all weathers—had nearly broken his neck once, in fact, trying to hunt in the ice, and almost ended as his father had.

"Evan, sit down." Guy indicated a chair across from him. "It's time we had a talk about this hodgepodge of dreadful deeds you've been perpetrating."

"Dreadful deeds? I?" Evan laughed, folding his arms across his chest as he sat and crossed one buckskinned leg neatly over the other.

Guy referred to a list he had been writing before his agent's visit. "Here we have it all laid out. Your first crime of this latest batch was offering to collect funds from our friends the Brangleys or else tell me of their meddlesome ways with little Harriet's money. That was a double game, for you knew I had already found out about their embezzling. Indeed, you'd found it out yourself from my papers before we even left London. Next, kidnapping Harriet, probably with the goal of selling her to the Brangleys; presenting yourself as me in letter upon letter; need I go on?"

Evan spread his hands in a helpless gesture. "A fellow's got to take care of himself, Guy. You haven't been the most forthcoming of brothers, a rich devil like you, and I'm all to pieces."

Guy ignored the excuse. "Tell me one thing: how did you discover the Brangleys were misusing Harriet's money? That seems a large leap for someone of your . . . forgive me . . . lack of intellect to make. You only knew those people from my one or two visits to their house in London."

Another shrug from Lord Marchton. "Mrs. Brangley is rather stupid."

"Quite a facer, coming from you," muttered Guy. "Go on."

"If you must know the whole, it has nothing to do with the fact she's stupid," Evan said. "She didn't let anything slip. I picked up the news from going through your things, is all. I make a habit of it; have for years."

"Why?" his brother asked in awful calm.

Evan seemed to look a bit chastened—not much, but the glimmer of conscience was there. "Well, stap me, a man must live, Guy. I told you, I'm sailing up the River Tick."

Guy rolled his eyes toward the ceiling. "Perhaps in future you could think in terms of asking me for a loan to repair your estates—plant some crops, return that tin mine you own to working order, that sort of thing. Too ordinary for you?"

"But you've never said you'd come down with that sort of blunt," Evan exclaimed. "Know you're rich enough to, but you're the veriest nip-farthing with the ready, old fellow."

"I'll think about your difficulties, and I'll propose a solution," Guy said, frowning. "After I extract myself from this latest coil you've got me into."

"What?" Evan asked, looking up from a thoughtful consideration of his brother's words.

"Nothing more or less than your telling Miss Percival I was the origin of her mother's sudden fortune. I know where you got the information, blast you, but did you have to go relaying it to the very person I wished most to hide it from?" Guy spoke bitterly.

The seriousness in his voice seemed to strike Evan. "She didn't know? She acted as though she didn't, but I thought it a pose. A female of her sort, the hypocritical sort, I mean to say, don't think much of it when her light-skirt ways are laid out for the world to see."

"Evan!" Guy roared, getting to his feet. "What do I have to do to put a leash on your tongue? Did you say that sort of thing to her?"

Evan shrugged. "Don't think so; don't know. But a Cyprian ought to be more easygoing. Thought it only fair to claim my own share of the filly, for 'twas I discovered her in that City den."

"Good lord," Guy groaned, "I can imagine what you said. Will you do me a favor now and get out? Go ride about in the rain, as you suggested. I expect it to turn to a driving sleet ere long, and I for one can't wait."

The worst thing about Evan, Guy reflected as his younger brother lounged his way out of the study, was that he probably still had not even the slightest inkling that he might have done something less than noble.

Caroline built on her story of the day before. She let it be known that she still had the indisposition that had struck her at the end of Christmas Day and remained in her room, only venturing out once, in her dressing gown, to play quietly with Harriet in the nursery. She told her mother's abigail, who came to inquire, that she was to be out to all visitors.

She had also luckily made it known that she was to be notified of anything that passed in the house concerning Harriet, and thus Mrs. Binberry herself came to tell Miss Percival that Harriet's cousins, the Brangleys, were waiting for the little girl in the drawing room.

"Good heavens!" Caroline had returned from Harriet's nursery to her room for a nap—she really did have the most shocking headache that simply wouldn't go away—but she shot bolt upright at this news and rushed around the room, looking for the nearest clothes to put on. "She isn't with them, is she?"

It was the quiet hour before dinner, when Harriet commonly lay down to rest. The housekeeper's broad face creased in concern. "No, ma'am, nobody is. Lady Percival is in her room asleep, and Baxter and I thought it best to tell you about this visit before letting the people see Harriet. They are her own cousins, but we're being especially careful of the little dear since the other night."

Seeing Caroline's struggles, Mrs. Binberry helped the young lady on with her clothes and even helped her with her hair. Then she left to tell Baxter Miss Percival was coming down.

Caroline stood before the cheval glass and wondered if she should have chosen a simpler costume. The readiest one to hand was the rich-looking red ensemble she hadn't felt comfortable in at first, but which had since become her favorite gown. She took a look at her reflection and shrugged. The Brangleys would think she was trying to dress above her station, but they might as well see her in all the glory of her new status.

She looked into her own eyes, stricken. What exactly *was* her status? Guy Constant had admitted to being the economic force behind her mother's new income; then what was Caroline's position in the world?

The answer came as a dull throb of shame. *Kept woman.*

She had been beginning to lose the shell of the governess personality she had put on so many years ago and worn too well; now what was she to do? She would doubtless be looking for some kind of a position within a very short time, for the thought of depending upon Constant's largesse was intolerable. Would she have to resurrect the governess?

The mere thought caused an overwhelming sadness to flow through her, but she lifted her chin in determination. The one thing to remember in all this was that she was quite capable of supporting herself without anyone's help. As for the Brangleys, she would not humble herself before them. She would be the baronet's wealthy daughter if only for one last time before her world changed back to the dismal place it had been before.

She entered the drawing room with this sense of purpose and came face-to-face with the couple who had figured in her nightmares and caused her so many suspicions. Mrs. Brangley, tricked out in furs and velvet of precisely the wrong cut and colors, stared at Caroline as though at an apparition. Thin, nervous Mr. Brangley had much less presence than his wife—it was one of his few charms—and he tried a quizzical half-smile as he bowed. Not a low bow by any means, but a bow nevertheless, and a courtesy Caroline had never got from him as his employee.

"How do you do?" she began the conversation with a bright and innocent smile.

"We wanted to see little Harriet, not some menial," snapped Mrs. Brangley. "Fetch her, please."

"Now, my dear, no need to be rude," Mr. Brangley put in, with an odd glance at Caroline.

She gave him another, more intimate smile, the sort of expression she knew would throw the jealous Mrs. Brangley into a fury. "I'm quite certain, sir, that your wife is incapable of being less rude."

"Why, you little *snip*," Mrs. Brangley cried. "Give us back our child, you monster. How dare you keep her here in a house of ill-repute? It's unheard of. And how Mr. Constant could ever have allowed it is beyond me.

You must have charmed him quite as you tried to beguile his poor, innocent brother. Oh, we're well aware of your crimes, you . . . you strumpet!"

Caroline had no ready response to such a tirade. Dimly she remembered that if the Brangleys had been communicating with anyone, it would have been Lord Marchton, with his pithy opinions on Caroline's relationship with Guy Constant.

"Why do you think that I, a notorious woman, would wish to keep a little child?" Caroline asked curiously. The logic in her supposed actions quite escaped her. That she should entice Mr. Constant into supporting her merely so that she could have Harriet made no sense at all—ah, but she was forgetting to think as they thought. "The money. You think I'm after her money. Of course."

"A hardened adventuress like yourself is doubtless already spending the poor little creature's money," sniffed Mrs. Brangley. "Arthur? We should be collecting Harriet. Perhaps we should simply go up to her room and get her. That poor child will have to be cared for night and day until she realizes that there are some people in this world who aren't to be trusted."

"You mean," said Caroline slowly, "that if I gave you the charge of Harriet you would talk to her incessantly, wear her down until she thought nobody could want her for herself. I know what you've been doing, you see; everybody knows you've been mishandling Harriet's fortune."

Mr. Brangley looked shocked; his lady's haughty expression didn't change.

"Bring the child to me, you miserable trollop," Mrs. Brangley commanded, folding her arms.

"Don't be ridiculous," Caroline returned, wincing in spite of herself at the harsh words the woman used; they brought back the dreadful days when she had had no option but to obey this harridan's every whim. "Will you do me the favor of leaving my mother's house? You were not invited, and you will not see Harriet. She is Mr.

Guy Constant's ward, and he must direct her movements. Good day."

"You're mistaken, Miss Percival. Someone had misled you," Mr. Brangley said, approaching Caroline with a modicum of respect. "We want the child back because the other little ones miss her so. Ask anyone. They're her cousins, and she should be with them."

"Harriet can hardly help who her relations are," Caroline said with a cold bow. "If she were to be given a choice in the matter, I doubt she would like to be returned to little Miss Amanda's mercies. Harriet is a forgiving creature, but I don't think even she could forget the time her dear cousin locked her into the wardrobe for half a day, or the incident at the Serpentine."

"Childish high spirits," Mrs. Brangley put in. Her husband looked blank, confirming Caroline's suspicions that he knew nothing of what passed in the domestic side of his household.

"Oh, get out." Caroline lost patience totally, turned on her heel and left the drawing room.

She nearly ran into Guy Constant. He reached out, in fact, to catch her by the arms and avoid a collision.

She stared into his eyes, at the mix of affection and hope in them. "Oh, no," she whispered.

"Caroline. Please talk to me."

"No." She jerked her head in the direction of the drawing room. "If you feel the urge to talk, there are two charming people in that room who are pleased to call me a notorious woman and who wish to take Harriet off with them." She paused and cast one despairing glance into his eyes. "I *am* a notorious woman, am I not? I'm most certainly being kept. No, sir, I can't talk to you. Not now."

And she ran up the stairs without looking back.

13

CONSTANT entered the Percivals' drawing room in his coldest, most supercilious manner, thinking this would set the coming interview off on the right path.

Even as he nodded to the angry-looking Brangleys, he couldn't help his thoughts straying to Caroline. How would he ever resolve the coil that had toppled her trust?

He had no idea. For now he would help her in the best way he knew; plain usefulness was something, though it was not the knight-errantry he would have preferred. "I'm delighted to meet you both here," he said to the couple. "It saves my looking for you at your hotel. You have been calling on Lady Percival and her daughter?"

Mrs. Brangley sniffed. "*Lady* Percival! Mr. Constant, you have been most shamefully taken in. As though that governess person is really living here with her mother, let alone that her mother could be a ladyship!"

"You will find her ladyship's late husband listed in the baronetage," Constant said mildly.

"Ha! That is, there may be lists of this and that, but people can change their names. No, we know the rig she's been running, and we're come to take dear little Harriet away from this soiled atmosphere. When we got your letter in Croydon we came instantly to Bath, though at the cost of a Christmas spent with our own dear little children, to beg you to reconsider. Then we found, once we arrived, that sweet little Harriet has been living with that low person, that governess. Now I insist, Mr. Constant. Give Harriet to us now."

The woman was speaking in tones Constant associated with the most amateurish examples of that new area of stagecraft, the melodrama. "You insist? Do you not remember the child is my ward?"

"We are her cousins," Mrs. Brangley said, putting on a soulful look. "Her nearest kin."

"Poor, dear child," put in Mr. Brangley, after being nudged out of silence by his wife.

"She is indeed unfortunate," Constant said in a dry tone, raising his eyebrows, "but I mean to remedy that serious lack in her life by giving her an atmosphere of security and care."

"How sensible of you, sir," Mrs. Brangley said heartily. "We will take her with us now. My sweet Amanda does long to see her dear little cousin. She had been so saddened by her loss."

"Harriet is not dead, though not due to any vigilance of yours." Constant felt his temper rising. "I found her at your closed home in London, the next thing to alone."

"Mrs. Stephens is the soul of good nature," Mrs. Brangley objected, the plumes on her bonnet springing at least two inches higher into the air as she straightened her back. "A treasure."

"A deaf treasure and on the verge of senility. When I found the child she hadn't been fed in at least a day," Constant said. "Let us cut line, shall we, good people? Brangley, if you insist on letting your wife speak for you, I suppose I have no choice but to address my insults to her, but I would prefer to malign you, as you've been the one responsible for this fiasco. As head of your household, all blame must fall on you if that child is scarred for life by your neglect."

"What?" Mr. Brangley's sharp chin, which had been nesting somewhere in his high cravat, sprang up, and he actually looked a little spirited.

"You can't let him talk to you like that, Arthur," Mrs. Brangley put in, glaring at Constant. "This gentleman is evidently deeper in the toils of that horrid governess than we thought. A governess, only think! A servant."

"Miss Percival," said Constant in a rigid voice those

who knew him well would have recognized as a danger
sign, "is too fine a lady to have her rooms swept out by
such as you. You call yourselves Harriet's cousins, yet
you mistreated her, ignored her, and used her money for
your own ends. Yes"—he faced Brangley, whose sharp
features had whitened at this clear accusation—"I've
found it all out. Shady dealing upon 'Change with her
trust; losses which I only hope I can repair. I've discovered how you got signing power over her money,
through bribing a law clerk, and that is at an end. You
don't need Harriet, Brangley, for the game's up. I doubt
you'd want her to live with you if you didn't have a fair
chance at her fortune, and I don't doubt it was the
Deauville fortune made you take her in the first place."

"Well!" huffed Mrs. Brangley. "We don't have to listen to this."

"As you wish." Constant stood aside from the door.
"You've trespassed on the Percivals' hospitality long
enough."

"Arthur! Aren't you going to challenge this man? He's
behaving in a most ungentlemanlike manner."

Brangley took a good, long look at Constant. A per-
ceptible shudder racked his slight frame. "No, my dear,
I'm not."

"Prosecution will follow," Constant said cheerfully,
gesturing to the drawing room door. "My man of business is looking into recovering Miss Deauville's funds. I
don't want you to think your little scheme has served."

Mrs. Brangley looked from her husband to Constant.
Then, tossing her head, she led the way out of the room.

Constant did not outstay them long. He had a feeling
that if he were to go upstairs and seek admittance to Caroline's room in an attempt to explain himself, none of
the servants would try to stop him. Baxter, who stood in
the hall, holding the outer door for the departing Brangleys, shot Constant a look that could be interpreted as
sympathetic. Mrs. Binberry, the housekeeper, hovered
near the green baize door under the stairs with almost a
hopeful expression. But Guy knew collusion with the

domestic staff was not the way to Caroline's heart. She would consider such behavior unforgivable.

She might as well have nothing more to add to her list of his sins. Taking his hat from the attentive Baxter, Constant left the house.

Caroline was ashamed of her cowardice, but as soon as she left Constant in the downstairs entryway, she retreated to her room and returned to her pose of invalid, taking off her clothes to point up the fact that she was not fit for company. She was putting on a warm dressing gown of softest cashmere when Harriet invaded her bedroom.

"I'm so sorry you're sick, Caroline," said the little girl, looking truly contrite. "Aunt Elinor is afraid you took a chill when you were out looking for me on Christmas Eve."

"Oh, nothing of the sort." Caroline hugged the child to her. "It's only a little headache. I expect I'll feel perfectly fine tomorrow, so long as I don't see any company or do anything too strenuous."

"Oh, good."

"I'd hoped you and I could take a walk if the weather clears."

"May we go with Mr. Constant? That is, with Uncle Guy? He asked me to call him so," Harriet said with evident pride. "And may we take the dogs? Lord Fred said anytime I wished a dog, I was to go to Lady Lambert's stable and tell the man."

"We'll see." Caroline sighed, thinking over all the dreadful things she had to impart. What would it do to her mother, the news that they were really not rich at all? Lady Percival might have to take to her bed; her improvement had been so marked since her change of fortune that a similar worsening was to be expected when she found out she really was only a poor widow with a tiny jointure.

Caroline looked at Harriet's innocent face. Surely it would be well to start hinting to the child that her life was to change yet again; the shock of another sudden upheaval might be too much for her. She would be honest with the little girl, Caroline resolved; she would respect her feelings though she was so young.

As for Caroline, when she walked out with Harriet on the morrow, she would have to mix practicality with pleasure.

The next day, before she could think too much about the issue, Caroline went to Henrietta Street to converse further with Mrs. Deschamps, the formidable headmistress of the highly regarded Mrs. Deschamps' Select Seminary for Young Ladies of the Quality. This was the woman who before Christmas had offered Caroline a post based solely, Caroline was convinced, on the genteel appearance her new clothes had lent her. She had to cringe now, remembering that every stitch of her modish appearance was owned to Guy Constant, but she determined to be hard and practical and use the advantage a look of fashion lent her. She had been given a taste already of the reception her poorly dressed self had received at the other ladies' seminaries.

Mrs. Deschamps remembered Miss Percival and welcomed her fur-trimmed pelisse into her office with due cordiality. She was all smiles when Caroline offered her services. "Why, yes, Miss Percival, you may start as soon after the New Year as you like." Mrs. Deschamps was a dark, plump woman dressed in jet-trimmed silks. She nearly rubbed her hands on seeing Harriet, who perched on a stool in the corner while the ladies were talking. "And is this little girl a pupil you are bringing to us?"

"I'm not quite certain," Caroline said demurely, "but I believe so." Placing Harriet in the same school she taught at would give them as much time together as could be possible in the circumstances. Perhaps she would convince Mr. Constant of this course—when she had calmed herself enough to talk to Mr. Constant.

"But, Caroline," piped Harriet, "Uncle Guy said I was

to stay with you always. He said I must object if someone wanted to take me away."

"Dear, I am going to be a teacher at Mrs. Deschamps'
lovely school, and if you come here as a pupil, we can
be together all the time," Caroline said, exchanging a
grown-up look with Mrs. Deschamps.

"Schedules permitting, of course," that lady put in
with a falsely tinkling laugh.

Caroline was used enough to servitude to know that
she would not really have much in the way of free time.
She glanced at Harriet and saw the child looking most
thoughtful. Well, school would naturally be a disappointment to one who had believed she had a secure home
with people who loved her.

I will be here. I will love her, Caroline promised
silently, then had to make some excuse to Mrs. Deschamps for not hearing the lady's latest remark.

"You may expect me on the seventh of January,
ma'am," Caroline told Mrs. Deschamps on her way out.
Surely it was not too much to ask, to give her mother the
rest of her Christmas holiday. They would need the time
to make arrangements for new lodgings and to dispose
of all their new effects, dismiss the staff . . .

Caroline sighed when once she and Harriet were back
on the pavement of Henrietta Street, being discreetly followed by one of Lady Percival's footmen who, unbe-
knownst to him, would soon be wanting a situation.
How, Caroline wondered, could she have been so silly as
to believe even for a moment in unexpected good fortune? It had seemed so true, that delayed legacy from
Great-Aunt Lucretia, yet all along Caroline had been
troubled by twinges of disbelief. She should have listened harder to that pessimistic streak of hers.

"Oh, Miss Percival! Caroline! Do let me take you up."

Caroline looked round and saw Lady Georgiana Stapleton leaning out the window of a sober, chocolate-col-
ored carriage with a ducal crest emblazoned upon the
door. Harriet ran up to it and stood jumping up and
down.

"We'd be delighted, my lady," Caroline said, summoning up a smile. Faced with Harriet's enthusiasm, she could hardly make a lame excuse and walk away, but she did not feel up to seeing someone who knew her under false pretenses. She wondered how long she and Georgiana would remain upon speaking terms. She knew her ladyship to be kind and charitable; she would probably not even cut Caroline's acquaintance once she knew all, but Caroline did not think herself able to bear the inevitable condescension of an unequal friendship.

When she was settled against soft velvet squabs, with Harriet perched beside her, she decided to open the matter for discussion. She would not hide her ill fortune and let one who had been a friend find it out from someone else. "Lady Georgiana, I have something to tell you. My mother and I won't be Lady Lambert's neighbors for much longer."

"Indeed, I hear her ladyship and Lord Effrydd plan an early marriage," Lady Georgiana said with a little questioning smile.

"Oh, I'm not gossiping about Lady Lambert's affairs," Caroline hastened to assure the other girl. "I mean to tell you my mother and I will shortly be moving house."

"But I was certain you had only recently arrived in Lady Lambert's neighborhood."

"True. You might remember we were able to lodge in the Crescent due to a sudden change in fortune," Caroline said. Trying to salvage some humor from the situation, she added with a shaky smile, "It has changed back."

"Oh, my dear, I am so sorry." Georgiana put out a gloved hand to clasp Caroline's.

Harriet had been watching and listening intently. She spoke up with, "Caroline is to teach in a school, and I am to go there and be with her. I don't know where Aunt Elinor will be."

"Close by us, no doubt," Caroline said with a note of false cheer. "But you mustn't speak of those plans as settled yet, my dear. We have to ask Mr. Constant what he prefers you to do. You must remember, he is your guardian."

"Yes," Harriet said sadly, "but he didn't tell me the truth. He said I should never bc taken away from you."

"But you won't be, sweetheart. If all goes well, you'll be right with me at the school."

"That woman," Harriet said with an eloquent shudder, "won't let me see you all the time."

Caroline exchanged a worried glance with Lady Georgiana. "Harriet and I met the headmistress of the school. Like many women of business, perhaps she seemed a touch more harsh than a little girl would find comfortable."

Lady Georgiana seemed to understand all Caroline could not say. "My dears, I call this a shame. If you have to earn your living, Caroline, can't I help you in some way?"

"I've already said yes to the position," Caroline faltered, sorely tempted to take the kindness so gently offered. Mrs. Deschamps, for all her smiling aquiescence, had the makings of a termagant. Lady Georgiana must know many great people; surely someone congenial, somewhere, was in need of Caroline's services as companion or governess. But then she could not have Harriet . . .

"Please promise to let me think on it," Georgiana said with such an animated look on her pale face that Caroline nodded, feeling that it was something to have aroused this level of interest in the habitually bored duke's daughter.

Lady Georgiana directed her coachman to the Crescent, and as the ducal carriage moved through the streets, the two ladies endeavored to entertain Harriet, who had grown uncharacteristically silent.

Suddenly, in the middle of an anecdote about Stubby, the pony Harriet was soon to meet, Lady Georgiana broke off with a smile. "Caroline! I have the best notion. You know I've been trying to open a school for the children on my father's estates. I've been having remarkably little success, for every time I start to organize, I'm thwarted by something or other. I suspect I'm simply not very good at details. Would you take on the position of choosing a teacher and all that?"

"Not be the teacher myself?" Caroline was uncertain, fully sensible of Georgiana's kindness in creating a job out of nothing.

"Oh, my dear, my notions are bigger than that," said Georgiana. "Father has given me leave to mess about as I will with education for the tenantry. He washes his hands of it, he says, but I'm to have free rein. You would be setting up schools in a dozen villages. It would take some time."

"Heavens." Caroline had to admit such a project sounded much more fulfilling than merely slipping back into servant status.

"Then you'll think about it?"

"I . . . I suppose I must," Caroline said. "You're so very kind, my lady."

"Georgiana. Please always call me Georgiana."

The two girls smiled at each other, well satisfied with their friendship if not with the turn Caroline's life had taken. By the time Georgiana dropped Caroline and Harriet off in the Crescent, Caroline was feeling almost optimistic about the prospect of earning her own living.

She couldn't find the words to tell her mother.

Cautioning Harriet to say nothing of their morning's business to her Aunt Elinor, Caroline wondered how in heaven's name she would ever tell her mother that they had been the objects of unwanted charity from a man they hardly knew. And she would have to tell her before many days passed.

What had been Constant's motives? Caroline couldn't begin to imagine, but she supposed he had some noble reason. For when all was said and done, she couldn't believe, Lord Marchton's opinion and her own suspicions notwithstanding, that a man as upright at Guy Constant would have given Lady Percival a spurious legacy in order to make her daughter yield to his dark desires.

Yet Caroline knew he was attracted to her; she had even believed he was coming to love her. What did this mean, when coupled with his actions? Was he only a more subtle type of seducer than his brother? She spent many a sad hour puzzling over this.

Meanwhile she was faced with Mama's continued Christmas spirit. The combination of Harriet's return and the first Christmas in a dozen years with something to celebrate kept working a heady magic on Lady Percival. She shopped incessantly for holiday trifles for Harriet and Caroline, insisted on going out to the holiday concert at the Lower Rooms, and somehow, through her new network of friends, found children enough for a noisy morning party in Harriet's honor.

Harriet, while continuing to be delighted at each attention paid her, had developed a pensive manner that Caroline felt guilty for, but couldn't see how to mend. Harriet was obviously looking forward with something less than joy to being deposited at a school, no matter if Caroline would be with her.

Caroline set her own sights on trying not to look sad, but she couldn't help picturing her mother's dismay on finding out that she had indeed been spending fairy gold.

By New Year's Eve Caroline was ready to end her silence. She would go to Mr. Constant, hear his explanation of his conduct, and then, on New Year's Day tell Lady Percival exactly where matters stood. Caroline chose an early hour suitable for a morning call and walked down the Crescent a few doors to Lady Lambert's house.

It had been pure luck that she had not seen Constant since that brief moment on Boxing Day; he had not been at the recent concert, all Lady Lambert's family being engaged to friends elsewhere, and for the rest of the week Caroline had unabashedly been hiding in her mother's house.

She had to give him credit for sensitivity. He had not

called on her again; he was evidently waiting for her to make the move to communicate with him.

Now she squared her shoulders as she lifted the knocker. She would have it out with him, and then she would never see him again. She had worked herself round, in the past few days, to a proper gratitude for his kindness in trying to make easier the lives of a couple of indigent women. Of course he had no evil designs on her virtue; inexperienced as she was, she had only mistaken a casual interest for something more.

She had come to realize he must have been motivated by disinterested charity. Perhaps this sort of good work was nothing new to him; likely he was kind enough to make a habit of such activities. One of his wealth and generous nature would naturally be a philanthropist. But he had embarrassed her very deeply by pretending to be on an equal level with her; she could never forgive him that.

When the butler let her in, she asked for Mr. Constant rather than her ladyship and was told he was presently engaged. Refusing all offers of refreshment, Caroline sat down in a chair in the hall to await the gentleman's pleasure.

"Madam, you must go into the drawing room to wait, indeed you must," the butler pleaded. He looked scandalized at Caroline's insistence on waiting in the hall.

But Caroline knew she was no more, really, than any other petitioner who had ever waited to see Mr. Constant on a matter of business. Deep into her role, she refused steadfastly to move to a more comfortable place.

The butler gave up and retired to his pantry. Caroline sat and waited in the silent hall, hoping she would not see Lord Marchton. Lady Lambert, she had been told, was out driving with Lord Effrydd.

A slight noise from the floor above alerted Caroline that someone was coming down the stairs. She was astonished when Lady Georgiana Stapelton descended into view.

"Why, Caroline," cried Georgiana, hurrying to the

bottom of the stairs. She blushed deeply; Caroline noticed the attractive effect a change of color had on her friend's serene face.

Caroline summoned a social smile. "I have business with Mr. Constant." She eyed the butler, who nodded briskly and started up the stairs with her card on a salver.

"I'm glad," Georgiana said. "I was afraid you were cross with him for some reason. I see I was wrong. I'm glad," she repeated.

To Caroline's eye Georgiana looked more embarrassed than glad, but she let this impression pass. She did not even ask what Georgiana had been doing in the house in Lady Lambert's absence; it was all too clear that the young woman had been visiting Constant.

Caroline wondered if Lady Georgiana had developed a more than casual interest in Guy. She knew by now that neither of the respective families were precisely pushing such a union—Constant had no title, after all—but she had no reason to believe either the Duke of Davonleigh or Lady Lambert would find the marriage repulsive. If Lady Georgiana and Constant were attached, then nothing could keep them apart. They were equals in all but station, and his vast fortune ought to count as an equalizer of sorts.

"Well, I must be on my way," Georgiana said, and nodded to the footman who had been awaiting her in the shadows at the other end of the hall. Caroline realized dimly that she ought to have noticed the man and marked his livery; she was certainly not very quick this morning. "Happy New Year, dear Caroline. I'll see you here tomorrow evening at Lady Lambert's ball."

Caroline agreed to this while not knowing if, by tomorrow, she would be wishing to attend a ball in this house.

The butler returned. "Madam, I will conduct you to Mr. Constant's study." Caroline nodded, swallowed hard, and followed the servant up the stairs.

"Caroline." Guy came forward to meet her as she entered his room. He had been standing at a window—

watching Lady Georgiana depart? Caroline wondered—and now he turned to her, gray eyes brimming with what looked like hope. He took her hands. "I couldn't have wished for more. Thank you for coming to me, my dear."

Caroline was nearly rendered helpless by this show of kindness. "I wanted only to ask you at last what motivated your actions," she said quietly, marshaling all her forces of built-up resentment, gently withdrawing her hands from his disturbing touch. "I'm faced with the task of informing my mother she's been living on your charity, and it's not easy."

He gave her a quizzical look and said something altogether off the subject. "Do you know who my last visitor was?"

"Yes, I saw Lady Georgiana leave. What has she to do with this?"

"Nothing much. She merely wondered if I could help you in some way. You told her you've suffered a reversal of fortune."

"Yes, I didn't know how else to describe it. I can hardly tell people that we've decided to stop letting you pay our bills."

"My dear girl, sit down." Constant led her to a sofa opposite a large desk and urged her down upon it. He sat next to her. "You're making this sound grim and rather sordid, and it's not like that at all."

"What is it like?" Caroline demanded, cheeks turning rapidly to a vivid rose. She had a natural streak of pessimism, and that had been her downfall many a time; but she could put no other construction on Guy's actions than the obvious one, the one most flattering to him: that she and her mother had been the pitiful objects of his charity.

A strange light burned in his eyes. "First you must forgive me for what I'm about to do. I'm sick of not seeing you; nearly mad with the need of you. Let that be my excuse." With no further ado, he grasped her by the shoulders and kissed her, hard and long.

Caroline responded. She couldn't help it; love and desire were so new to her, so magical, she couldn't cast them aside merely for sensible reasons. Logic and pride demanded she wrench herself away; dignity insisted upon it. Yet she couldn't even begin to do so.

When he let her go, it was to undo her bonnet strings. "This confection is terribly in the way," he murmured.

Caroline noticed his eyes had changed; now they were glazed over with some emotion—passion, she had no doubt. How dear he was to her in spite of his deception. If only they could always kiss, never talk or live in the world. The bonnet fell to the floor beside the sofa, and he kissed her again.

Not that there was anything less than full cooperation on her part, she had to admit as they finally drew apart. "Oh, Guy," she said softly, touching his cheek. "What did you mean by it? Must you be the lord of the manor, dispensing your bounty to one and all? Must you control the world? What is it?"

"Will you listen to me and hear what I say, without protest, without telling me what it is I really meant?"

Caroline was injured by such a remark. "I hope I'm capable of listening. Please do go ahead."

"Thank you." He drew her close beside him, turning to look into her eyes as he spoke. "When I met you, I learned something I had never known before. Do you know what it was?"

"I'm not to ask," Caroline said with a little smile.

"That's right. Well, my dear," and his arm tightened about her shoulders, "I had never met a governess."

"Such a lowly being would naturally not have been in your sphere," Caroline interjected.

"My love! You promised not to interrupt."

"Forgive me."

He kept looking at her; even reached out to touch a curl that had escaped from its pins and was nestled at her throat. "I was the typical arrogant man of means, I suppose, who had never given much thought one way or another to the persons beneath me in station. Then I saw you, and I learned you had been brought up to expect as much of life—as much ease, as much opportunity—as ever I had. Yet your life had taken a different path, a difficult path. I was touched by the lengths you had to go to, the indignities you had to endure to earn your living. When I learned to love you—don't interrupt, Caroline— and this happened early in our acquaintance, I hit upon the foolish notion of wanting to be loved in return."

Caroline said nothing, but she looked at him in amazement. Who could not fall in love with him?

He smiled, acknowledging the unspoken compliment. "I imagined myself asking you to marry me and you agreeing; but I thought you would have to say yes if a rich man asked you that question. You had a mother to think of. I didn't want you to take me in order to escape a life of drudgery."

"Oh." Caroline held her breath as he continued the story.

"I thought that if I settled some money on Lady Percival, then you would have a free choice in the matter of marriage. I had hoped you would never have to know how I pulled the strings behind her ladyship's income: finding a likely relation of hers to take the role of benefactor, having a will made up. Now my plan is spoiled, thanks to Evan's wandering tongue."

"Guy," Caroline said slowly, "now it must be my turn to talk. I don't think I've ever heard anything more noble, more touching in my life. And to think I construed your motives as something less! I ought to be horsewhipped."

"Not whipped, merely loved into a proper realization of what's due to you," Guy said, very near her ear. "Let me ask the question anyhow, Caroline, even if the circumstances are changed. I thought you were learning to love me. Was I completely wrong? Can you bring yourself to marry me?"

"I believe I have to," Caroline said demurely. "Such thoughts as I have now would certainly be the height of impropriety if I didn't marry you."

Again they lost themselves in each other's arms; Caroline eventually pulled away, but only to tell him how happy she was.

"And can we leave your mother believing that her fortune is an inheritance? Or will you insist on telling her all?"

"I see no occasion to tell her," Caroline said. "I must simply ask you to accept my thanks on her behalf. And I can think of some novel ways to thank you if you give me a chance."

"Delighted, my love. I think you've made the right choice. Unless I mistake the matter, Lady Percival will keep in much better spirits as an independent woman. She is independent anyway, you know. I settled the income on her absolutely."

"Not knowing whether or not I'd choose to marry you?" Caroline was astonished anew at her lover's generosity.

"I wanted it to be a free choice, remember,"' Guy said, shrugging his shoulders. "Speaking of Lady Percival, may we go and tell her now? And I believe little Harriet will be pleased as well."

"Harriet!" Caroline thought of the little girl for the first time since she'd been in the room. "She may live with us, then, and be secure of a home? Oh, Guy."

"We'll make a good home for her," he said, and it was both a promise and a statement of fact.

"Then you aren't the gentleman you once warned me about? You said, if I recall, that I might meet a man who wouldn't be happy at the prospect of a ready-made family."

He looked self-conscious. "I admit I said those words with myself in mind; but I didn't know Harriet. It should have been enough for me that you loved her, but now that I love her myself I can't imagine our life without her."

"Harriet will be thrilled," Caroline said. "As will my mother. But why spread the news so soon?" A part of her wanted to cherish this delightful secret in her heart before telling the world.

"For an excellent reason, dear Caroline. I want to make sure you don't change your mind."

As though she would! Again the scene dissolved into a flurry of kisses and fond assurances. Caroline didn't know how her bonnet got back on her head, but it did; and on her left hand was a sapphire ring Guy said would match her eyes if it were a little brighter. She walked on his arm down the street to her mother's house, wondering how anyone could be so happy.

From being ashamed of her willful misunderstanding of Guy's motives, she soon passed to forgiving herself. After all, who in her right mind would have had the conceit to think a man so far above her touch would have done so much on the off chance she would marry him? Caroline had never ranked her own attractions nearly that high.

"Do you know," Guy said as they walked, "Lady Georgiana advised me to propose to you anyway. She suspected how it was with me and didn't want me to be put off by your poverty. She gave me a wonderful lecture, which I wish I'd had the presence of mind to write down, on how money isn't everything. She listed your amiable qualities, too; didn't know she was speaking to one who had twice as long a list of his own. How will you explain to Lady Georgiana and anyone else you might have told that you were mistaken about this latest reversal of fortune?"

Caroline shrugged. "Oh, a groundless fear over some stocks, I suppose. Would that be adequate?"

"I don't see why not."

"Or," Caroline said with a slow smile, "since I've spoken of this to no one but Georgiana, I could tell her the truth. Georgiana would never tell my mother, and why shouldn't she know what a truly generous prince of a man I'm marrying?"

"Do what you think best," said Guy.

Caroline thought she saw him reddening under the

bronze of his cheeks, and she began to tease him for his modesty as they opened the door of her mother's house.

Within servants were running about in a panic.

"What is it?" cried Caroline, intercepting a frantic-looking Mrs. Binberry, who was wringing her hands as Baxter waved his arms and shouted incoherent orders to a footman.

"It's Miss Harriet, ma'am," said the housekeeper. "She's vanished."

14

"NOT AGAIN," Caroline cried, looking in anguish from Binberry to Guy.

"She can't be found, ma'am. We've turned the house upside down and inside out," Mrs. Binberry said in a mournful tone. "This time her nursemaid is here, and the lass didn't see the child go out. In hysterics in the nursery, she is, ma'am, if you wish to question her." So saying, she rushed off belowstairs, cap ribbons flapping behind her.

Caroline was left alone with Guy in the entrance hall. She made no move to go upstairs, for she didn't think much good could come from an interview with a vaporish nursemaid. Had Harriet gone away by herself, or had someone taken her? Caroline knew the Brangleys had left Bath, and Lord Marchton had been sternly warned against any further antics.

"Where is your brother today?" she asked Guy nonetheless, turning worried eyes to his.

"He and a party of young men went to Wells to place bets on a bout of fisticuffs. He isn't expected back till the small hours," Guy said. "Not that I'm discounting the possibility he could have gone in for further mischief, but since I've revealed all his actions, he hasn't much incentive for making trouble in this way."

"I suppose not. But where could she be?"

Guy took a deep breath. "Before, she was taken away. Can we at least consider the possibility that this time she might have left on her own?"

"But why?" Caroline cried. "She was happy here; she

was—" She cut off her words, on the point of saying that Harriet was secure. Was she really? What had happened to her sense of security in the past few days?

Harriet had been an oyster on the matter of Caroline's search for work; she hadn't breathed a word to Lady Percival. What had that reticence cost her?

"What are you thinking?" Guy took Caroline by the arm. "Do you know where she could be?"

"No," Caroline said slowly, dully, "but I fear I know why she might have gone."

In a halting voice she described her mood of the past few days and how it might have affected Harriet. She had told the child they would be together, yes, but she hadn't really held out much hope of a happy future. Harriet had seen for herself the small likelihood of their being much together at a school; and she had heard other plans of Caroline's, none of which seemed to include her, such as Lady Georgiana's kind scheme for Caroline to direct the village schools.

"I'm so very stupid," Caroline said with a sigh. "Why didn't I keep all my worries from her? She's only six. But I had some idea that getting her used to the change gradually would help her when the moment came."

"My fault," Guy said in what Caroline interpreted as an excess of gallantry. "I ought to have stormed after you on Christmas Day, forced my way into your room and demanded that you listen to me. Then we might have had this all sorted out days ago."

"It isn't your fault," Caroline protested. "It's all my lack of trust and faith. But let's not waste time apportioning blame. We must find Harriet. At least it's full daylight."

"I'll start out at once. Does she have a favorite place where the two of you go on your rambles?"

Caroline stopped to think. Harriet had liked Sydney Gardens, but that was so far away she would never find her way there. She had been much taken with the view from Beechen Cliff; but would a little child be likely to walk all that way? Caroline tried to remember the day she and her mother had taken Harriet to the Pump Room; had she enjoyed that experience much?

"I think someone should go to Beechen Cliff in case she might have decided to walk there," Caroline said. "One of the footmen—she likes Tony best. Then I believe we should go to the Abbey. I took her there to hear the singing, and she was enthralled by the place. She had never been inside such a big church before—or any church that she could remember—and anyone could direct her there. From certain streets she would even be able to pick out the tower by herself."

"A good thought," Constant agreed.

"I must see how my mother is faring before we leave," Caroline then said, and while Constant saw to sending Tony up Beechen Cliff, she made her way into the drawing room. Lady Percival wasn't there, nor was she in the smaller sitting room she sometimes used. Caroline found her mother in the ground-floor bedroom, reclining against the pillows of a duchess bed and looking white and resigned.

"Oh, Caroline." She held out her hand to her daughter. "This is beyond anything frightening. Harriet is gone again!"

"I know, Mama, and Mr. Constant and I are off to find her."

"Ah! You're speaking to Mr. Constant again? Capital," said Lady Percival.

"Mama! What gave you the idea I was not speaking to him?" Caroline was shocked; she thought she had been quite adept at hiding her distress of the past few days from her mother.

"Caroline, there is one thing I know about you, and that is this: you are never ill. On the rare occasions when you are, you must be tied down to your bed in order to take a proper rest. I remember well from your childhood, and you can't have changed that much. In the past days you've been feigning indisposition and avoiding Mr. Constant. Give a mother credit for some discernment."

"Oh, heavens." Caroline was appalled that all her efforts had been so transparent, but she recovered quickly. "My silly behavior doesn't matter, Mama. Mr. Constant and I are going to be married. But the important thing now is to find Harriet."

"You're going to be married?" Lady Percival sat upright, eyes lively as they hadn't been a moment before. "What wonderful news. Mr. Constant is the finest young man in Bath, and he loves you very much, you know. I see it in his eyes every day. You must get Harriet back instantly, and we'll pick out the most delightful dress for her to wear as your bridesmaid."

"Mama, do you have any idea where she might have gone?"

Lady Percival frowned in thought. "We spoke of going into the Labyrinth at the Sydney Gardens. And of course she has been excited about going out to Davonleigh to ride Lady Georgiana's pony. Harriet has been quiltier the last few days, though. I've thought she was sympathizing with you in your illness." She gave a certain inflection to the word "illness" that made Caroline feel guiltier than ever.

"I'll send someone to the Syndey Gardens, though I do hope she wouldn't try to go so far," Caroline said.

"Caroline," Lady Percival said, "when a child runs away, the ends of the earth is not too far. Don't underestimate how overset she might have been, or how far her determination might have carried her."

"You do think as Guy does that she's run away, don't you, Mama?"

Lady Percival nodded. "There has been something not quite right with the dear child; I believe she's still getting over the fear of her abduction. But I certainly can't fathom why that would result in her running away by herself."

"Yet you think she did. So do I," Caroline said, and, giving her mother a quick kiss, she left the room.

Constant was awaiting her in the hall. "My curricle should be brought round at any moment. The streets are crowded, but I believe we'll make slightly better time than we would on foot." As he spoke, he ushered her outside to the pavement.

Caroline thought the curricle was the most abominably slow vehicle she had ever been in as it tried to work its way around carts and chairs. Passing through the Circus, they drove down Gay Street, Caroline using the time to peer carefully at every child she saw in the street. There were so many children, too, from ragged urchins selling wares to well-dressed mites clasped firmly by the hands of their nurses or governesses.

"Oh, Guy," Caroline said with a sigh, "if only we find her. If only she's safe."

"We'll find her," he answered, speaking more roughly to her than he had that day. She took this as a measure of his concern for his little ward; she half wished he would snap at her, she felt so guilty for filling Harriet's head with new fears at such a sensitive time in the child's life.

In the churchyard Caroline jumped down from the curricle almost before Constant brought it to a halt. He followed her, tossing the reins to the tiger who had been riding up behind them. They hurried into the huge medieval bulk of Abbey Church; it was not time for service, and the place was quiet but for a couple of worshipers, anonymous dark shapes near the altar.

Caroline had walked in at a very quick pace, but she came to a stop just inches inside the great doors and went forward at a slower speed more appropriate to the religious hush. Constant came up close beside her, and she put her hand on his arm as they paced the perimeters of the place, on the lookout for anything unusual. They examined the shadows of each monument on the old walls, cast curious glances up at the wooden galleries that some purists said disfigured the place, and mounted to search through these. All was quiet.

They finally arrived back at the church entrance, and Caroline whispered, "I don't know where to go next, Guy. What shall we do?" She looked into his face. Tomorrow was the New Year and would mark a new beginning in her life. How could she face it if something had happened to Harriet? Guy's eyes were worried as he drew her close.

She had about settled it within herself to pray for some sign when a loud bark came from outside the church door.

She and Guy looked at each other, then nearly ran out into the gray daylight.

In the middle of the churchyard stood Harriet, looking very tiny in one of her new pelisses and the grown-up bonnet her guardian had bought her. Beside her, teeth bared, was one of Lord Effrydd's dogs. A sinister-looking old lavender woman was backing away from the pair in apparent terror.

"Harriet!" Caroline ran forward. "What happened?"

"That old woman said she would take me to a lovely place and care for me, but I told Gruffydd I didn't want to go, and he told her," Harriet said, looking up at Caroline with wide eyes.

"Dear child." Caroline crouched down despite the dirty cobbles, and Gruffydd licked her face enthusiastically. Harriet was giggling before Caroline remembered to dislodge her bonnet and give the dog an ear, after which she was allowed to go on with her questioning. "I'm so glad you had a dog to protect you, but what I meant to ask is what happened to make you go from home without telling anyone?"

Harriet took a deep breath. One of her hands was clasped in Guy's, and the other rested on the dog's head. "I wanted to come here and ask the vicar why I must leave you, Caroline. Uncle Guy told me not to let anyone take me from you, and I didn't know what to do if you were the one separating us. Now that you're going out to work, you won't need me, and so I thought the vicar could tell me what I must do."

"Have you met the vicar here?" Caroline asked, puzzled at this reasoning.

"Oh, no," Harriet said, looking up at the huge tower. "But if he has such a beautiful church, with all those angels walking up and down on the front, and such lovely singers as we heard the other day, he must be a great man who knows the answers to many questions." She paused. "And I didn't know who else to ask."

"Oh, my darling child. Why didn't you ask me or your Aunt Elinor or your guardian, your Uncle Guy?" Caroline asked sadly.

Harriet looked surprised. "The question was *about* you, Caroline. I could scarcely ask you. And Aunt Elinor is your mama, and besides, you had asked me not to tell her anything about—about the school, or working for a living and moving house, and I do keep my promises."

"Why didn't you ask me?" asked Guy, bending down.

"I didn't want to hear the answer," Harriet said in a very soft voice.

Caroline understood. Grown people were forever pulling Harriet this way and that, and she had never until quite recently got much satisfaction from the voice of authority.

Hugging the child, Caroline said, "You have nothing to worry about, my dear. Nothing. We are not to move after all. That is . . . I suppose we'll indeed move sooner or later, but you and I and Aunt Elinor will pass a most delightful winter here in Bath, all of us together."

"Truly, Caroline? You aren't pretending this time?"

Caroline winced at this.

Guy cleared his throat. "Will you include me in your winter's plans, dear Caroline, or am I to wait and be put on like a new hat in the spring season?"

Caroline smiled, shaking her head. "I assumed you would want to be engaged for a while: to make arrangements, to get used to the idea."

"Is that your wish?"

Harriet and Gruffydd both looked on in puzzled concentration as Caroline rose to clasp her arms around Guy's neck. "I have no interest in a long betrothal."

"And I have every interest in shortening my own period of frustration," Guy said, squeezing here waist and moving his hands to her hips in a manner than really shouldn't have been tolerated in the pubic street. "I'll allow you three weeks for banns, but that's as far as I'll go. Much better if you let me get a special license at once."

"We'll have to ask my mother. She had some extravagant plans about a bridesmaid's dress for Harriet, and I can't disappoint her."

"It's settled, then. The time it takes to make one gown. You had better be married in something you already have; I can only give you the time required for one little dress, and I know a grown woman's outfit would take too many days."

"What's going on?" Harriet asked, tugging at Guy's coattail. "Am I to have another new dress?"

"Yes, dearest," Caroline said, laughing, and at that opportune moment the church bells began to chime.

Lady Percival sighed in pleasure. "A New Year's Day wedding after all. I was so hoping you would let Guy talk you round to it, Caroline."

"For now we must make do with Lady Lambert's. How odd it will be to call her Lady Effrydd."

"Fanny has been called many things in her time. Her friends will soon get used to it," said Lady Percival.

She made some infinitesimal adjustment in her headdress, and then Caroline wheeled her mother into the small, ornate ballroom of Lady Lambert's house.

Caroline had on her white and silver ball dress, and when Guy came up to her, as soon as they were announced, he took her hand and looked at her from all angles. "You would make a beautiful bride this moment, my love. Are you sure you won't reconsider?"

"I'm sure. You said Harriet might have a new gown for our wedding, and that's how it is to be. The poor child will be worn out with acting bridesmaid before January is over."

Lady Lambert's New Year's ball was in full swing, all her most intimate Bath friends gathered either on the dance floor, where a quadrille was in progress, or on the sidelines. The event would be termed by its more aristocratic attendees rather mixed; Lady Lambert had even invited the Duttons. Caroline could see Desideria in a low-cut gown of bright rose silk, weaving in and out of the quadrille figures with Lord Marchton. That young man wore his habitual expression of boredom, tempered only a little by the interest he was taking in his partner's décolletage.

Lady Georgiana was there, too, in the same set with Desideria and Marchton. She was dancing with someone new, a dashing officer, and looked happier at the prospect than Caroline remembered seeing her.

An unusual excitement buzzed in the air, and at the end of the dance all eyes turned toward the door. The musicians played a little fanfare, and two liveried footmen threw open the doors.

To have a wedding in the middle of a ball was one fantasy Lady Lambert had not yet attained in her career of marrying, and this time she had elected to surprise her guests while she fulfilled her heart's wish. However, she had not been able to keep her own counsel, and those of her friends who had not precisely been told she was marrying Lord Effrydd this evening had guessed.

Guy's mother stood on the threshold, magnificent in a new gown of mauve with an overlay of white lace. The costume was most appropriate for the heavy rope of pearls she wore, the latest gift from her husband-to-be. Beside her stood her son's ward, in a little mauve silk gown that Lady Lambert had but that morning given Harriet as a New Year's gift without telling her it was to be a bridesmaid's dress. Both Lady Lambert and the little girl carried white roses, Harriet's in a basket. The child's eyes shone with excitement, and Caroline noticed how becoming the mauve was to Harriet's dark hair. They would have to remember that color in future years.

Lord Effrydd stepped forward, beaming through his bushy beard. He was distinguished in his evening gear, a blinding white satin waistcoat setting off the severe black of his superfine coat. A clergyman stood by his side.

Lady Lambert and the child moved through the crowd, her ladyship smiling and even winking at certain of her friends. She reached her betrothed, gave over the flowers she carried to Harriet's charge, and put her gloved hand in Lord Effrydd's. Harriet jumped up and down.

"Leave it to my mother," Guy said into Caroline's ear. "This is what she calls being married privately in a simple little ceremony, you know."

"I think it's beautiful," Caroline replied, her eyes on the four giant dogs in an orderly rank near one of the windows. Several of the more timid lady guests had looked at them in alarm, but Lord Effrydd insisted his Fellows should witness his marriage.

The clergyman cleared his throat and began to read the service.

"I'm glad you're in the mood for a wedding. See that you stay that way." Guy put his arm around Caroline's waist and held her close. "My mother could coach you in your lines if you're afraid of forgetting the responses."

"Guy!" Caroline shook her head at his levity.

He was bending toward her for a kiss when Lady Percival's whisper interrupted them. "Oh, Caroline! I've done it! I've finally remembered where I met Mrs. Dutton. I simply knew that if I stared at the woman long enough, I could do it."

"Where was it, Mama?" Caroline brought herself back to reality with difficulty, but could not summon up much interest in Mrs. Dutton.

"She was married to the smith in our village. I must have carried soup to their cottage a score of times. Their names was Dubbins. Dutton does sound more genteel, does it not? My word, he must have been a saving sort of man to leave her so well-placed."

"The smith. Fancy that," Caroline murmured.

"You don't think it shocking that I've been entertaining a former member of your father's tenantry quite as though she were our equal?"

Caroline shrugged, still smiling at Guy as she bent

down to answer her mother. "Why should you not, Mama? The world is changing."

"My sentiments exactly. I was afraid you would be disapproving, Caroline. You are sometimes so stodgy." Lady Percival smiled quite serenely. "Oh, listen, they're coming to the 'wilt thou' part. This always makes me cry. How sweet little Harriet looks. We'll have to teach her not to keep hopping about on her tiptoes for your wedding. It's distracting the dogs."

Caroline passed her mother a handkerchief. Then she allowed her attention to wander from the ceremony as Guy kissed her cheek and said, low, "Happy New Year, my dear love. And now that we've practiced the wedding, perhaps we could sneak away to my study and practice the honeymoon. I've had a kissing bough hung over the sofa in anticipation."

"Guy!" Caroline pretended to be scandalized, though his words made her heart race with something other than prudish indignation. Several heads were turning to look at them in disapproval, for their whispering was interrupting the most sensitive moments of the marriage service.

"Don't worry, my darling. I won't try your sense of propriety more than you wish."

"More than I wish!" Caroline repeated with a mischievous smile. "I'm afraid that would be too shocking."

As the final words of the ceremony rang out, she let her lips meet Guy's in a perfectly silent, perfectly communicative kiss.